The House on Russian Hill

A Novel

Thomas Hofstedt

Table of Contents

The First Murder

The Rio de los Americanos (1857)

The man was ragged, cold and gaunt, just short of starving and so long encased in his own misery as to be unmindful of any other possible state of being.

A small part of his misery was that he was from a big city in the East and had little experience or aptitude for living in a country where one had to shoot or catch his dinner, a country that seemed as hard and unchangeable as the granite boulder at his back. But the far more important factor was the seemingly consumptive effect of simple greed, the lust for gold that had drawn so many men to this area, driven by a hopefulness that caused them to neglect their own welfare as they dug their way into the slopes of the Sierra foothills. There were not many overweight miners coming out of the hills.

It was not the end of the California Gold Rush, but it was the end of the boom times. By 1857, finding and extracting the seductive yellow metal required capital in all its forms. It was becoming a business instead of a quest, leaving thousands of miners wondering what had happened to them.

They had come from all over the world, mostly unskilled laborers with visions of instant wealth. Among them, the Chinese stood out with their pigtails, strange language, darker skin, and tendency to stay with their own kind. They were, at first, valued for their willingness to work hard for low wages in less desirable jobs, those that the whites did not want. Those who were more daring became miners, but even they did not stake out their own claims but worked those claims abandoned by white miners when it required too much work for too little gold.

The ragged man sitting hunched against the granite boulder on the riverbank was not Chinese, but he had lived on the fringes of their camp for the last year, driven by his low circumstances. He had been trying for almost eight years and had lived through the entire gold rush cycle. At the start, the lucky ones – but not him -- picked up loose gold from rivers and streams, some occasionally large nuggets and then tiny flakes panned from the gravel. But, inevitably, the yellow metal became both harder to find and, once discovered, far more difficult to extract. They built ever-larger dredges and sluice boxes and then began to dig tunnels and shafts, first with shovels and picks, and then using more sophisticated equipment. Then they brought in huge hydraulic pumps and washed away entire hillsides in the search for the ever more elusive yellow wealth, leaving denuded landscapes and sludge-filled creek beds.

The man, like most of those who came, worked like a dog and came up empty. The combination of his persistent failures, the falling price of gold, and the prospect of yet another bitter winter had worn him out. He was done, with only one last desperate card to play. If that failed, he was headed home to St. Louis and a questionable job on the Mississippi riverboats.

Despite his low circumstances, the man was strong-willed and proud, reluctant to accept his failure. Being forced to live with the Chinese was the last straw, the ultimate humiliation that could be inflicted on a white man with his upbringing. He maintained the veneer of superiority, but both he and the Chinese understood the reality. Other than one man, they did not speak to him or even appear to notice him.

Ah Yang was different. He spoke broken English and, as the obvious camp leader, consulted the man about how to deal with other white men, seeming to take his thoughts seriously. Inevitably, it was an uneasy alliance, one with mistrust at its core.

The man sat on the riverbank at the foot of a homemade pier, a makeshift affair that jutted only a few feet into the slow moving current. The first snowflakes of the season pelted him, sharp wind-driven dots, more felt than seen in the darkness. His only possession – a highly dubious one, both legally and functionally – was the boat at the end of the rickety pier, an unwieldy shallow draft keelboat that he had found nearby, half-imbedded in a mud bank. The man marveled at the amount of work it must have taken to manhandle the boat upstream to this point on the north fork of the Rio de los Americanos, only to be abandoned by its owner in his haste to get his share of the yellow metal that he had been assured was lying around waiting for someone to pick it up.

And it has only one more trip to make.

Ah Yang had approached him two days ago. The accent was thick, but his ear had become accustomed to it in the months that he had lived on the fringes of their camp.

"We need boat. To San Francisco on river. Will pay."

A boat! So they're not going to risk another encounter with Schultz or his crew. But I'm not supposed to know about that, so ... The question was an obvious one. To not ask would seem suspicious.

"Why not a wagon? Faster, easier, cheaper."

"Too dangerous. White devils watch road. Take gold. Murder Chinaman."

An expression of sympathy was neither expected nor offered, so it was easy for the man to conceal that he already knew this.

Six Chinese miners were killed three days ago on the stage road to Sacramento. Schultz and a half-dozen others – the white devils that Ah Yang was referring to -- were waiting for them and shot them down after they had handed over the several bags of gold dust that represented years of backbreaking labor. What Ah Yang does not know – Thank God – is Schultz knew they were coming because I had told him.

The man rubbed his fingers together in the universal gesture. "How much?"

"One hundred dollars. In San Francisco."

A fair price, even for the gold camps, where the prices of ordinary goods and services were anything but ordinary. Not so high a price to make me think it's a special cargo. A hundred dollars for two days, downriver to the bay and then some hard rowing. But, if it turns out like I want it to, the hundred dollars won't matter.

The snow flurries stopped and a full moon came out just as he heard them coming. It turned out to be a single cart drawn by a lone and very old horse, led by Ah Yang on foot.

He was alone, a fact that the man took as a sign that his luck had finally turned. The rickety cart was loaded with wooden crates, which Ah Yang and the man wrestled with difficulty into the boat. They were surprisingly heavy. The man saw to their precise placement on the flat platform in the middle of the boat, barely leaving room for him and the oars. There were modest rapids during the first few miles and cargo had to be both balanced and lashed down.

Some of the crates were not covered and he could see some of the topmost contents: a birdcage, rolls of cloth, stacks of mugs and plates, pans, even a small sewing machine.

"What is this stuff?" he asked Ah Yang.

"Women's things. Cloth. Dishes. They say must go."

Women's things. Sure. Loaded late at night and using a leaky boat instead of a very dull – and much cheaper -- wagon trip on known roads. Women's things. And something else that must not be mentioned.

"It will take me two days. I will meet you –"

"No. I go." And Ah Yang sat down on the narrow plank bench in the bow. When the man cast off the single rope holding them in place and the boat began to move with the current, Ah Yang removed a large revolver from inside his tunic and placed it alongside him on the bench.

The man set the oars and took his place, looking downstream and at the vague dark shape that was Ah Yang.

"One hundred dollars, yes?"

"In San Francisco."

"The river? It can be dangerous, especially at night."

Ah Yang said nothing, but placed his right hand on the revolver, making it clear where he thought the dangers rested.

The moonlight persisted, making it easy to navigate in the luminescent waters even with the unwieldy and heavily loaded boat. The current was sufficient to keep them moving at about the pace of a fast walk. The man stood in the middle of the boat, facing downstream and using the oars mostly as rudders, to keep the boat positioned in the mainstream. Ah Yang was absolutely still, his back to their direction of travel and all of his attention focused on the man at the oars. It was as if he knew the direction of the man's thoughts.

The revolver is a problem. Unusual for a Chinaman to have one, let alone show it to a white man. He obviously doesn't trust me. I wonder if he suspects that I was the one who tipped Schultz?

He worried about that for a few minutes, mainly because it meant that his plan for Ah Yang would be much more difficult to achieve. Then he was struck by the much more important implication of Ah Yang's possible suspiciousness.

Maybe he's thinking to get even! Just him and me, late at night on a dark river, and he's got that gun ...

It took only a few minutes for the speculation to become fact in his imagination and for Ah Yang's immobile figure to become a mortal threat rather than merely a moveable obstacle to his own schemes. He tried to put himself in Ah Yang's place, to think like a man with vengeance pushing him.

Where? And when? The 'how' is pretty clear. Shoot me and toss me in the river. Nobody's going to miss me and, even if they did, they're not going to get excited about another murder in the camps, and nobody knows that we left together. But he can't do it until we get to calmer waters, somewhere where anybody could steer the damn boat past the rocks. For the moment, he needs me.

The irony did not occur to him. If he was right about Ah Yang's motives, then each of them had the same malevolent intention toward the other. Perhaps, if weighed on some cynical moral scale, Ah Yang's cause was more justified, given that the white man had caused the death of six of his countrymen and was intending to steal an entire community's collective wealth. But after their several years of scrabbling for gold, the topic of morality would not have entered into either of their calculations. The only question was which one of them would act first and what the outcome would be.

The man's newfound fear determined his course of action. *It must happen in the next few miles. Before the calm waters.*

It was as if the river heard and conspired with him. A row of jagged rocks appeared about fifty yards ahead on the right, well apart from his intended course. But he dragged one oar briefly, so that the bow of the boat scraped the rocks as it slipped by. There was a significant jolt and a very satisfying loud sound. Ah Yang was startled and gripped both sides of the boat, looking around wildly.

It helped the man's cause that they were approaching an obvious set of rapids, with quite apparent white water and visible rocks that appeared to be much more threatening than they actually were. There was an easily navigated channel through this particular stretch of white water, but Ah Yang did not know that.

The man tried to sound afraid and uncertain. He stood tall, straining to see ahead of the boat, holding the oars out of the water.

"Rocks! Very dangerous in this section! You must watch for them! Warn me so that I can steer around them!" He gestured excitedly, pointing first to his eyes with two fingers and then downstream. "Watch for rocks!"

His simulated fear worked. Ah Yang turned around and stood up in the bow, facing forward with both hands braced on the sides of the boat. He stood as tall as he could and peered downstream at the oncoming white water.

The man, still standing, braced his hip against the nearest crate, raised the right-hand oar out of its oarlock and swung it behind him in a huge arc. Then he pivoted and swung it around his body as hard as he could, concentrating to keep the blade of the oar accelerating, parallel to the water and at the right height. It was like swinging a scythe with a ten-foot long handle. The noise of the iron-edged blade cutting through the air was masked by the sound of the approaching rapids.

Ah Yang was raising his arm to point downriver when the oar's blade struck him in the side of his head. He was slammed into the side of the boat, half over the edge, but then slid down into the bottom of the boat like an empty suit of clothes slipping off of its hanger.

The man beached the boat on a mud bank about five miles downstream and just before the first outbuildings of one of the shantytowns that had sprung up along the river to serve the swarms of miners that had come. A rock wall was being built along the bank about ten feet back from the high-water mark and the builders had conveniently placed piles of stones along its intended track. The man added another two yards to their incomplete wall, four feet of rocks on top of Ah Yang's shallow grave.

He finished just as the first rays of the rising sun touched on the river. He considered that a good omen.

An Urban Crime Scene
San Francisco (2015)

The underground garage at the Civic Center Plaza in the middle of San Francisco never failed to depress Martin Kline. The phrase 'dark and dank' popped into his mind every time. It seemed to him a gigantic grey concrete bunker that had its own special quality of light; a uniform murkiness punctuated by strobes of light where daylight penetrated through the ramp openings and the occasional encrusted skylight. Somehow, it made all the parked cars seem unwashed and even sinister. The atmosphere was unpleasantly moist, in part because of the shallow puddles that seemed a permanent feature even in drought years. It didn't help that the stairwells served as public bathrooms for the hundreds of homeless that roamed the aboveground plaza on any given day.

As was usual at eleven on a weekday morning, the garage was full. He was sitting in his idling SUV near the end of one of the long ranks of cars, waiting hopefully for a spot to open up. His present hopes were pinned on the tall woman who had just entered his level by walking down the far entry ramp. She was reaching into a large shoulder bag and clearly rummaging around for car keys.

I guess she missed the big red letters that say "No Pedestrians on Ramp." Or, more likely, she has an unaccompanied woman's healthy paranoia about using stairwells in underground parking facilities.

Watching her, Martin realized that he'd seen her before. Just yesterday. She'd been one of the so-called stakeholders in the Mayor's public hearing on the Brookings House. She was easy to remember because she stood out in that group, at first because she was quite good looking, and then because she had been the single most aggressive questioner of the entire lot.

Reminded me of a crusading journalist on a mission for truth and justice.

From fifty yards away, he had a clear view of the unfolding felony. The woman was walking slowly with her head down, clearly focused on sorting through an assortment of irrelevant objects in her purse to find the keys. The man stepped out in front of her from between two cars. From Martin's vantage point, he was just a shape in dark clothing. The woman stopped and then sidestepped to go around him, but the man swung at her, a wild roundhouse right hand. As her head snapped back from the blow, he grabbed the strap of her shoulder bag and yanked it away, sending her spinning hard into the side of a parked van. He turned and ran directly at Martin, clearly focused on the exit doorway immediately behind him.

The next few seconds were a blur, and it wasn't until an hour or so later that Martin could place all of the separate sounds and sights into a coherent reproduction of what actually happened. The man was running head on at Martin, the awkward sprint of someone not accustomed to running. He was small, probably white, clean-shaven; wearing sunglasses and a dark sweatshirt with a floppy hood and some kind of stocking cap. Everything about his appearance screamed "homeless purse snatcher."

He heard a shout from the woman. "You son of a bitch! That's my bag!"

And she's chasing him!

Much later, Martin would recognize that the very absurdity of her pursuit was the initial attraction; that the woman was either crazy or – at the very least – oblivious to her personal safety. But, in the moment, all he could do was to watch her try to run while simultaneously trying to take off her high-heeled shoes!

The end was as quick as it was impromptu. The man was in a dead run as he approached Martin's car, looking back over his shoulder at the crazy woman hopping on one foot and screaming at him. Martin timed it perfectly, pushing his driver's door wide open in the man's path at the last second. The collision sent him sprawling and slammed the door back against Martin's shoulder. By the time he got the tire iron out from under his seat and was getting out of the car, the man was sprawled face first on the concrete and the woman was standing on his arm with both feet and prying her bag loose from his fist. The guy was groggy but not out. By the time Martin got within a few feet of them, he was kneeling and looking like he was going after the woman.

When Martin said, "Stay there" and showed him the tire iron, he shoved his hands into the pockets of his hoodie and stayed on one knee, his head drooping.

The woman was standing in her stocking feet with blood dripping from her nose onto an otherwise white blouse. She had a slightly dazed expression; not so surprising given the last twenty seconds. Her bag was back on her shoulder and she was fumbling around in it, maybe recalling that she was needing her car keys. Instead she came out with a cell phone and stood looking at it as if it would tell her what to do next.

Martin waited. *I wonder if Siri is programmed to deal with purse snatching?*

He said, "It won't work underground here. No reception. Trust me, I know."

She looked at him as if seeing him for the first time. Then she put her hand to her face and stared at the blood on her fingers with a puzzled expression.

Just a touch of shock, I think.

"He hit me."

"Yes he did. You may have a broken nose."

Then she surprised him again. "Is he OK?" She gestured at the man, now watching the two of them with what Martin thought was a very composed demeanor, given his situation.

"I think so. What do you want to do with him?"

She clearly thought about the question, long enough that the man stood up, still with his hands in his pockets. He was short and pudgy, middle aged at least, although the sunglasses made it hard to tell. *Definitely not your ideal purse snatcher profile.* Martin thought of Emilio, the kid from the Tenderloin who bragged about his one-hundred and eighty-seven snatches. *Shock and speed, man. Shock and speed.* They'd spent a few days together in a holding cell in Oakland. Emilio had it down to a science. If he hadn't tripped over his own shoelaces, he'd still be out there.

This guy should stick to sitting on Market Street with a cardboard sign reading "Please Help." But Martin kept a firm grip on the man's sweatshirt sleeve and tapped him on his shoulder with the tire iron to remind him of his status. But then the woman surprised both of them yet again.

"Let him go, I think."

He looked at her closely. Other than the bloody nose, she seemed fine.

When he didn't respond, she added, "He's got more problems than I do. And a lot fewer solutions. And I've still got my bag."

It was a series of declarative sentences, but he thought he could hear a very slight appeal in her voice, an acknowledgment that Martin had earned the right to have a vote.

She's probably right about that. At least that bit about whose got more problems. And I'm tempted to go along. But the guy punched her and slammed her into the car. He needs some down time to think about that. Who knows? Maybe he'll run into Emilio and get some professional coaching.

He realized that both the man and woman were watching him closely. Somehow, the three of them had become linked in some strange way.

Martin sounded apologetic. "I'd like to. Let him go. I really would, but –"

The word "but" caused the man to take a step back and take his right hand out of his pocket. It held a small but definite gun. *Probably a thirty-eight, maybe a Beretta. An expensive weapon. Not something that your average homeless guy carries around. But whatever it was, it sure as hell trumps my tire iron.*

The man kept the gun pointed vaguely in their direction. "Give me the bag. Then you two can continue to work out your issues about the underclass in San Francisco."

Not so homeless, I think. Something more substantial. The diction as much as the sarcasm startled Martin and made the man seem far more dangerous.

The woman put both hands on the strap to the bag. She seemed to be engaged in an internal debate about how to respond and Martin remembered the angry shout, "You son of a bitch! That's my bag!" and the ensuing chase scene.

She's actually weighing her options. Like she has a choice! Who the hell is this woman anyway?

He reached out and took the bag from her shoulder and handed it to the man. She looked at Martin accusingly, but didn't say anything and – thankfully – stood still.

The man took the bag and considered the two of them.

"I'm leaving. And I have this" – he showed them the gun – "and I don't want you to follow me." He walked rapidly away, into a nearby stairwell. They were left standing looking at one another.

Martin thought about following but quickly discarded the idea. *Well. That was interesting. And there's something I'm missing about the guy. Something's off.*

The woman walked back to pick up her shoes and returned to where Martin was standing. She handed him the cell phone that she was still carrying and put her hand on his shoulder to steady herself while she put her heels back on. To Martin, it struck him as an incredibly intimate act. When she stood erect again with her heels on, he realized that she was taller than he was.

"How about a cup of coffee?" he asked. "And some ice for that nose of yours?"

She grinned. "You'll have to buy. You seem to have given away my purse."

Coffee Shop Conversation

Paul Campos walked for three blocks before stopping to look behind him. Fast, but not fast enough to look like he was running away. He kept the hood up and hid the woman's bag under his sweatshirt, which also altered his profile.

Not that it matters. Those two won't be chasing me.

What a fuckup! I told him, goddammit! "Mannie, purse snatching is not my kind of thing. You can hire a kid off the street for twenty-five bucks and he's a lot better at it than I am."

"Don't want a kid off the street. Want you."

"Mannie –"

"She carries a laptop in her bag and I want it. And it's got to look like your everyday mugging. And you can rough her up for the sake of realism, but nothing serious. That's important to my client."

It should have been easy. Christ, a woman alone in an underground garage! Then the hero with a tire iron shows up. Good thing I brought the gun.

He stopped just before going underground at the rapid transit escalator and stood looking at his phone, thinking about what to tell Mannie. It didn't take him long to work it out.

He wanted the laptop and I've got it for him. He doesn't need to know all of the details.

The call rolled to voice mail, which suited him nicely. "All done. Piece of cake, but with some interesting twists. Got the laptop and I'll drop the bag where you said."

At the other end of the call, the person called Mannie listened to the incoming message, wondering about what the caller was leaving out.

Some interesting twists, he says. Shorthand for, 'I screwed it up, but you don't want to know the details!'

Part of Mannie's distaste was because he was looking forward to being done with what he thought of as 'this legbreaking shit,' his characterization of the line of business that had been his bread and butter vocation in his early days. The Green Fence Project – he always thought of it in capital letters – would make him respectable as well as rich, enabling him to leave the seedier parts of his operations to others. He had taken on the purse snatching only as a favor to his powerful patron.

A simple job. But a perceptive biographer might title it "the beginning of the end" for Mannie.

"My name is Martin Kline."

"I know who you are. I'm Natalie Weiss. And I know we've only known each other ten minutes. But given what happened during that time, I think we can use first names, don't you?"

They were in Philz Coffee Shop, a block from the Civic Center. They were probably the only two customers in the place to order plain black coffee. The barista smiled at them in a kindly way that made Martin feel improbably old and obsolete. That feeling was compounded when he noted that he and Weiss were also unique in that they were actually talking to one another rather than hunched over laptops or cell phones. Weiss had used paper towels to wipe the blood from her face and stop the slow bleed. She held a plastic glass filled with ice against the side of her nose.

"Is it broken, do you think?" She asked, without seeming to care very much about the answer.

"I don't think so. And I'm kind of an expert." He gestured at his own nose and looked at her head on, so that the very slight change in direction would be apparent to her. "It'll be swollen for a couple of days, though."

"Not a problem. I'm already marred for life." And she traced with her finger a faint two-inch-long scar on her cheekbone.

She asked, "Should we call the cops?"

He thought about it. "It's a little late for that, isn't it? Not much that we can tell them. And, frankly, purse snatching won't get a lot of their attention."

"Not even if he's flashing a gun?"

That same thought was bothering him. *He wanted it to look like your everyday smash and grab operation ... a target of opportunity, not a deliberate holdup of a designated person.*

The gun was a last resort. He wanted that purse ... didn't even bother to take my wallet or drive off in my fancy new SUV.

He ignored her question. "What was in that bag? He seemed kind of fixated on it."

She shrugged. "The usual hodge-podge of essential personal trash that women carry around these days. The thing I hate to lose is the laptop. It's a MacBook Air with my entire professional life on it."

"Backed up?"

"Oh, yeah! I may be a victim, but I'm not stupid."

"I'm sure you're not, but you did a really dumb thing down in that garage."

"Going after the guy, you mean?" She smiled in a way that told Martin that this was not the first time she'd been scolded for her rashness.

"There's an old joke about a dog who wouldn't stop chasing cars. What's he going to do if he actually catches one?"

"Pretty stupid, I admit. Pure instinct on my part." She was absentmindedly stroking the scar and Martin wondered if that was the result of an earlier surge of 'pure instinct.'

"A bad instinct, I'd say. And then you wanted to let him go. What was all that about him having more problems and fewer solutions?"

She leaned back and looked at him closely and – for the first time – he got the sense that she was thinking about how to respond, that this was the kind of question that required a serious answer and that its exact phrasing depended on her reading of her audience. He tried to look open-minded, but gave up since he really had no idea what open-minded people looked like.

"That was before he brought out the gun, and when I thought I was getting my bag back. I thought he was one of the homeless types looking for a few bucks. No harm, no foul, y'know?"

"He hit you. He shouldn't be on the streets. I'd call the cops but we can't give them much to work with. What do we say? 'He was a white guy with a dark sweatshirt?'"

"Well, I've got his picture."

"You took his picture?"

She held up her cellphone. On the screen was a dark snapshot of a dark figure, but the white face stood out nicely. Even then, given the sunglasses and hoodie, a positive ID would be tricky.

It was his turn to sit back and look, wondering again who this woman was and how she managed to continually surprise him.

Nothing like the direct approach.

"Who the hell are you, Ms. Natalie Weiss? You chase muggers, forgive them after you catch them, take their picture and don't seem to care very much about whether your nose is straight or not!"

She pulled a business card from some back pocket of her cell phone and slid it across the table at him. "I'm a consultant. Specialize in civic preservation and affordable housing. Deal with a lot of clients that probably aren't much different than the guy with the gun."

"Are you –"

"Oh. And the nose? It's already been broken once. But enough about me. What were *you* doing in that garage at this time of day and how come you're so eager to help damsels in distress? And where did you learn to improvise self-defense tactics using car doors and tire irons?"

"C'mon! I just –"

"And don't give me that 'aw, shucks' Jimmy Stewart kind of bullshit that you're about to trot out for me. I saw you when he pulled out the gun. No fear, not even surprise, just recalculating the odds. So, who are you, Martin Kline? Other than somebody who wants to buy a house for thirty million dollars?"

So she also remembers the Mayor's conference on the Brookings House.

He thought a bit about all of the different – and mostly truthful – answers he could use. In the end, he kept it simple. "Let's just say I've had a lot of experience with people like him. As to why I was in the garage, I have an appointment with a guy at City Hall."

He looked at his watch and winced. "That is, I *had* an appointment. Took me a long time to get it too. Guess I'll have to go to the end of the line and start over."

"Maybe I can help."

"I doubt that. This guy? My missed appointment? He doesn't take bribes, has tenure and gets mad at no-shows. Unless maybe you know the mayor?"

Natalie grinned. "Actually, I do. Know the mayor. She's a real bitch. But she's my mother, so maybe I can do you some good."

'She's my mother!?'

Martin called up images from yesterday's meeting. The older woman, a Chinese-American politician with a world-weary expression and the younger thoroughly Caucasian beauty sitting opposite him.

"The mayor's your mother?"

He tried to hide his incredulity, but his stammering betrayed him. "Uh … the Mayor doesn't …. Janet Li is … You're not … "

She waited, still grinning, perfectly willing to let him dig himself deeper. She was impressed when he stopped, laughed at himself and came right out with it.

"You're adopted."

Very good, but he doesn't get off quite that easily.

"What? You think that I'm adopted just because she and I are different races and I'm two feet taller than she is?"

"No. Because I remember the stories about Janet Li. The way she took in teenagers who were having difficulties. Eventually adopted four of them, as I recall."

"Three, actually. All girls. One white girl – that's me -- one black and one yellow … although Molly was more brownish than she was yellow. Every one of us oozing pathologies. The kind of kids you manage with a whip and a chair."

Something changed in Martin. It was if he had pulled a shade down over his eyes. The smile faded and at the same time he regarded Natalie with an intensity that made her start to fiddle with her coffee cup.

She asked, "What's the matter? You got something against orphans?"

The smile came back, but a very rueful one.

"Nope. I am one. But nobody adopted me."

It stopped her cold. What had started as playful bantering with emerging sexual undertones had just become deadly serious.

OK, Natalie. You spent two years in therapy dealing with this. Time to reassess. You met this guy in strange circumstances in an underground garage. He prevented you from doing something really stupid ... Maybe saved your life. Bought you a cup of coffee. Shared some personal tidbits. Ignited some promising early stage chemistry. Then he pulls that rabbit out of the hat.

He watched her, wondering what she was thinking.

"That's a great pickup line, isn't it?" he asked. "The orphan ploy?" Late at night, in a bar, near closing time."

"Have you tried it?" It was a serious question, and he knew it.

His response was instantaneous. "Nope. In fact, I think that's the first time I've ever used the line in my entire life. It's not something that I talk a lot about."

Sadness had settled on him like the shadow of a passing cloud. It made her want to change the subject, but she couldn't.

"I was lucky," she said, very softly.

"Strange line for an orphan," he said.

"I only spent six months in foster care. Then Janet came along. How about you?"

"Foster care? Better part of six years. All I could take. Life on the street was a better alternative, and I took it."

He shook himself, literally. When he spoke again, Natalie knew that the topic was closed. She was also sure that they would come back to it.

He looked at her closely. "You called her a bitch."

"Huh?"

"We were talking about the Mayor. You said – and I quote – 'she's a real bitch.'"

Natalie laughed, relieved to be back on safe ground. "It's a term of affection between her and I. And if you're a politician in San Francisco, it's probably a compliment."

He pushed his chair back. "Can I lend you money or drop you somewhere, given your purseless condition?"

"City Hall is around the corner. I'll borrow some cash from Mummy. And, while I'm at it, I'd be glad to lobby for a meeting on your behalf. Who is it that you're trying to get some face time with?"

"Thanks. I can use the help. His name is Edward Albans. He's the head of –"

He stopped when he saw her quick reaction to the name, a sudden flash of suspicion. "Oops! Never mind. I can –"

She shook her head. "It's funny. Your man Alban? It's him that I was visiting this morning. Just before that little drama in the parking garage."

"That's a bit of a coincidence, isn't it?"

She nodded. "It seems to be a morning for coincidences."

She's right about that. Yesterday, I didn't know this woman. Today, we seem to have a lot in common. Including broken noses and a soft spot for felons.

His next question surprised her. "What were you trying to see him about? This Albans guy?"

"It's Alban, without the s. As you know, assuming you were listening yesterday at City Hall, I'm pushing the city to give us the Russian Hill property for our Affordable Housing Coalition. The one you want to buy. Alban is opposing the idea and I wanted to lobby him just a bit. Why?"

He stood up with an amused expression. "It seems we are in competition with one another for the hearts and minds of city officials. You were at the hearing yesterday, so you know that I'm trying to buy the same property from the city for my personal residence. I was hoping to talk Mr. Alban into supporting the idea. But your having the Mayor as your mother seems to give you an unfair edge."

Even while talking, he was recalling the image of her at the microphone with her list of questions, one for each of the hapless city staffers sitting meekly at the side of the room. He remembered feeling a twinge of sympathy for them as they tried – unsuccessfully -- to appear responsive to her relentless interrogation.

She chases muggers and terrorizes city officials. Who is this woman, anyway?

A Public Hearing

It was only yesterday and easy for Martin to recreate the image of Natalie Weiss at the microphone. He remembered his relief when her questions were directed at others rather than him. *One of those rare things ... feeling good about being ignored by a really good looking woman!*

Martin Kline's prior experiences with city government had been with its judicial arm and he had always been cast as its designated target, so he went to the 'Brookings House Forum' reluctantly and with low expectations. He would have been intrigued to know that the presiding officer – the Mayor of San Francisco – shared those same emotions.

As she looked out over the room from the small raised dais at the front of the space, Mayor Janet Li thought, *I've complied with the letter of the law, but pretty well violated the spirit.*

Given that it was a legal document, Stephanie Green's Last Will and Testament was a model of clarity. It clearly set out three conditions concerning the disposition of the Brookings House. First, the property was to be used 'for the benefit of the City of San Francisco.' Second, the decision as to the final use or disposition of the property was reserved 'to the Mayor, without restriction.' Third, the Mayor was 'required to convene a public hearing to entertain proposals for the use of the property and to give due consideration to all alternatives.'

The meeting taking place in the large conference room at City Hall was designed to serve as minimal compliance with that third condition. She'd scheduled the meeting for eight AM on a Monday morning, the absolute least favorite time for meetings in the heart of the city. She had published a very limited agenda with a tight schedule and made sure to seed the crowd with individuals that were bound to disagree. She'd required written proposals in advance.

She'd even planned the physical setting to suit her purposes. She sat alone at a small table at the front of the room, facing the tall windows looking out on Civic Center Plaza. Directly in front of her, three individuals – the official 'petitioners' -- sat at a long table, facing her, with a single tabletop microphone in front of them. Along one side of the room, in a single row of uncomfortable straight chairs, she had arrayed staff members from each of the city departments that had any connection whatsoever with her pending decision. They were window dressing, and they knew it.

They'll sit quietly, partly because I told them to, but really because they know that they can walk into my office and lobby for their pet projects without being subject to public scrutiny.

The symmetry was maintained by a similar row of individuals arrayed on the wall opposite to the city representatives. That group was made up of what her aides liked to call 'stakeholders,' individuals representing wildly varying views of government and its roles. Li could identify representatives from the neighborhood association, taxpayer's union, homeless coalition, affordable housing mandate, PTA, Safe Streets for Our Children, the Historical Society and three low-level staffers from the Board of Supervisors. The Audubon Society was even on hand, for reasons she could not imagine. Beyond those she knew, there were another dozen or so individuals.

Probably realtors. Their 5% commissions on a deal like this would be more than I paid to buy my first house!

However, she could not control everything and despite what she hoped for, there were two reporters near the door. But, thankfully, there were no TV cameras. She had learned long ago that the cameras brought out the worst in people, particularly if their jobs were dependent on public opinion.

The other bothersome factor was the presence of Natalie, her daughter, staked out in the chair nearest the freestanding microphone in the middle of the room.

The whole bloody circus. Democracy at its best ... and worst. And all you have to do is listen and seem attentive. You've done this a thousand times. Thank God for that second clause in Green's will. Ninety minutes from now, you can start thinking about what you want to do and all this noise will be just that – noise.

At precisely eight AM, she banged the gavel on the bare table in front of her.

"The meeting is called to order. Our only agenda item is the Brookings House utilization issue. Thank you all for coming. First, I want to acknowledge the City's enormous gratitude to the late Stephanie Green for her generous and civic-minded gift. Second, I would like to remind everybody that it is my intention to adhere strictly to the agenda. Our first presenter is Mr. Kenney."

The mousy-looking man at the center table looked startled, but pulled the microphone into position in front of him and opened a shiny leather folio that contained a single sheet of paper. He was a mid-level accountant in the Department of Finance, as comfortable with columns of numbers as he was uncomfortable with the notion of public speaking. The Mayor had selected him for that reason and given him a strict admonition.

Just the script. No adlibbing, speculation, lobbying or working of agendas.

"Your Honor. The Department of Finance has submitted a formal written proposal, which you have before you, and I shall not take time in this setting to go over the various points and recommendations. In summary, we believe that 'the highest and best use' clause in the City Charter and the citizens of San Francisco will be best served by retaining the Brookings House under City ownership, either for direct use by relevant city-sponsored programs or as an administrative facility for City offices with a neighborhood focus. Thank you."

A masterpiece of bureaucratic obfuscation. Seemingly responsive while leaving all of the original options open.

"Thank you for your brevity, Mr. Kenney. I hope our other presenters can do likewise. Ms. Garcia, I believe you're next."

No doubt she'll be brief. The people she's representing want as little time in the public eye as possible. I suppose the New Yorkers think they're being clever in sending someone like her, a woman, a Latina who looks like – and maybe is, in fact – a lesbian.

Suddenly and to her surprise, Janet Li felt a surge of sympathy for the woman, remembering all of the times she had been used as a token by white males needing to seem sensitive to gender, race or unpopular points of view. *And in my case, they got all three at the same time… an affirmative action trifecta!*

Garcia didn't look much like the kind of person that would care very much about what some other person thought of them. She was a stocky woman with short hair, wearing a severely cut, black pinstripe suit and an impatient expression. She pushed the microphone away and stood up to speak. Her voice carried quite clearly throughout the room.

"Thank you, Mayor Li. Like Mr. Kenney, I shall not spend my time repeating what is set out in our formal proposal. I am an associate in the New York law firm of O'Malley and Simpson. We have submitted to you a formal all-cash purchase offer on behalf of a fully qualified buyer to purchase the Brookings House for thirty million dollars and to fully comply with all city and neighborhood codes. Our client wishes to remain anonymous, but – as set out in the written proposal – we believe that your constituents will derive far more benefit from thirty million dollars properly reinvested in public services than from Mr. Kenney's 'retention' program. Thank you."

A low buzz of conversation began as soon as she sat down, and the Mayor allowed it to run on for thirty seconds without interrupting. *Even in San Francisco, the sale of a single family residence for thirty million dollars deserves some time for wonderment to be expressed. Even without knowing that the anonymous buyer has said that, if there are competing buyers – which there are -- their 'fully qualified" and highly anonymous buyer will offer a million dollars more than any other bona fide offer.*

The thought of where those millions were likely coming from made her unexpectedly angry, and she rapped the gavel more sharply than she intended, twice. "Thank you, Ms. Garcia. Our third presenter is Martin Kline. Mr. Kline, you have the floor."

Hearing the name 'Martin Kline' stopped the background noise far more effectively than Li's gavel. Virtually everyone in the room focused intently on the man sitting in the middle seat at the table. Janet Li could almost *feel* the change in the room, as if curiosity took on a physical force.

So this is our famous – no, infamous – billionaire. The one who hangs out with parolees and ex-cons. Mayo's project.

Kline looked like your standard issue tech executive, the sort that seemed so pervasive on the City's streets the last couple of years. All he lacked was the three or four day growth of facial hair. Youngish, probably late thirties. Dark, short curly hair, unruly and in need of a trim. About six feet tall, lean with good shoulders, a body type for a swimmer or rock climber. He was wearing a black turtleneck, blue jeans and a sport jacket. When he leaned forward to speak into the microphone, he placed both hands palm down on the tabletop and Janet was disproportionately pleased to see that he was wearing what looked like a quite plain watch with a leather band, clearly not a Rolex.

"Mayor Li. I am representing myself. I want to buy the Brookings House because I need a place to live and I like the Russian Hill neighborhood. You have the terms of my offer in my proposal in front of you. Thank you."

When he sat down, Li could sense the disappointment among the onlookers. *They wanted more. Hell! So did I. It was like we invited Warren Buffett for dinner and all he said was 'Buy low, sell high.'*

She also could feel another mood shift in the group of stakeholders as they realized, along with her, that the three speakers had taken less than five minutes and that the remainder of the time was theirs. Several of them were edging forward on their chairs, clutching index cards with their 'talking points.'

Great planning, Janet! You've provided a ninety minute forum for thirty people who think they can do your job better than you, and you have to listen politely.

Two more raps with the gavel. "The floor is open for questions. Please speak using the standing microphone in the center of the room and direct your questions either to one of our three presenters or to me. And please be mindful of the time limits. We have a number of individuals who wish to speak."

She sat back and closed her eyes briefly, slipping into what she thought of as her 'Yoda mode,' the semblance of absolute calmness in the face of provocation. When she opened them, she was pleased to see the two reporters leaving the room, knowing there would be zero news value in the Q&A segment. But that momentary satisfaction was quickly offset by the sight of otherwise dignified citizens scrambling to be first in line at the microphone. To her chagrin, she watched one particularly aggressive woman – who happened to be her adopted daughter – elbow her way past a septuagenarian birdwatcher to be at the head of the line.

Christ, Natalie! It's just a house! No need to flatten little old ladies!

The House

But it wasn't *just a house.*

It even had a name – 'The Brookings House' – apparently merited by its age, size and having been lived in by four generations of Brookings. Even more of its cachet arose because of the house's rebirth after the 1906 earthquake and fire. One could view it as a metaphor for the resilience that is always invoked after disasters, even as the dazed survivors are stumbling out of the rubble. And it helped that Russian Hill had become one of the 'in' places to live in San Francisco, a thoroughly gentrified cross section of the city's middle and upper classes, the kind of neighborhood that valued its past as yet another proof of its present superiority.

It was over eighteen thousand square feet of floor space, with a dozen bedrooms, a ballroom and dedicated rooms for a library, billiards and media. On the other hand, it had no yard and was engaged in a constant battle with mice and termites. Like many of the city's famous dowagers, the house was probably at its pinnacle. The question was no longer "How can this be made better?" but rather "How can we preserve this in its present state?" The city passed quasi-ordinances, declaring it to be 'of historical interest,' thereby ensuring that some Hollywood enfant terrible or a recent beneficiary of a high-tech IPO would be precluded from seeing a 'teardown' or even doing a significant remodel. These days, it would be difficult to even paint the exterior some color other than pastel without the approval of an army of bureaucrats.

It stood on top of one of San Francisco's seven prominent hills, taking up half a block in two directions and occupying some of the most prized frontage in the Western world. Being on a corner lot on one of the high points in the city, it had magnificent views, particularly to the north and east. The northern-facing side was particularly spectacular, with tiny Alcatraz Island strangely prominent, perhaps because of the grim sand-colored concrete structures that seemed almost a continuation of the rock formation.

It was the kind of residence that a strolling tourist expects to encounter in a city such as San Francisco. At first glance, that tourist might guess it to be an embassy or consulate of some minor country, or a boutique hotel catering to rich foreigners, or a museum dedicated to some obscure form of art. Pedestrians tended to look closely and in vain for a discreet bronze plaque alongside the ten-foot-high entrance doors that would provide a clue about the inhabitants.

The house was commissioned by the youngish widow of Hiram Brookings in 1906 and four generations of the family had lived there until 1995. Donald Brookings, the last descendant of Hiram to own and reside in the house, was a real estate developer who was politically connected and frequently pictured on the society pages of the Chronicle. He liked to describe himself as the great grandson of one of the Gold Rush era pioneers who helped to create the modern San Francisco. In June, 1995, he was found savagely beaten and shot to death in his home. The police called it a 'home invasion robbery scene,' but there were rumors that a grand jury was considering an indictment at the time of his death for various frauds and the press was cautiously hinting of gangland involvement.

Donald's widow listed the house for sale within a week of when the police were done with it. Notwithstanding the bad publicity that went with murdered tenants, the house sold almost immediately. It helped that San Francisco was in one of its crazy upward real estate spirals. Homes were sold for all cash, no contingencies and usually well over the asking price.

It also helped that the new owners of the house were prone to impulse, a trait common to the newly rich. Moira Malloy had inherited an unexpectedly large amount of money from her parents and she and her husband bought the house and moved in thinking that this would be their residence for life. At first, it seemed a reasonable decision. John and Moira Malloy were at least as respectable as any of their neighbors. John was a Professor of Religion at the University of San Francisco, a man who not only taught but lived by a strong Jesuit code. Moira was a social worker with the City and

County of San Francisco, working almost entirely with 'at risk' kids. They were white, native San Franciscans, highly cultured with excellent educations and liberal biases. On those dimensions, they fitted into the neighborhood.

However, the realities of living in such a place very quickly taught them they'd made a mistake. For them, it was absurd that the annual upkeep of the house – taxes, utilities, maintenance – was almost the exact equivalent of their combined salaries.

"The house is bankrupting us," said John. This was a gross exaggeration, as Moira's inheritance amounted to enough to sustain even extravagant life styles and the homes to go with them.

The more important reality was that they simply weren't the kind of people who sought status or defined themselves by where they lived and how much money they had. They were fundamentally uncomfortable with the trappings of wealth, not the kind of people to live in such a house. And their neighbors would have agreed.

"It's just not us," Moira said. The expanded version of that short characterization involved their shared feeling that it was morally wrong for two people to have such an abundance of space in a time and place where others were sleeping in garages, doorways and public shelters.

The cure was an obvious one. They began interviewing real estate brokers with the intention of selling the house. More importantly, they began the planning of what they called 'the next phase.' They talked of 'going off the grid' and began exploring ashrams in India, trekking in Bhutan and sheep ranching in New Zealand.

They also found a way to ease their conscience about the social inequities all around them. They became an informal drop-in center for the kind of at-risk kids that Moira encountered throughout her workday. Such kids were plentiful in San Francisco. Some were local, from the usual sources – broken homes, juvenile courts or merely extreme poverty. However, others came from other parts of the country, runaways who were drawn to the city of free love, with its legendary Haight-Asbury neighborhood and longsuffering tolerance for the homeless.

However, given the Russian Hill address, isolated from the slums or even the Tenderloin, and the informal nature of their sanctuary, there were relatively few kids hanging out at any given moment. Presently, there were three.

But that was three too many for the neighbors.

Back in the Midwest, a neighbor would have knocked on the door and begun an awkward conversation by saying something like "Some of us wanted to share our concerns ..." However, this being Russian Hill and San Franciscans being San Franciscans, the Malloys received a quite-formal letter from a lawyer enclosing a petition signed by seven other families on the block and a one page excerpt from the city ordinance governing zoning and the occupancy of single family residences.

It was if the letter triggered their disappearance. Two weeks went by before anyone approached the house. Then it was the police, who found the front door unlocked and the house unoccupied. They'd been approached by coworkers of Moira's and John's who became concerned when neither of them showed up for work and attempts to contact them by phone or through other friends didn't work.

The last person to talk to them before they left was their lawyer. He said, "It was ten days ago. They came in saying some very unkind things about their neighbors. I believe they used the word 'fascist' quite a lot. When they calmed down a bit, we signed some papers giving me the power of attorney to act as their financial agent. They told me to settle the contract issues, sell the damn house – their words, not mine -- and give the proceeds to St. Ignatius. Since he's been dead for about four hundred years, I assumed they meant the Society of Jesus."

Among their friends, the consensus was that they had launched their "off the grid" experiment and gone off on their extended round-the-world trip. This was reinforced by the fact that they left all of their credit cards, driver's licenses and checkbooks scattered on the massive dining room table along with dozens of colorful brochures promising 'carefree adventure travel.' Their passports weren't there.

The TV and newspaper media made it a story for a few days, pushing a 'Local Couple Disappears' kind of theme, with the added teaser that they had been sheltering kids with questionable backgrounds. Cops made some phone calls, checked airlines and other standard things. They got some vague descriptions of the three kids, but nothing that enabled them to locate any of them.

It became a non-story. Neither of the missing individuals had any apparent family and the only traces of concern after a week or so was on the part of the realtor community, who sought ways to spin the facts so that the house's history stayed positive. After all, their commissions were at risk.

The Russian Hill house sat vacant for several years after the Malloy's disappeared, tied up in courts while questions of its title, historical significance and – a new buzzword – its 'environmental footprint' were fought over by a mélange of claimants who saw the house as symbolic of something other than as a place to live and raise children.

It was finally sold in 2005 to a couple that actually liked the notoriety that went with ownership of a 'historic' house that was reputed to be 'unlucky' or even haunted. In many ways, the new owners, John and Katherine Green, were like Hiram Brookings and his new young wife, reincarnated a century later. They needed a house to accentuate their status; a residence with enough history and gravitas to overcome the unpleasant reality that they were from Texas and their wealth from oil wells. For them, the search was simple: they simply bought the highest-price house that was on the market, viewing it as a stepping-stone for their social aspirations.

Katherine Green was a natural snob, but she was born in the wrong century and country. In a different time and place, say in England a hundred years ago, she would have been automatically enrolled in the aristocracy by virtue of her being the daughter of Lord somebody-or-other or the wife of the Duke of something. But in the twenty-first century and in

San Francisco, she was merely a second-tier socialite; the kind of person that is on the board of the opera or symphony because her husband is rich. Unfortunately for her, the source of the wealth was not "old money," arising as it did from investing in an asset class that the A-list socialites neither understood nor valued. Even worse, the husband was now gone, having dumped Katherine for a much younger, prettier and far more congenial woman. He left Katherine with the house, several million dollars in securities, and fifty thousand dollars a month in spousal support.

She made do. Partly by enforcing a degree of magical thinking that your everyday underachieving pot-smoking teenager would have admired, and partly by the far more practical strategy of making ever-larger donations to the right causes. As a salve to the short-run pain of rejection, she decided to do what many newly divorced women do. She would remodel and redecorate the house, thereby furthering two objectives. First, since the house was already notable in San Francisco history, the redo would attract lots of attention from exactly the kinds of people she wished to impress. Second, it would enable her to expunge the last traces of the husband that had dumped her.

Aside from the pettiness of her motives, it was a good plan. The house was old and needed some attention. But her plan quickly ran afoul of city government.

"It's classified as 'of historical interest,'" was the first hitch. That led to months of delay and enormous expense while plans, drawings and environmental reports were commissioned, submitted, reviewed, modified and resubmitted. Katherine left the details to the lawyers, realtors, architects and engineers, but still was both infuriated and daunted by the expense and delay. In her mind, it confirmed her second-class standing in society.

The City Planning Department ruled on the remodel plan, requiring an earthquake retrofit of the house "upon the next transfer of ownership or significant structural work." The ruling particularly noted that, according to the original drawings, the house sat on a steep hillside and was not anchored to its foundation. The ruling meant that Katherine's sale or remodel would require significant work on the foundation and add millions of dollars of cost. An independent consultant hired by the city estimated the cost of such a retrofit to be "somewhere between three and fifteen million dollars, depending on findings from core samples."

As recently as ten or fifteen years ago, such bureaucratic rulings would be of purely local interest, invisible to the rest of the world. Now, with the internet and a growing third-world appetite for trophy properties, the Brookings House was a pawn in a global capital market.

At first, Green was sorely tempted to sell when the New York lawyer called to make an unsolicited and totally unexpected purchase offer. She did not know it, but the offer was timed to coincide with Katherine's point of maximum frustration. It was well above any reasonable estimate of its market value, a 'take it or leave it' cash deal with no contingencies. The buyer had a name – the Petrel Foundation – but operated in a highly anonymous fashion, working through a large New York law firm. Realtors and others assumed that it was a Chinese or Russian oligarch needing a financial safe haven, working through a shell company.

Katherine was tempted but said "no." She didn't need the money and knew quite well that her social mobility would go only one direction – down – if she sold to an anonymous foreign buyer, particularly if that buyer turned out to be Chinese or Russian.

It was as if her decision not to sell triggered a sequence of carefully choreographed events. Certainly a conspiracy theorist, a novelist or even a historian would be intrigued by the degree of "coincidence" inherent in what happened in the ensuing month. After all, San Francisco is in many ways a small town with a fixed amount of real estate, and there are close ties between politicians and certain important citizens.

At about the same time that she turned down the offer, Katherine was asked to have lunch with three other women. Each of the women was in her eighties and each had a surname that was featured prominently in California history books. They were everything Katherine aspired to be, other than old.

The day after the lunch, Katherine met with her attorney and revised her will. Upon her death, the house would be given to the City of San Francisco "for use or disposition as the Mayor sees fit, subject to maintaining the character and historical integrity of the Russian Hill neighborhood." The society page of the Chronicle featured a long article in its Sunday edition with numerous photos of both Katherine and her house.

She was pleased. Her social calendar quickly filled up with the kind of names that she valued and she was basking in the limelight that automatically accrues to someone who has just given away approximately twenty or thirty million dollars.

"That will is the best thing I've ever done," she confided to her lawyer.

She could not have known that 'that will' was also her death warrant.

She was not alone in her ignorance. There were others who failed to understand that the house was not 'just a house;' that it harbored secrets that could not be contained and, in their unraveling, lives would be irrevocably altered.

The Cop

Thirty-three days. But who's counting?

Mayo Marsh was retiring from the SFPD on his sixtieth birthday, thirty-three years after graduating from the academy and putting on the badge. But in his mind, he was already out the door. And the prospect scared him to death.

He was one of the most senior Detective Lieutenants on the force and probably had more experience across the spectrum of policing than any past or present officer in the Department. The last few years had been in a unit called "General Investigative Unit #2", which was responsible for a grab bag of major crimes – homicide, arson, terrorism, hate crimes, auto and others.

When he hit the sixty-day mark, the Deputy Chief told Mayo, "Go home. You've got enough accumulated vacation and I'm not going to assign any of the new stuff to a short timer like you. If anyone asks, I'll tell them I've got you working out-of-town. Go home and start practicing to be a civilian."

But he couldn't do it. At first, he tried to fool himself that he was staying in the office because 'he was on the payroll' and going home would be a kind of fraud. But the three decades of being a cop would not allow that kind of self-serving excuse to stand. *Face it. You don't want to go home because you don't know how to do anything else except to be a cop.* He still had not confronted the real question: *So what are you going to do with yourself thirty-three days from now?*

So he hid from the Deputy Chief, conning Hector Ramirez, the head of Homicide, to give him a desk in a vacant office. Hector didn't like the fact that he was retiring with unsolved cases and used him as an errand boy, a handy lame duck body that could be sent out for the odd job; the kind of police work that requires neither judgment nor risk. Mayo figured that it was his way of getting even with him for not taking the sixty-day offer. *Or a way to make the point that I'm a cop who doesn't know how to be anything else.*

He'd spent the last couple of days going over open case files, sorting them into two piles, what he thought of as "toss" or "pass on to the next poor sap." When he came across the tattered cardboard box labeled "Mission Street Murders, 1995," he stopped, as he always did, and allowed the anger to rise and then recede slowly, seeing the images that remained as sharp and accusative as they were twenty years ago.

The killing spree did not get the initial press coverage that ordinarily would have been its due. In that part of 1995, the news media were sufficiently preoccupied with Bosnia, the OJ Simpson trial, and the bombing of the federal office building in Oklahoma that a few West Coast murders did not get much attention. But it had nevertheless been a bad week for a city that thrives on its tourist trade. Four murders were not a record, but it's not a statistic that the Chamber of Commerce likes to see in the news. In a way, they were lucky.

The first murder was on a Sunday. Wanda Whimsy -- her street name -- was a black prostitute, slashed to death in the Tenderloin by a schizophrenic customer who faithfully did what his voices told him to do. It was not an 'interesting' murder for the police and press, merely a sad and even predictable end to a sad life. The killer was quickly apprehended and confessed.

The trio of killings that eventually became "the Mission Murders" began on Tuesday of that week. The first of them started out as an unremarkable event, especially because the police did not disclose the details of the brutality that had been practiced on the body. The story of the murder got two inches below the fold on page four of the Chronicle, alongside the story about President George Bush's dislike for broccoli.

It was, however, a major occasion for Mayo Marsh: his last major crime scene while working as a street cop and the one that motivated his transfer into the Homicide Division. The body was in a dumpster down an alley off of Mission Street and he was the first cop on the scene, pulled along by a wino who'd been dumpster-diving and come across the unrecognizable mess of blood and gore. Mayo played a minor part in the initial investigation, mostly doing crowd control around the scene and then some fruitless interviewing of neighbors who were totally unaware of what had happened. But he would never forget the horror or the flood of anger that transfused him when he first looked over the rim of the metal box.

He's a kid! And I know him! And this was my beat! I will find and kill the bastard that did this! He did not know it then, but that vow would be with him for the next twenty years, unfulfilled but never forgotten.

The second murder in the series was two days later and it loosed all of the pent-up irrationality and fear that lies so close to the surface in a city with so many diverse people in too small a space. The impact was greatly magnified when it became clear that the two murders were linked.

The similarities were striking. Both victims were young men, eighteen and nineteen respectively, from solidly middle class families and without any history of criminality or gang involvement. They lived about three blocks apart in the Mission District and had been friends with one another, from Kindergarten through their graduation from Mission High School.

They died in the same ugly way, their throats slashed from behind in a rat-infested alley late at night. Then came another twenty or thirty stab wounds, most of them after they were already dead. The largest share of the wounds was around the genitalia and the face. To the police and the press, it looked like the act of an enraged psychopath, one with some form of sexual dysfunction.

Theories were plentiful, particularly in the press and on the street. The victims were close friends and even looked somewhat alike. Both were white, young, blond, blue-eyed, and athletic. Neighborhood gossip and tabloids quickly popularized the idea that some unspecified 'non-white' cult was targeting Aryan youth. That theory faded when it was disclosed that the two boys were avid players – 'Dungeon Masters' -- in the Dungeons & Dragons game. So a different set of crazies argued that the murders were some kind of deranged extension of the game. The SFPD 'tip line' was overwhelmed.

As for the Homicide veterans working the case, they were convinced that the motive for the killings had something to do with the boys' common activities; that they had done something to somebody that decided to get even in a lethal fashion. Mayo and a lot of his colleagues spent sixteen hours a day tracking down leads, canvassing the neighborhood and interviewing everyone that knew the kids. It was a dead end. No motive, no witnesses, no reason for them to be in alleys late at night, no enemies. Nothing.

The third murder in the series did put San Francisco briefly on the front page of most of the major newspapers in the country. It came four days after the first murder and both the victim and crime details were eerily similar to the earlier two murders. The only differences were that the victim was a seventeen-year-old Chinese-American and that he died defending himself. He had defensive cuts on his hands and arms and was clutching a piece of fabric, presumably torn from his attacker's clothing. Perhaps that is why his body was mutilated even more savagely than those of his two childhood friends.

The other difference was that, this time, there was a witness. Ironically, it was the same wino that had discovered the first body.

He was drunk but unshakeable. "It was a woman that he went in that alley with. A woman in a bright yellow dress."

The fragment of fabric that was clutched in the dead boy's grip at first seemed promising, but other than noting that it was yellow silk of an unusual weave and probably from the sleeve of a woman's dress, the police laboratory could offer little tangible support.

He did not know it at the time, but that scrap of fabric would make Mayo famous within the SFPD, for sheer doggedness. He spent twelve days walking the streets and knocking on doors, showing the piece of fabric to women, dry cleaners, tailors and retail dress shops; always asking "Have you seen a dress with this kind of material?" It was the most basic form of police work imaginable. No spectroscopes, DNA tests, or carbon dating; just slogging from door to door.

And he found it. Not the dress, but its owner. She was the most unlikely looking serial killer he could imagine. Her name was Abigail and she lived by herself in an assisted living complex in the lower Mission District. She was eighty-four years old and confined to a wheelchair. Mayo had been directed to her by a woman who volunteered in the serving line at Saint Anthony's.

"I once had a dress made out of that material. It's raw silk, you know."

"Do you have it now?" Mayo asked, halfway dreading that she would say, "Yes."

"No. I finally had to admit that it was hopelessly out-of-date. Florence said that I looked like a Victorian old maid. I put it with several other dresses and left it outside the door of the Salvation Army resale shop. In a big plastic bag."

"When did you do that?"

"On June 30th. I go through all my clothes and throw away what I don't want. Every year on the thirtieth of June."

She gave Mayo a year-old picture of her wearing the dress. He did not tell her, but he thought Florence was right: it did make her look like a colorized version of something from an earlier century.

A white-haired octogenarian at the Salvation Army confirmed that such bags were picked up each morning and the contents dutifully logged in, with a brief description of each item. He and Mayo went over the records for two or three days on either side of June 30 and found an entry for "a bright yellow, semi-formal woman's dress," but that was the end of the trail.

"We're looking for a woman that gets her wardrobe from the Salvation Army," Mayo told the Lieutenant that was in charge of the investigation.

After that, it was open season on the 'bag lady' population of the city. They pulled in and questioned most of San Francisco's female homeless population, particularly those that frequented the Mission District. It drove the detectives nuts and got exactly nowhere.

Eventually, the fear died down and the press lost interest. The Mission Murders remained unsolved. But Mayo didn't forget.

A Series of Related Events

The California drought had gone on long enough that meteorologists began to talk about historical records. By 2015, it served as evidence for scientists and politicians who were just beginning to appreciate the impact of climate change. At a more practical level, it caused Central Valley farmers to reduce their acreage or seek new crops. Sinkholes appeared and some fields sank by several feet as wells drained the underground aquifers. Mandatory rationing was imposed and the citizens of San Francisco, Los Angeles and Palm Springs took shorter showers and their golf courses developed unsightly brown spots. Californians began to get used to the idea of getting by with less.

But the drought had some benefits as well. The receding waters of the lakes and reservoirs exposed entire swathes of the past. Folsom Lake was created in 1955 when the American River was dammed and entire towns that had existed on its banks were deliberately flooded. For sixty years, the lake was an aquatic playground for the citizens of Northern California. But as the drought stretched on, the waters receded and the outer walls of the town of Mormon Island reappeared foot-by-foot. The local papers and news programs reprised the colorful history of the boom-and-bust town that was created by the Gold Rush and inundated by both water and modernity.

The newspapers called it the 'Chinese Corpse,' but, technically, it wasn't really a corpse, but a skeleton. It was discovered by a landscaper who was expropriating old, hand-hewn stones from a newly exposed rock wall on the riverbank, despite the threat of severe penalties for anyone touching – let alone taking – artifacts from the newly-exposed site. Some of the overwrought preservationists even drew analogies to Pompei and Ephesus in their outrage. In the end, the man was forgiven because he called the authorities' attention to the fact that the pile of rocks covered a skeleton with a caved in skull.

There was a burst of attention because a state legislator had disappeared while kayaking on the upper part of the river at about the same time the island was flooded. But that possibility was quickly dismissed when a forensic examination declared that the age of the bones was approximately one-hundred-and-fifty years. Further, the pathologist opined that the cause of the death was a sharp blow to the head with a blunt object, that the man died about a century earlier when he was approximately sixty years old, and that he was probably of Asian descent. The police reinforced this by noting that they found an amulet at the site with a Chinese symbol on it.

They also found a crudely fashioned belt buckle and half-a-dozen large buttons scattered among the bones, fashioned out of almost pure gold. They turned the items over to the Gold Country Historical Society, who announced their intention to devote some space to exhibits that documented the role of Chinese miners in the California Gold Rush.

Nobody was quite sure what happened to the skeleton.

The woman standing looking out at Singapore harbor was almost nine thousand miles from Mormon Island and had no way to know that the Chinese corpse would change the trajectory of her life. Even if she had known, however, it would not have mattered. In her world, premonitions and similar omens were for other people, the ones that she preyed on.

Emily Connors was at the top of her chosen profession, a highly intelligent and ambitious woman. Unfortunately for society, she chose to apply her considerable skills toward criminal acts.

She liked the irony of living in Singapore, one of the most law-abiding countries in the world, with its draconian penalties for criminals. Not very long ago, they hanged careless tourists who brought their recreational drugs with them on vacation. The irony was that she was one of the *least* law-abiding individuals in the world.

The advantages of Singapore were substantial for her. First, that very legal system repelled her competitors and shielded her from those of a more violent nature. Also, Singapore was a city that honored wealth and would tolerate much from the wealthy so long as they inflicted their criminality on other parts of the world. It was also very much a Chinese city, making it easy for her to build her clientele among the race that was second only to the Americans in their commercial dealings, but – perhaps because of their second-place status – had fewer scruples about extra-legal methods.

Her eyes were the first feature one noticed, and the last to be forgotten. They were exceptionally large, seemingly lidless and bulging out from their sockets as if to emphasize that they were spherical bodies. Those in conversation with her or even close proximity did not make eye contact after the first glance, and that made it unlikely that they would notice that, except for that deformity, she was an attractive woman.

The irony was that Emily had spent a fortune and endured much pain to make herself attractive. She was Narcissus in an era where cosmetic surgery was highly advanced and readily available. But there was nothing she could do about the onset of hyperthyroidism – formally labeled Graves Disease -- only a year after her once-in-a-lifetime makeover. The resulting hyperthyroid imbalance was easily cured, but the ophthalmic malformation was permanent and unfixable.

She was a tall woman with broad shoulders and a slight physique. She wore her hair long and spoke in the sort of husky voice that one associates with lifelong smokers. She had a tendency to daintiness in gestures and posture that misled some into thinking that she could be treated lightly.

That would be a mistake. She was quick to sense – or to imagine – feelings of condescension in others that she encountered.

She was in her late thirties and at the top of her profession, but she had started at the bottom, learning her trade the hard way, beginning with a five-year apprenticeship on the outskirts of hell. No one knew of her or where she came from until she first surfaced in the Padpong sex district of Bangkok, working as a runner and prostitute for a Thai gangster who liked having white flesh on display for his patrons, especially for those who were largely indifferent to gender.

One of those patrons, the son of a major drug dealer, found her combination of compliance and creativity so compelling that he took her home with him. It was not long before she cajoled him into setting her up with her own sex club in Padpong, nor was it very long before both she and the club became notorious, a specialty venue for sadists of either gender. Fortunately for her, it was a time and a place where notoriety was good for business.

She was both young and a somewhat exotic foreigner, cast in a role where respect had to be earned. For her role as proprietress of a sex club, she perfected the art of physical intimidation. It featured her as an occasional raging maniac, terrifying those around her with the ferocity and the randomness of her violence. The rages were unfeigned, fits of screaming and seemingly uncontrolled personal violence that came without warning and were over quickly, like earthquakes or avalanches, sweeping away bewildered victims. In those cases where others acted for her, she made sure that the survivors understood the true source of their pain.

Unfortunately for her drug lord patron, she learned that he was skimming larger and larger amounts from the shipments and – even worse for him – she knew where he was stashing the cash. His body – or at least what was presumed to be his body – was found in the ashes of his house.

It was a clear turning point within her documented existence. There was little threat from the police: one of the advantages of murdering a scumbag was that the authorities did not try very hard to ascertain what started the fire or even to specify the cause of death. Nor did they expend time or effort making inquiries about the protégé/consort that slipped back beneath the surface of the Thai underworld.

She reemerged a year later with a new name, appearance and business model. She quickly became an essential force in an urban Asian sub-culture that flourished on the misery of its own inhabitants and the pathologies of Westerners that craved access to exotic pleasures, a subterranean market for goods and services not readily available in the highly developed and increasingly prudish economies. So a German or English tourist could do horrible things to a ten-year-old girl or boy without fear of consequences, or a Mexican tycoon could buy a healthy kidney from a highly suitable but involuntary donor, or an ex-Venezuelan banker living in Miami might require a pair of compliant teenage girls as indentured live-in 'maids,' or a Korean politician might requisition a retarded Chinese immigrant to assassinate a local businessman and thereby foment a race riot that was beneficial to his own interests.

She excelled in such highly specialized markets, almost always involving an underground and cross-border exchange between cultures and nationalities. She found patrons: Thai and Japanese and Chinese criminals and psychopaths who needed a special nexus for such one-off transactions. She became a broker with a reputation that cut across cultures, gaining access to wealthy clients with specialized needs scattered around the world.

The markers of her success were simple – money and what she called 'respect' but was really fear. The metrics were clear, at least the 'money' part. Wealth was a concrete number, and – even better – it could be exhibited overtly. In her present case, for example, she was standing in a penthouse at one of the most expensive addresses in Singapore, wearing a designer dress that had been modified by her personal tailor.

The 'respect' indicator was more subjective, but it was the more important barometer for her. She looked for it in every interaction, from the waiter pouring her coffee to the local politicians who came asking for favors. She recognized that respect was automatically accorded to wealth, and so she mistrusted the words and gestures that she encountered in her everyday world. So she made it a point to instill a simple, primeval fear in those around her. For most everyday encounters, an arbitrary, even random, application of power would do the trick – a controlled tantrum about some trivial slight, occasionally throwing something. But such stagecraft was ineffective in her other world; the arena where an ancient law of the jungle still applied. *I can kill you. Fear me.*

Gary would be pleased with me.
The thought took her by surprise. She no longer thought very much about Gary, but when the memories came, they were intense. And they could be triggered by almost

anything – a TV ad, a song from the eighties, even a glimpse of a tie-dyed T-shirt. Today, it was the sight of a teenage boy huddled within his baggy hooded sweatshirt with ear buds in place, being shouted at by his enraged father.

He was such a misfit. It's funny how others could see it so much more clearly than he did. In his world, 'they' were the ones that were screwed up, not him. He didn't dress the way they did, play the kind of games they played, didn't think right. Maybe it would have been easier for him if he had tried to adapt, to somehow play their game with their rules. He could have done it. He was smarter than they were, better at playacting, at pretending to be something that you're not. Especially compared to his father, a throwback to a time and culture where roles were engraved in stone and handed down from generation to generation. But Gary made it into a contest, one that had survivors rather than winners, faceoffs where irrationality and stubbornness prevailed. The worse they treated him, the more superior he felt.

He caused the two us so much pain. And it went on and on. I didn't think we would get through it. But it shaped us, made us stronger. That was his final gift to me, the pain. It made me into who I am today. What I am. Not quite human, but nothing else either. Some would say 'monster,' but they're like his father ... incapable of appreciating, even accepting, someone who doesn't fit their idea of normal. People who advise turning the other cheek, of being grateful for what you've got rather than trying to change.

They learned, though. All of them. The father, the perverts, even all the do-gooders. Anybody who refused to accept what he was. At the end, each of them knew what was happening to them – and why.

Maybe he's alive somewhere. Maybe after all the contempt, the drugs, and finally even the knives, Gary survived and is still out there somewhere.

Gary

San Francisco (1995)

He was always a troubled child.

It was evident from the first day that his liberal adoptive parents brought him home from the orphanage. They were bursting with a sense of possibility, oblivious to the iron laws of genetics. In his case, it seemed that virtually all of the developmental milestones for infants and children were delayed or achieved only with great difficulty – the transition from crawling to walking, the acquisition of language, toilet training, sleeping through the night, or any of the other conventional markers that parents use to reassure themselves that their first child is normal.

At first, the parents blamed themselves. They were the type of people and it was an era that believed that a newborn child was a malleable bit of humanity to be shaped and molded by a careful mix of parental love, discipline and controlled exposure to risk. Such purpose and optimism is particularly acute when the parents have been told that they cannot have their own children; that she, the would-be mother, is 'barren.' Over time, science and their own experience would prevail, so they would learn that genetic factors can -- and usually do -- overwhelm both the intentions and the actions of adoptive parents.

He cried for much of the first eighteen months, seemingly in pain from an ailment that could be neither diagnosed nor alleviated. They were told, "he's just a colicky baby." The only thing that seemed to help was to be in motion, so the sleep-deprived parents took turns walking with him. Miles and miles, developing strange swaying motions while babbling nonsense lullabies.

The preschool years were difficult. At first, they blamed it on him being the only child of overly concerned parents. He was steadfastly sullen, except for the sudden, apparently random outbreaks of aggressiveness, often bordering on assault. There were numerous incidents where the day care center called and asked the parents to reclaim him, cautiously suggesting that he was at least mildly autistic.

The behaviors did not change very much after his sister was born. He was almost nine years old by then; old enough to see and resent the outright joy that his parents felt during the unexpected pregnancy and birth and the inevitable shift of their attention from him to her. To their relief, he did display an intense curiosity, even protectiveness, toward his new sister, often sitting for hours just looking at her or playing with her on the floor.

He was a misfit from the very beginning, an unattractive, unathletic and unhappy boy with imaginary friends. He preferred dolls to toy trucks, color crayons to hammers. He liked fabrics and was extremely sensitive to what was touching his skin. When he started having a say in what he wore, he was obsessively concerned with matching colors and fabrics.

During preschool and the primary grades, he would hang out with the girls rather than the boys, particularly on the playground. "I don't like the other boys," he insisted. "They're not like me." And eventually, his parents stopped their efforts to enforce conformity, and even became enthusiastic about the faddish arguments by the child-development specialists for gender-free child rearing.

Most disturbingly, he seemed hard-wired for violence. In the early years, it presented as temper tantrums, acted out with screams, hitting, biting and kicking. His earliest fingerpainting projects in preschool featured gory scenes; crudely drawn people and animals in pools of blood, impaled by knives and spears. He watched violent TV cartoons over and over, especially those depicting superheroes and villains in deadly combat. He tore the heads off of his sister's Ken and Barbie dolls and exchanged them for one another, creating a pair of make-believe transgender friends for himself.

He did not do well in high school. He was a natural target for the bullying and taunting instincts that seem so natural to adolescents, and he had no defenders. He was the peculiar combination of an intensely shy adolescent with a smoldering rage just beneath the surface.

Some of the incidents were nasty enough to warrant what the school termed 'therapeutic intervention.' The worst was when a small group of boys circled him in the shower after gym class, taunting and poking at his nakedness, then hiding his clothes and locking him naked in the steel cage where they stored sports gear. His parents took him to a court-ordered child psychiatrist when he was twelve, after he had been expelled for attacking a teacher by stabbing her with a sharpened pencil multiple times. When asked why, he said, "She embarrassed me."

The therapeutic sessions were brief, ending when he assaulted the psychiatrist, throwing his heavy medical books at him one-by-one until he drove him from his office. The doctor's mandatory report to the juvenile court judge was predictably grim: *"Gary shows little empathy for others or remorse for his own actions. He exhibits predatory behavior patterns that stem from callous-unemotional tendencies. He is prone to violence, risk taking and incapable of learning from punishment. He exhibits a suite of symptoms consistent with a psychopathic personality."*

He attended a series of expensive private schools that catered to 'troubled' children lucky enough to have enabling parents, offering high-priced babysitting disguised as a high school curriculum. Even then, he dropped out at age eighteen just before graduation and became part of the small army of homeless in San Francisco, fending for himself in a city that was a fabled destination for troubled and runaway teenagers, thereby ending both his formal education and the remnants of his tattered relationship with his family.

As if to confirm the dissolution of the family, his father died three days after Gary dropped out and went on the street. For Gary, his father's death was a classic case of "good riddance," meriting neither mourning nor reunion with his surviving family members. He would come to view it as the opening act in what would be his last three weeks in San Francisco.

Gary's most pressing need was for some capital and he knew where to find it. He'd read about gangs that monitored obituaries and burglarized homes during scheduled funeral ceremonies. *Should provide me some cover. But she wouldn't call the cops even if she caught me in the act.*

He went through his father's home office and grabbed the obvious stuff. The ten thousand in cash was first. *The schmuck insisted on what he called 'mattress money' for emergency use. But I don't think he had this in mind!* He pawned the two watches and laptop and sold the collection of gold coins that his father was so proud of. The coins turned out to be far more valuable than he had guessed ... a nice surprise. He kept the handgun, a 45-caliber semi-automatic that his father brought home from Viet Nam.

He also needed a place to stay, a problem that was solved when he found Zinni. It was a stupid made-up name, but she had chosen it when she ran away and wouldn't tell him her real name. *Or even where she was from. Has to be some Podunk town in the Midwest, somewhere where they grow corn and all the girls have big breasts.*

He'd come across her about two days after she got off the bus. She'd gone straight from the Greyhound depot to the Haight, of course. Sleeping in shelters and panhandling during the day. Wayne at the pipe shop was the first to tell him about her.

"Got a newbie. Fresh off the boat. Kinda makes me long for the sixties."

He found her in Golden Gate Park, trying to buy some weed from anybody that looked like her Midwestern image of a hippie. She seemed close to closing a deal with a skinny kid in a tie dyed T-shirt and love beads, a caricature of a time and place that no longer existed. Gary knew him to be a Berkeley graduate student who spent afternoons in the Park, trolling for just such innocents.

He stood watching until Zinni became aware of him. He gestured at the kid in the retro T-shirt, who was already edging away. "This cool-looking guy and his so-called Mexican gold? He's selling you parsley."

The kid grinned, flashed a peace sign at him and took off, leaving her holding her fistful of dollars and looking dismayed.

Gary fished in his shirt pocket and came up with a half-smoked joint. He held it out to her. "Here. It's good stuff."

When she hesitated, he smiled and said, "View it as a gift … kind of like a welcome wagon kind of thing."

When they started walking, she said, "My name's Zinni." Without thinking about it, he said "I'm Ken."

It's too bad her name is Zinni. 'Barbie' would be so much better!

They went to his favorite place in the park, a small hollow among a stand of cypress trees close to the beach. Nothing was really private in the Park, but mid-morning on a weekday was as close as it came. She sat smoking the joint and he leaned back on his forearms and watched her, trying to judge her age and level of desperation.

"Where are you coming from?" he asked.

"The middle class." Those were the first words she had spoken since "My name's Zinni' when he interrupted her transaction with the parsley dealer.

She smiled dreamily. Then she pushed him down against the warm and soft sandy earth, unzipped his pants, and gave him one of the best blow jobs of his still young life. It caused him to rethink the history that he'd been imagining for her. And their near future together.

It was Zinni that found the house. "It's like a Transylvanian hotel, y'know? Cobwebs and secret passages … Take your pick of bedrooms … eat whatever you can find …"

"Overrun by squatters?"

"Nope. Just me and two others. The girl's a real mope from the East Coast. The other kid is local, I think, but I don't know anything about him."

"I need a place for a few days, somewhere I can stash some stuff and hang out. Think I can join you?"

"I promise you: they won't even notice."

"They?"

"The owner's a social worker and her husband ....
some kind of professor. She reminds me of my bitch mother.
Thinks she knows what I need ..."

A blank look settled over her face and he watched her
float away from the conversation, back to a time and place
where the bitch-mother was very real and San Francisco was
just a bunch of stories. *She won't talk about it, but she can't
let go of it. We can use that.*

Her eyes gradually came back into focus. When he
asked, "Where to?" she smiled in a way that once again made
him wonder how old she really was.

"Russian Hill. It's the in place for runaways these
days."

Hidden Spaces

Zinni and Gary neither appreciated nor cared that the house was unique, even a little bit famous. For them, it was shelter, nothing more. And the Malloys were like their parents, only slightly more tolerable because of their acceptance of them. Neither of them knew that their presence in the house would trigger a neighborhood squabble that – as it played out – would make the house even more notable.

The Brookings house was controversial long before the Malloys made it into an improvised shelter for troubled kids. It stood out, partly because of sheer size and partly due to its oddball architecture. It was as if a series of boxes had been bolted together. The first stage of construction was to simply level off the top of the hill and build a very large two-level house. It had a magnificent front entrance on Hyde Street, with massive white columns flanking the door. Stage two was to move downhill and carve into the fifteen-degree slope to create a level dirt base on which a three-story addition – essentially a very large rectangular box --was erected so as to link to the stage one construction. Stage three was a repeat of that procedure another fifty feet downhill, this time with a four-story addition on top of the site where Hiram Brookings had died.

The construction technique was not all that creative. Man had been building houses on steep hills for some time and the method was cheaper and easier than using a pier-and-beam system or designing massive cantilevered spaces. And it had the unintended benefit of making the house very resistant to the earthquakes still crouching far below the surface of the street.

From the side street perspective – the one that ran down the hill to the northeast – the house resembled a set of blocks. That and the hodge-podge architectural style made the house look, at the very best, unimaginative, like something assembled by a two-year-old playing with blocks. The original builder quit, offended by the owner's insistence that she be involved in every aspect of the design and construction, and his successor seemed to favor a haphazard combination of the Craftsman and other styles, distorted even more by Hiram Brooking's insistence – enforced posthumously -- that any self-respecting house had to have pillars at the entrance.

Another distinctive feature of the construction was the interior stairway that ran from the highest level down to the lowest level, uninterrupted except by small landings at each of the four levels. Among other things, the stairway enabled Zinni and Gary to travel throughout the house unnoticed by the Malloys.

The landings were accessed from an alley that was bulldozed out on the side away from the street. The grade – over fifteen percent – was too steep for vehicles, so it was quite narrow and limited to pedestrians. The interior of the staircase was poorly lit, unadorned and quite narrow. Its original role was to provide access to each of the four floors for servants and tradesman. The family and their guests entered through the ornate and massive front doors flanked by the columns that Hiram wanted.

Maybe it was the proximity to the one-time Russian cemetery, or perhaps that the house was born out of the destruction of the city, or the tragic deaths of Hiram and the widow's three children, but what came to be called 'the Brookings house' was saddled with a reputation that persisted through time. Nothing like being haunted or suffering from a curse; more like a sense that nothing good would happen to those who lived there.

For Gary in 1995, the house was a solution to his need for a staging platform, the means whereby he could set the last pieces of his master plan in place.

She was right. This place is like an old hotel fallen on hard times.

Zinni had gone through the motions of asking the owners if it was OK for him to spend a few days. She introduced him as 'Ken' and made up a story about a scorched earth divorce in LA; alcoholic parents, neither of whom wanted him; a need for a place to crash. She went on long enough to make the point that he needed and deserved some of their attention. Zinni was really getting into it, going on about physical abuse, but he kicked her ankle to shut her up, wondering if maybe this was her story and she needed to tell it.

The owners – "Call us John and Moira" -- were a pair of fortyish anti-establishment types. To Gary, they seemed more interested in thumbing their nose at society than they did in helping a couple of alienated kids.

"Sure, a few days is no problem. Make yourself at home."

They were into planning for some major foreign trip. When he asked about it, they corrected him. "Not a trip, it's more like a migration to a new planet."

There were four of them for a few days. What Zinni had labeled the 'mope from the East Coast' was the first to go. She moved in with a bunch of stoners in Berkeley. The other kid spent most of his time with John and Moira and had little to do with either him or Zinni. Even with their limited interaction, it was quite clear that he disapproved of everything about Gary, particularly his domineering treatment of Zinni. To Gary, he seemed a fugitive, definitely on the run from someone or something.

John and Moira seemed intimidated by their own house. They lived at street level, using very little of the space available. The vast remainder of the house was effectively for Zinni and him. They explored it together. At first, Zinni announced her personal goal: "I want to fuck you in every single room!" But her enthusiasm waned, mostly because he had begun introducing her to heroin and she spent most of her time zoned out in random spaces.

It was easy to keep her supplied. He was in the process of acquiring inventory, using the money from his father's coin collection. Pills, opiates, painkillers, tranquilizers, cocaine, heroin, marijuana, even a little meth … whatever he could buy from dealers who preferred to deal in larger quantities rather than setting up networks of street runners to deal with the retail trade.

During one of their early walkthroughs, he asked Zinni, "You said something about secret passages. What's that about?"

She led him to the corner of a bedroom on the second level of the house. The space was about twenty feet in either direction with a highly polished wooden floor and windows that looked out onto the steeply pitched side street. She put her back to the far wall and said, "Listen carefully."

She took an exaggerated high step and put her foot down with some force. The result was a dull 'thud.' She repeated this a half-dozen times and then stopped, about eight or ten feet from the opposing wall. Her actions reminded him of a vague childhood game whose purpose he could not quite remember.

She looked at him, clearly disappointed by his lack of curiosity about her strange behavior. She said, "There's nothing but dirt and rock below this floor. These two levels are built on a shelf cut into the hillside. But get this …"

She took one more giant step. This time, the sound was more resonant, faintly drum-like. It was the same with each following step until she was stopped by the wall.

He was unimpressed. "So there's space below us? We know that. It's a four story house and we're on the second level."

"But this wall" – she touched the one facing her – "is also the wall for the room immediately below us. That leaves about ten feet of hollow space" – she stamped her foot for emphasis – "unaccounted for."

They went down one level and he confirmed it. They were in a very large laundry room. The floor and the bottom half of all the walls were white tile except for the wall in question, which was floor-to-ceiling built-in cabinetry on one half and a long deep sink on the other half. When he thumped on a blank part of the wall with his fist, he thought the sound had the kind of hollow tone that signaled empty space on the other side.

Zinni was looking at him with the sort of 'See what I can do' expression that he hated. It reminded him of his stupid sister, always looking for his approval when she did something for the first time. It made him mad.

"Big fucking deal! You're living in a house with a couple dozen rooms and discovered some closed-off empty space! You want a medal?"

She grabbed his sleeve and pulled him close, looking up at him from three inches away with red-rimmed eyes. Her breath was rancid and her hair was greasy and tangled.

She's going down real fast. But I need her and her connection to this house and these people until I get a big enough stash.

She was almost shouting. "Closed off? Not for me!" She pushed him aside and lunged at the cabinet immediately behind him, slamming into its edge with both hands. He backed away.

She's nuts! Completely round the bend!

She banged into the cabinet twice more before he heard the faint click and saw a six-foot wide section of the floor-to-ceiling cabinet move quite perceptibly a couple of inches. Zinni slipped her hand into a narrow slot at the side that was now exposed and started to pull, her feet slipping on the tile. But the entire section came with her, pivoting soundlessly out into the room. Where it had stood was a dark hole, the size of an outsized door.

A week later, Gary was ready to go. If only he hadn't stopped by the house for one last check, his future almost certainly would have turned out dramatically different.

Stupid damn bitch!

Zinni lay sprawled in the corner of the laundry room. All she had on was a ratty terrycloth robe with large splashes of coffee stains, vomit and other unidentifiable substances. It gaped open and was bunched under her, somehow making the nakedness far worse, an obscenity.

Gary saw the syringes. Two syringes – one for cocaine and the other for heroin. He knew immediately that what he had intended as a warning was taken as a sales pitch.

He'd laid out all the paraphernalia. Then he told her. "It's called speedballing. And it can kill you. You're mixing a stimulant with a depressant. It's the most intense rush you'll ever get... But if you don't get it right …"

Even while he was talking, however, she was twitching to get started and he knew that nothing that he had said had gotten through.

When he squatted beside her to check for a pulse, she stirred. Her one hand flopped weakly, trying to pull the robe over her. Her eyes were rolled back in her head and vomit was seeping from the corner of her mouth.

Stupid damn bitch! Time for us to part ways. See who else you can find to get you what you need ...

He was ready. His inventory was safely stashed and everything he needed was in his backpack. As if to confirm his change of plan, he was carrying the 45 – his father's handgun -- for the first time, tucked into the back of his waistband under his shirt. He stood, considering the girl at his feet and marveling at the transition from their first encounter in Golden Gate Park. The fact that he was the cause of her total dissolution did not occur to him; and the idea would not have bothered him if it had.

Safe enough to leave her. Even if she hasn't fried her brain, she knows nothing about me.

He turned to leave. And then all his plans went to shit.

The two goofballs – John and Moira – were standing in the doorway, their eyes fixed on Zinni with horror.

His first reaction was simple anger.

You were supposed to be gone until Monday. Something to do in LA. 'Getting our affairs together,' was what you said. 'Then we're gone gone. 'Three days,' you said!

Moira took two steps toward Zinni, stopping short and stretching out her hand like she was going to help her up.

"Is she … is she alive?"

"For the moment," he said, realizing as he said it that both his matter-of-factness and the callous phrasing condemned him as surely as if they had watched him injecting the stuff into her veins. He felt the familiar calmness settle over him, a mantle of absolute assurance about how this was going to end.

John was frozen in place, looking wildly from Zinni to Moira to him. His wife knelt alongside Zinni and arranged the robe to cover as much of the nakedness as she could. She turned and looked over her shoulder at Gary and in that single withering look, he again experienced the full depth of his parents' disappointment and, eventually, disgust.

"Call the police."

When John just stood there with his mouth open, she said it again, much louder. "John! Call the police! And tell them we need an ambulance!"

Gary reached out to them, trying to sound urgent and scared. "Wait! You need to see this first. What happened to Zinni."

He turned to the cabinets behind him, leaned his full weight against the key shelf and pivoted the mechanism to expose the dark doorway. The startling sight drew them as he knew it would, as surely as a magnet attracts iron filings. When they hesitated at the threshold to the darkness, he said, "This is what happened to Zinni. In this secret room. You need to see it."

He switched on the flashlight they kept on the nearby shelf and pointed it into the darkness. The couple stepped into the space very tentatively, with Gary trailing. The wobbling flashlight seemed to trigger answering gleams from the glass and ceramic shards imbedded in the dirt wall that sloped down to the dirt floor before them. When he pointed the flashlight down, they found themselves standing on the edge of a square hole, perhaps eight feet deep and about ten feet on all sides.

It would be their grave. Gary fired a single shot into the back of John's head and the second round into Moira's right eye as she was whirling around. Both of them pitched forward and down into the moist earth at the bottom of what was intended to be an elevator shaft. He tossed the flashlight after them and it imbedded itself at an angle that highlighted the undamaged side of Moira's face.

He walked back into the laundry room and considered Zinni, thinking about options. Finally, he shrugged and took the hand that she seemed to be holding out to him. He dragged her across the tile floor and to the edge of the large hole. He stood to one side so that the florescent lights from the laundry room enabled him to see what he was doing and fired a single shot into her face. He poked her several times with his foot to tumble her into the common grave.

Stupid damn bitch! Not much of an epitaph, but the only one she'll get. Now, still one more thing to do.

Chao Zhu

The ringing phone startled Emily and jarred her out of the reverie. She stared at it for a few seconds while the images of Gary faded. It was the special phone, the one that very few individuals knew of.

"This is Emily."

"Hello Emily. We haven't talked for a while."

She recognized the voice immediately.

"No, we haven't." *Three years. Since your 'special board meeting' in Kuala Lumpur that required five young boys, along with some highly specialized cameras and a skilled technician to operate them, one that wouldn't be missed very much if he didn't return from the meeting.*

The caller went immediately to the point. "There is a project that you may be interested in. Very unusual, and I know you appreciate novelty. And profitable, of course."

"Are you the client or speaking for someone else?"

He knows the rules ... what happens to him if the client turns out to be something less – or more – than what he represents himself to be.

"I have a friend, a man that is very important to me. His name is Chao Zhu."

"Tell me about the project."

"I can't. But I'll set up the meeting."

It took a while to make the arrangements. The man named Chao Zhu apparently was traveling a great deal and 'still working on some of the details' for the project where Emily was being considered.

In fact, he was in Las Vegas, an ideal venue for the type of negotiations he was engaged in. It was a city that understood the need for an occasional anonymity on the part of visitors, especially those from foreign nations whose religious or political values were suspect. And it was close to San Francisco, with excellent international flight schedules, so it was convenient for both parties. By meeting in one of the lesser casinos away from 'the Strip,' they minimized the odds of running into someone that knew them, and they got more work done.

The negotiators operated in secret. Neither side could afford the slightest glimmer of transparency at this stage. If it became known that they were even talking, all of the interest groups on both sides – political, economic, cultural – would lobby for 'most favored' treatment and would unleash television ads, law firms and armies of lobbyists to get their way; or, equally important and far more likely, to prevent anybody else from getting *their* way. In such a fishbowl, the negotiators would be forced to pay attention to 'matters of principle' and to publicly disdain compromise.

And compromise was essential. Each faction had much to gain. And to lose, especially the vital commodity called simply, 'face.'

They had been meeting for the last six months, two or three days at a time, always in a different venue. The same two people were at every meeting, with a rotating crop of another six or eight analysts or bureaucrats in attendance as necessary. The meetings would start at nine AM and continue through dinner. A good part of the day would be spent in a conference room with the larger group, always with a great number of documents being discussed. But the two main negotiators would also spend time with just the two of them, at lunch and dinner, and occasionally walking through the neighborhood where the casino was located.

To a disinterested observer, they could appear to be father and daughter. The age difference was about right, they were clearly both ethnic Chinese and they were continuously in close conversation with one another. However, if one looked more closely, they behaved toward one another with a degree of formality more closely associated with business associates than family members, and the elderly Chinese gentleman was conspicuously deferential to his younger companion.

After their last meeting, the man said just before boarding his plane, "I think we're very close."

The younger woman nodded. "Yes. Most of the big issues are agreed on. Price, location, financing, ownership …

but we still disagree about who will manage the facility. That is also a big issue. And it must be settled before we make a public announcement."

She paused, obviously troubled, and went on reluctantly. "And you know what my problem is with your candidate."

The man bowed very slightly to acknowledge her concerns. "Yes, I do, and it is your problem to solve. And, frankly, I do not understand your concern. You have already lived with this person – and what you call 'your problem' – for twenty years. You have – how do you Americans say – a 'wink-wink' relationship. He pretends to obey the law and you pretend to enforce it. Surely that can be continued in our proposed arrangement? Especially if our preferred candidate can deliver the labor unions that are so important in your democratic society."

The younger woman was shaking her head before he finished speaking. "Our waste management contracts are unglamorous, very much below the radar. That allows us to negotiate and tolerate certain, shall we say, *dubious tradeoffs* for the good of the citizens without anybody getting excited. But when we announce a state-of-the-art billion-dollar facility, the first of its kind, we'll be under a microscope. And so will the vendors. The politics will be vicious."

The man smiled. "You have a democracy, so politics are required. Our methods are much better, more efficient. Protest against such decisions is, shall we say, more restrained?"

They were approached by a Chinese woman in a blue blazer and grey slacks. "It's time to board, sir." The man stood and picked up his attaché case, but his companion stopped him. She said something that he thought nothing of until much later.

"Maybe I should use your 'more efficient' methods to solve my problem with your candidate?"

Emily met Chao Zhu two days later, in Macao at a time and place brokered by one of her oldest and most trusted clients. The flight from Singapore was three-and-a-half hours, long enough for her to read through and think about the report that she had commissioned on the man she was to meet. It was a thicker report than usual. Typically, those who wanted to engage her services operated well out of the public view, leading to quite thin dossiers. However, despite the added detail, there was nothing in the report that helped her identify the threats or vulnerabilities that he offered, or the nature of what he might want from her. On the surface, he was a construction contractor and real estate developer, living in Shanghai but with projects all around China. He seemed to be important, both because of his wealth and his family. He was the eldest member of a prominent family that could trace their lineage back hundreds of years to ancient and royal dynasties.

The Banyan Tree Resort and Casino in the Taipa District of Macao was massive, with a manmade beach and computer-controlled waves. *The kind of excess that would appeal to a real estate developer.* When she asked at the VIP Desk for Chao Zhu, the clerk immediately picked up the phone and a distinguished Chinese man in a business suit appeared within ten seconds, introduced himself as the hotel manager and escorted her to a suite on the top floor. A man sat by the window reading a bound document that – from the doorway – looked like a very thick prospectus. He stood up when they entered and bowed slightly and he and Emily regarded each other intently until the manager closed the door behind him.

His first words were very strange. "Do you know that America's biggest export is trash and that China has been the largest buyer?" He spoke English with almost no accent. He raised the document and Emily could see the title – in English and Chinese -- quite clearly: *The Green Fence.*

Before she could respond, he bowed again. "I am Chao Zhu. Thank you for coming."

"You were highly recommended. I could not refuse my friend."

He is very old, probably in his late seventies. English is excellent. I don't think he's well ... something in his expression or posture.

He smiled. "You also are highly recommended, although your skills are not so much valued by some of those who encounter your services."

He gestured to two chairs facing one another across a low table. As soon as they were seated, she said, "How much did your friend tell you about me?"

Chao Zhu smiled again. "The words I remember were 'expensive, discreet and dangerous,' and he illustrated them with stories that he has heard about you. Very compelling stories. He also said that I should be very careful about making commitments to you."

"Good."

When it was clear she was not going to add anything, he said, "I want you to go to San Francisco for me."

Her expression did not change, but everything about her became momentarily still, even her breathing suspended. *I wonder if he knows about San Francisco. I wonder how? And what else he knows? I think this man is someone to be careful with.*

"And what will I do? In San Francisco? If I decide to go?" She carefully stressed the word *if.*

He answered none of her questions. Instead, he leaned forward and watched her even more intently.

"Do you believe in honor?"

Strangely, the startling question made her think of Gary. *He understood the concept. Not in the same way as most people, but that was what made him do what he did. The others – the normal ones – they would call it vengeance, not 'honor.' But what he was avenging was their taking away his pride, his dignity, and his... yes ... his honor.*

He mistook her silence for contempt and sat back, seeming saddened. "It is not important to what I ask you to do. But for me, it is everything. That and family."

Family! I worry about clients that are motivated by concepts like 'honor' and 'family.' Soft and fuzzy motivations that can turn out to be more important than the contract that they negotiated.

He went on, unperturbed by her thoughts that he had provoked but could not be aware of. "I have a granddaughter in San Francisco. She is important to me. She is young and ambitious. A good combination, I think, in America. But she needs both guidance and support, which I would like you to provide."

"Chao Zhu, I do not think –"

"That someone like you could be a suitable mentor for a young woman?" He smiled broadly. "Normally, I would agree. But what if I told you that she aspires to be rich, as quickly as possible and by whatever means is available? That she already is second in command of what the American police would call 'an organized criminal activity' if they knew about it, which they don't? That she is threatened in ways that cannot be addressed with lawyers or mediators? That the full extent of your *special* skills will be called for?"

Emily inclined her head, an acknowledgment of his arguments.

"And there's more," he said. "I need an agent in San Francisco to represent my various interests. Someone who is versatile and ruthless, but trustworthy. Someone like you."

"Go on. What are the interests you need me to represent?"

Again, he did not answer the question directly. He said, "You will need to establish yourself. There are elements there that will not welcome competition with someone with your history. I have associates in Chinatown –"

She shook her head. "I do not need your help. I have the necessary connections already in place."

She had dealt with the man Gruber twice before; the man in San Francisco that she thought of as the big fish in a small pond. Smart enough to know that he needed outside talent to do what he needed. The first contract was an easy one: provide a pair of twelve-year-old boys, preferably Thai but Chinese was OK. Their target – a member of the California state legislature with strong sadomasochistic fetishes and incredibly naïve. He played an involuntary starring role in a film that – so far – only he and her client had seen. Her client insisted that the boys be done away with after the film. She thought that was unnecessary, but the contract called for it.

The second time, it worked in reverse. She had employed him – the word "outsourcing" popped into her memory – when she was asked to do away with a relatively low-level member of the Japanese yakuza when he was visiting San Francisco. She had called Gruber. The target was bludgeoned to death in his hotel room. She remembered thinking that she would have done it differently, but it was timely and effective.

She tried the same question a different way. "You say you want me to 'be your agent in San Francisco.' To do what?"

Zhu held up three fingers. "There is a woman that owns a house that I wish to buy. She does not wish to sell to me. I need you to fix that. Second, I would like you to buy the house on my behalf, anonymously and in such a way that ownership cannot be traced back to either of us. I suggest a highly anonymous foundation as the vehicle for such a purchase. Third, I want you to meet with my granddaughter and counsel her on how to achieve what she wants."

She started to speak, but he raised his hand to stop her. "I leave it to you as to the best way to do these things. And I am sure that other problems will arise in the course of these projects, problems that I expect you to deal with."

"Why do you want to buy a house in San Francisco?"

She knew such a question would be impertinent to a client like Zhu, but – for her – it was an important test. If he refused to answer or was offended, she would walk away and take the next flight back to Singapore.

He passed the test, although not in the manner she had intended.

"Your question is not a simple one. To answer it, I must tell you a story," he said. And he leaned back in his chair, clasping his hands together on his lap, as though preparing for a long conversation. "It is a story with monsters, lost treasure and, of course, villains and heroes. It is also a story about honor, and my family...."

An hour later, Emily made a series of calls. The first was to set up her travel itinerary – a one-way, first-class ticket on Singapore Airlines from Hong Kong to San Francisco. The second was to Daniel in Hong Kong and the third to a man named Gruber in San Francisco to carry out the first of her three projects on behalf of Chao Zhu.

Call on an Advisor

Emily made the trip from Macao to San Francisco in two parts. The first leg was only a three-hour ferry ride across the South China Sea to a luxury hotel on Hong Kong Island. The purpose of the short trip was to visit with the only person in the world that she feared.

Daniel Wong knew all there was to know about Emily Connors – her origin story, the victims strewn along her rise to the top of her profession, who her customers were, and what she was afraid of. She had known him since her beginning.

Bangkok, the mid-nineties. A room above one of the busiest go go nightclubs in the Padpong district ... at that time the 'sex capital of Asia.' On that night, the club was closed for a private party, a group of English lawyers – barristers? – being 'entertained' in the main room downstairs by twenty naked adolescents, a few of them boys. I was serving tea to five men in the upstairs room. One of them was my patron. He and three of the others, between them, ran most of the nastier criminal operations in Southeast Asia. The fifth man was Daniel. I spilled some tea on the Laotian with two missing fingers and he hit me with his closed fist. Hard enough to put me on my knees.

Later, downstairs, Daniel came up to me and said, "You should kill him for that."

When he turned away to leave, I asked him, "How can I do that? He is powerful and I am weak."

The question seemed to please him. He turned and looked at me for a long time, and then he told me how. Not very much later, I learned that his advice was calculated, a test, that he needed a 'source' in the Thai underworld. When the Lao turned up dead a week after our meeting, he called me and we struck a deal.

Daniel Wong was half Chinese, half Russian; the result of a liaison between a KGB agent and a Chinese diplomat posted to Moscow. Each of them believed they were seducing the other to recruit them for counterintelligence purposes. Ironically, each of them was shot in the back of the head by their respective government during the bloody power plays that marked the Soviet and Chinese intelligence services during the 1980's. Somehow, Daniel wound up with all of his parents' talents for clandestine work, but with none of their misplaced patriotism. His only client was himself.

They did not compete. Emily operated at a transactional level. She did 'projects'; well-defined one-off jobs with short timelines and clearcut objectives. Daniel, on the other hand, was more like an ambassador-for-hire; a well-connected 'facilitator' that a country or an organization could hire to open channels of communication with a competitor or even a hostile agency. He enabled entire new lines of business, joint ventures, treaties and cease-fire agreements between covert parties, mostly criminal in nature but every now-and-then leading to an arrangement that could be sold as socially beneficial. Emily knew of one case where he negotiated a sharp reduction in opium production in return for the disbanding of a paramilitary government-sanctioned death squad.

Unlike that first meeting in Bangkok, the setting this time was at the opposite end of the social spectrum, in one of the most exclusive downtown clubs in Hong Kong. She was directed to what they called 'the library,' although there was not a book to be seen in the entire vast room. She found Daniel seated in a secluded corner.

"Good evening, Emily. It's been a while."

She sat down in the very soft leather chair opposite him. "Twenty-three months, I think. You were in Singapore when the American trade delegation was in town. The deal that nobody thought could be pulled off because of the intransigent American dockworkers."

He grimaced. Emily knew that he didn't like talking about – or even worse, hearing about – his various engagements. *Why do I have this need to provoke him? He has so many ways to make my life difficult!*

He promptly confirmed it. "How's Gary doing these days? Still in touch? Or have you erased him from your memory banks?"

She smiled to acknowledge his comeback. *Does he expect an answer? I don't think so. I wonder how extensive his networks are, whether he could possibly know the entire story?*

He spoke again, as if he knew of her internal debate. "I understand you're moving to San Francisco. At the request of Chao Zhu. A homecoming for you, I believe?"

Emily nodded. She knew Daniel too well to be surprised by the timeliness or the accuracy of his information.

"What can you tell me?" she asked.

"About Chao Zhu or about San Francisco?"

"Both. But let's start with the man. I trust my referral source but I don't know this Chao Zhu, other than the official record."

Daniel leaned back and stroked his short greying beard. "He's like an iceberg: there's much more to him than what you see on the surface. He's very hooked in with the power brokers in Beijing, particularly with the Chinese intelligence services."

Emily thought about their meeting. "When we met, he was reading an official-looking document, and he wanted me to see it. Its title was 'The Green Fence,' apparently about the trash importing business."

She saw the sudden surge of interest that he could not quite disguise. *So Daniel doesn't know quite everything after all.*

He shifted into a recitation style. "The title refers to a program begun by the Chinese government in 2013. Up to then, China was accepting recycled trash from the U.S. and reprocessing it into a manufacturing-ready material, mostly plastic. But the Americans did a poor job of cleaning and sorting, leading to the stuff winding up in landfills in China, which are both toxic and prone to landslides. So the 'Green Fence' campaign was launched to force quality control. Among other things, it has pretty well stopped the trade, so the nasty stuff now winds up in American landfills rather than Chinese ones. Nobody likes the arrangement in its present form."

Daniel watched her closely as he asked, "Does that have something to do with what he wants you to do in San Francisco?"

"No. My assignment has nothing to do with trade, or even with business, as far as I can tell."

Daniel seemed satisfied with that, but she knew that there would be a follow up.

"I presume he gave you his lecture about honor and family?"

She nodded.

"It's real, not an act. He means it. And it goes both backwards and forward for him; he reveres his ancestors and he is highly protective of his children and all of their offspring."

"His granddaughter in San Francisco?"

"Especially her. Her mother – Chao's daughter – was the first of her generation to leave China for the U.S. He encouraged the move but it was hard for him. He's made it a special project to make sure she – and her children – are OK."

"Even when they're engaging in criminal activity?"

Daniel laughed. "Especially then. Chao's one of the biggest conduits for Chinese flight capital into the U.S. And other places, but San Francisco's a major honey pot for him. All those new millionaires and occasional billionaires needing safe parking places for their new wealth."

"I've got a contact in San Francisco –"

He cut her off. "Yes, I know. Manfred Gruber. The king of garbage and the go-to crime boss unless you want to deal with the Chinatown tongs or the street gangs. Mostly a one-man show with a few muscle bound thugs for backup. His real strength is his influence over the labor unions. They're still a real power in San Francisco."

"I gather San Francisco is not exactly a mafia stronghold."

"It's got less organized crime activity than any other major American city. Makes a place like Des Moines or Fargo look crime-ridden by comparison. The high point was when Alioto was mayor, but that's a long time ago. Right now, the mayor is a very tough ex-cop – a Chinese woman of all things

-- and there's zero corruption until you get about three levels down in the city hierarchy. Gruber makes a nice living on medium-sized graft and knows his limits."

"Any room for competition?"

Daniel considered the question. "Not from the various crime families in other cities. Really only two possibilities. The Asian and Hispanic street gangs ... but they're pretty far down on the sophistication scale. Chao Zhu could be a contender, but only if he wanted to be. So far, he's been content with a purely Chinese agenda, usually with a real estate focus."

He looked closely at Emily. "You're not thinking about competing with him, are you? Moving up from subcontractor to something more managerial, maybe?"

So he doesn't know about the other agenda. Good.

She said, "Most definitely not," and stood up. "Any other thoughts, or advice?"

"Yes. Don't trust anybody who values 'honor' or 'family' more highly than money."

Homecoming

Emily deliberately avoided thinking about her conversation with Daniel Wong until she was settled in her first class seat on Singapore Airlines and she'd finished her traditional Manhattan. Only then did she replay their conversation. But she couldn't get past his first comment after they had said their hellos … "How's Gary these days?"

He knew what he was asking and how it would affect me. Damn him and his games!

It was more than fifteen years ago. She and Gary had been inseparable until then, so close together and yet so different. Each of them at war with others and, most of all, with themselves. It ended only because Emily was stronger, the one who was able to declare it to be over.

Gary had to be irrevocably gone. He had to die. Only one of them could survive. But he had not just to die, but to be utterly erased, as though he had never been. They were like Siamese twins who shared vital organs. One of them, Emily, would suffer terribly, both physically and emotionally, as long as the other lived. The other, Gary, must cease to exist, a sacrifice to enable the other's full potential.

It would not be her first, but it would be Emily's single most important act of murder.

The funeral ceremony was unrecorded and entirely unofficial. Emily and four of hers and Gary's closest friends gathered in the courtyard of a small temple on the banks of the Chao Praya River on the outskirts of Bangkok. There was no body, but an ornate bamboo box held those few possessions that served as his identity. His passport, a favorite silk shirt, a lock of hair, and a single tattered photograph of him as a child, with his family. The box was small, about twelve-inches square and shallow, with a deep luster. They laid it on top of the knee-high pyre and Emily used a ceremonial torch from the temple to light all sides of the wooden pyramid. The cedar logs had been soaked in kerosene and burned fiercely.

The funeral ceremony seemed to work for her. She still thought of Gary, but now it was with feelings of nostalgia for their common past rather than the competition that had been the nexus of their relationship. Fifteen years was a long time, but a single remark from Daniel Wong somehow restored all of the anger and guilt.

Going back to San Francisco can only make it worse.

She used two hours of her flight to read through the single document that Chao Zhu had given her.

"It's an assortment of notes taken from the laptop of a woman who is trying to acquire the house that I wish to buy. She is a competitor, so I thought it would be useful to do some research into her intentions and resources."

Emily frowned and said, "But if she knows you have them –"

"She thinks it was an everyday mugging. Just another incident of the street crime so common in the capitalist paradise."

The notes were mundane in the extreme. The woman was the spearhead of a 'preservation campaign' seeking to acquire what was referred to as 'the Brookings House' for the City of San Francisco. In reading the disjointed narrative – apparently a rough journal of the woman's efforts over a two week period – Emily formed the impression of a slightly fanatic and elderly spinster chronicling a series of endless meetings.

Emily tossed the pages into the trash cart in the first class galley area. *A not-very-interesting woman pursuing an even-less-interesting artifact.*

She could not have been more wrong.

It was a clear day and Emily had a great view of San Francisco Bay and the city as the Airbus flew just west of the Golden Gate before circling back for its on-time landing at SFO. Even from ten thousand feet, she could see the changes.

A lot of tall new buildings, especially in the financial district. The new span on the Bay Bridge. A downtown baseball park. The city seems denser somehow. Not so surprising, given that you're surrounded by water on three sides. No wonder real estate prices keep going up.

SFO had a new international terminal, but the lines for immigration and customs were long, winding through their manmade switchbacks and filled with strangely quiet people clutching their documents. Even Emily, with her pristine documents and faultless passport, did not stop feeling anxious until she came out into the vast hall and saw the uniformed driver holding the sign saying 'Ms. Emily Connors.'

The traffic was worse than she remembered, so she had plenty of time to note the small changes paralleling the Bayshore Freeway. More office buildings, the BART station and – a shock that she didn't expect – Candlestick Park being torn down. She was amused to realize that she felt offended by the way history was being altered, as if the city should have been frozen in time once she had gone. Once on city streets, she felt an even deeper stirring of nostalgia. It was a sentiment that surprised and worried her.

The real estate agent met her at the door of the building and led her on a quick tour of the penthouse. "You have the entire top floor and access to the rooftop garden. As you requested, we've negotiated a year's lease, prepaid, with a renewal option for another year." He gushed over the view of the Marina and Alcatraz.

The agent tried several times and in several ways to elicit 'what Emily did' that enabled her to live in such style. He made it a point to emphasize that the previous tenant was the founder of some internet company with a name that seemed to be composed purely of consonants and was worth more than a billion dollars. He called it 'a unicorn.' Emily ignored him and he left thinking that she must be the wife of an obscure but very rich corporate mogul.

As soon as she was alone, she dialed the number for Manfred Gruber. She stood at the twenty-foot-long window looking out at Fisherman's Wharf and whitecaps on the Bay. A huge container ship stacked high with multicolored boxes seemed to dwarf Alcatraz Island as it moved from right to left across her vista. When the answering machine came on, she started to say, "This is Emily –," but she got no further before it was picked up.

"I apologize. I didn't know it was you. Didn't recognize the number." He did not sound apologetic, despite the language.

"I'm here, in San Francisco. This is my residential line."

There was a long interval. "You're living here?"

"For a while, yes. But I'm maintaining the same business lines. Same pricing and service levels."

"Is there anything more I can do for you? Other than what we talked about most recently?"

The Katherine Green contract. Project number one on Chao Zhu's 'to do' list.

"No. I just wanted to let you know that I'm here and that I may be calling for some local support if certain situations arise. How close are you to closing out the Green contract? There is some urgency."

He sounded slightly offended. "I've got a specialist working on it. Should be within a day or so."

There was a long few seconds before he continued. "You know, don't you, that this is my turf?"

My turf! Turf? The man's an idiot.

She kept the exasperation out of her voice. "Of course. I'll keep you fully informed if I start any operations. As you say, it's your turf. To start with, you should know that I've been asked to represent Chao Zhu's interests. I believe you know him."

She disconnected the call before he could reply.

Alcatraz was already emerging from behind the massive container ship. How can something that big move that fast?

She looked at her watch, realizing that she hadn't slept for more than twenty-two hours. She thought about going to bed, but knew that she wouldn't sleep until she ran one more errand that would make her return to the city an irreversible fact.

Time to put Ali to work.

The Killer CPA

Mannie Gruber sat looking at the phone that he had just placed face down on his desk and thinking about his very unsatisfactory conversation with the woman he knew as Emily Connors.

She's here in San Francisco. Could be some complications. And she sure as hell doesn't sound like somebody that's content to stay on the sidelines. We'll see. First step ... Get Campos moving on the Green assignment. He picked up the phone again and started dialing. *Time to talk to my accountant.*

Paul Campos had a thriving CPA firm, with his name on the door. He was good at it, so he had a lot of satisfied clients, perfectly normal people with perfectly normal financial profiles – doctors, lawyers and such. But he also had a subset of clients whose financial success was achieved through other means and who required an accountant and tax expert with two key attributes. The first was an ability to convert money from 'dirty' to 'clean' without giving away too much of it in the process. The second attribute was the ability to maintain a profound silence concerning those particular clients or their revenue sources.

It was this need for silence that led to his other line of business – killing people for hire.

It was an accidental career. Four years ago, he was approached by one of his temporary employees, a college student hired to help him get through the chaotic tax season. The kid was an accounting major at the local community college and Paul had put him to work on one of what he called his 'shoebox clients.' The term was coined for the type of person that would come in – usually about three days before the April 15ᵗ filing deadline – and dump a shoebox full of credit card receipts, utility bills and god knows what else on his desk, saying something like, "Here's all the stuff. Figure out what I owe."

Paul always turned them away. "That's not what I do. Go to H&R Block!" But this particular guy was Mannie Gruber's nephew and Mannie was one of his important and profitable clients, an upstanding local citizen who ran a garbage collection company for local municipalities and large corporations. About half of his revenue was legitimate; the rest was from extortion, union fraud or various other kinds of scams. So Paul scowled at the nephew, telling him "OK, but next year you bring me the stuff in January!" But, the kid being Mannie's nephew, he took the job. He gave the shoebox to the college kid and told him to code all the paper slips into the tax software, a tedious but simple job.

But the kid was smart, very detail oriented. He would have made a good CPA. He spent a couple of hours on the job before he approached Paul, looking both excited and worried.

"Something's funny with this client. He's making up numbers, writing his own credit card slips, claiming business deductions for fur coats and 'escort services' ..."

Where's this kid been? Doesn't he know anything about how things work in family businesses? But he recalled his own innocence when he took his first summer job and the memory disposed him to think kindly of the kid. He started to say something about how the real world might be slightly different from what he was learning in his college courses; one of those "It's OK, don't worry about it" kind of talks. He reached out to pat the kid's arm.

But his options for avuncular advice quickly narrowed dramatically.

"He's drawing paychecks from his uncle's company under eleven different names and social security numbers. And getting Worker's Comp payments under three other aliases. This guy's a one-man fraud machine."

Paul's alarm level jumped about three levels. *Time for damage control. But I think it may be too late.*

"Are you sure? Maybe –"

"All the checks are deposited in one of four different bank accounts, but all of them are in his name. And then once a month he writes a major check to his uncle."

Paul tried again. He shrugged and asked, "So what's the harm? He swindles his uncle and then pays him back. No harm at the end of the day. Probably some family politics behind it all... an angry ex-wife or a brother-in-law looking for a piece of the company ..."

"Yeah, but the people paying for it are the customers, mostly local townships. Those are cost-based municipal contracts, so the taxpayers are the ones getting swindled."

"Look, this stuff you're making up, these stories –"

But the kid was on a roll. "I'm not making it up! And that Worker's Comp scam? People get sent to prison for that kind of chiseling."

"OK. Give me the box of records that you've been working with and show me the coding you've already done. I'll take a look."

The result was at first a disappointed look; and Paul realized that the kid had enrolled himself in a campaign for truth and justice. That impression was immediately confirmed when the disappointed look clearly shifted to suspicion.

"You're not going to ignore this, are you? The guy's a crook."

Great! A self-appointed vigilante against white-collar crime! Why did he happen to me?

"I promise you that I will not ignore what you've told me. *That is for god damn sure!* But I need to see it myself. I want you to go put in a couple of hours on that receivables confirmation project that you were working on before the shoebox guy walked in."

He watched the kid walk back to his desk, indignation showing in his abrupt movements, even the way he walked.

He picked up the phone and dialed a number, his reluctance showing in every way. "Mannie. I've got – we've got – a problem. It's your idiot nephew."

Thinking back on the phone call, Paul was amazed to recall his absolute certainty that Mannie would solve the problem. His past interactions with him had always been pleasant, businesslike exchanges. He did not present as a mob figure, someone who was dangerous to be on the wrong side of; more like a harried small businessman who didn't like paying taxes and would pay well above the going rate to those who enabled him to avoid doing so.

Mannie took the call in stride. "I agree that he's an idiot. Most of my sister's kids are idiots. So what specific act of stupidity did he commit today?"

"He brought his financial files in and asked me to do his 1040."

"So? Do it. And then charge him three times your usual rate. The one for idiots. I pay him enough that he can afford it."

"It's not that simple. I gave the job to one of my seasonal temps. A good kid."

A barely perceptible impatience crept into Mannie's tone. "So? I still don't see the problem."

He tried to be as delicate as possible. He had discovered the hard way that clients like Mannie did not appreciate open-air discussions of their business practices.

"The records that he brought in? Your nephew didn't go through them very carefully. There's a lot of stuff about … of some payroll and Worker's Comp transactions that … that were not fully documented … involving employees other than your nephew."

There was a long silence on the other end of the call. With each second that passed, Paul found it harder to resist the urge to say more. Something reassuring. But he couldn't think of what that might be.

"This 'good kid' that you assigned? Did he know what he was looking at?"

The moment of truth, isn't it? Say "no" and let it slide. Maybe the kid will go meet his girl after work, get laid in a spectacular fashion, and forget all about it. Maybe I can convince him that it's just sloppy bookkeeping and I'll make sure to report it to the authorities.

No good. That leaves me on the hook if the kid has an attack of conscience or starts to brag about his forensic skills to his buddies. And he will, sure as hell.

Mannie was silent. Paul pictured him sitting patiently, probably knowing what kind of internal dialogue was going on and willing to let it run its course to the only acceptable conclusion.

Paul said, "Yeah. He did. Know what he was looking at. Got all righteous about it."

The silence, if possible, deepened.

"And?"

"Uh, I was wondering what you wanted to do about it?"

"It?"

"You know … the problem?"

"Me?"

That was three one-word answers in a row, with each of his responses sounding lame even to him.

"Well, I thought since he's your nephew …"

He let the phrase dangle in the air, hoping to stir up some kind of family bonding type of reaction.

"Yes, he's my nephew. But he's not the *problem* you keep referring to. Except the part where he's an idiot."

"Mannie, I –"

"Look, Paul. It's pretty simple. You've got an employee who's come across confidential and sensitive business information; information that would destroy my business should said employee share it with anyone. I think it's your problem at the moment."

"But what do you expect –"

"I don't *expect* anything. But I can tell you that – if it becomes *my problem* – you won't like the outcome."

Which is how Paul the CPA became a contract killer.

The phrase 'accidental death' had always seemed redundant to Paul Campos. After all, very few people intend to die, so from their perspective, the sudden end must surely be accidental. For the same reason, he objected to the notion that such involuntary endings are 'random' or 'mindless' or 'for no apparent reason,' the kind of language often used in the context of car bombs, airplane crashes or drive-by shooting scenes.

Paul was a believer in chaos theory. He liked the idea that what we call 'random' is merely our inability to see through apparently disconnected chains of events to the underlying causality; that what seems to be chaos is just an extraordinary level of complexity. The analogy of a butterfly flapping its wings in Brazil and – eventually – becoming a hurricane in Asia was appealing to him.

He did not analyze whether he liked the theory because it enabled him to avoid his responsibility for murder. After all, if he's just the final and fairly mechanical factor in a long and tangled sequence leading up to a murderous act, then surely it's not 'his fault?' Such sophistry might have been important to him when he began, but by now he just focused on solving the problem and doing the job in a professional manner. In a way, it was like his day job as a CPA – transforming the chaos of business into order and neatness, the messy details of getting deals done into balanced columns and rows of numbers.

He had gotten into the business involuntarily. *If he hadn't hired the college kid, and if he hadn't given him the idiot nephew's shoebox, and if the kid hadn't been a goody two shoes about a few deposit slips ....*

But then there was the biggest "if" of all, the one that launched his second career, the one that was like a cosmic prank played by some lesser Greek god who was bored and needed a harmless diversion.

Mannie had said, "If it becomes my problem, you won't like the outcome."

Paul was a CPA, but he had a vivid imagination. He also watched the local news and read the papers and was therefore well aware of the various allegations against some of his clients, including Mannie. He knew of colorful stories – urban myths, maybe – about missing subordinates and ex-partners. He spent twenty minutes thinking about all of the possibilities imbedded in the not-so-subtle threat. For a while, he spent the time cataloging the harm to his client base if Mannie was upset with him and thinking of ways to mitigate the damage. Then he was struck by a completely new set of possibilities.

The man's a gangster. He has goons that break people's legs if he doesn't like them. Maybe even kills people.

So what do I do?

To his credit, Paul came up with a civilized solution; an only slightly illegal set of actions that would satisfy almost everybody. *Just get the kid to keep his mouth shut. For everybody's sake, especially his own.*

As if to confirm the rightness of his decision, the kid walked up to him just then. He was exceptionally nervous and Paul wondered if he too had been imagining the possible outcomes of his actions.

"Uh. Mr. Campos, I –"

Paul stopped him quickly. "Before you say anything, I need to tell you something. That shoebox of receipts? You never saw it. No such client ever came in the door."

"But Mr. Campos! You can't let him –"

"Yes I can. And so can you."

And then he used the words that he would regret forever, words that would have an effect exactly opposite to what he intended.

"You could get both of us killed if you don't keep quiet. I can't let you go around telling people about this guy's business."

He watched the kid freeze up. *Good! He's scared. Maybe we can make this work out after all.*

Paul was right about him being frightened. What he failed to appreciate was *who* the kid was afraid of. His entire history to that point in time had not prepared him for the idea that he – a balding, pudgy accountant – might actually frighten someone.

The kid backed up a step and looked around the office for an escape route.

"I need to go. Got a class at SF State this evening."

Paul headed to the door. "C'mon, I'll give you a ride. I want to make sure that we're together on this thing. And I want to give you a little something extra for your cooperation. A performance bonus. C'mon, my car's in the garage."

Again, he failed to see the effect of his words; how his encouragement became – in the kid's mind – code words for something quite different. The phrase 'a little something extra' taken for a lethal threat.

He nudged the kid toward the door, but failed to notice the rigidity in his posture and the way he was looking both left and right, everywhere but at him. He was not yet familiar with the symptoms of suppressed terror and the way that it made every word or gesture appear as a sinister confirmation.

They were driving slowly on Market Street in dense traffic when Paul reached into his coat pocket for the 'little something extra' that he had put together, a thin sheaf of ten one-hundred dollar bills.

"I told you I have something for you. To help you forget about that shoebox."

To his astonishment, the kid lunged for the door handle and jumped out of the moving car. Paul slammed on his brakes and watched as the kid's forward momentum sent him tumbling ahead of the car, arms and legs flailing. He stumbled to his feet and took off in a clumsy lopsided run, staring back over his shoulder at Paul and straight into the path on an oncoming Muni bus.

Paul sat frozen for about twenty seconds, still holding the hundred dollar bills and watching a small crowd begin to form, peering under the front of the stopped bus. Then he drove off.

Two days later, Mannie called.

"I wanted to congratulate you on how you handled the *problem* that we discussed last time. I don't know how you did it, but it was a nice touch."

"It was an accident."

"Sure it was. I must admit I am just now beginning to appreciate the range of your skills. In fact, I'd like to talk to you about a couple of projects that call for someone with your special abilities. How about lunch tomorrow?"

That was four years ago. At first reluctant, by now he valued the second career that Mannie had steered him into and he was beginning to think of himself as a professional, a specialist in odd jobs that required both improvisational skills and judgment. He looked forward to the infrequent assignments and to visualize different roles for himself. He bought a gun in Nevada and began to work out at a gym.

Without knowing it, he had become the evil twin to Walter Mitty.

He did not know Emily Connors, but her arrival in San Francisco was about to cause a surge in his second career. As usual, it started with a call from Mannie.

Death of a Socialite

Mannie was quite brief. "There's a woman named Katherine Green. I think she needs to have one of those accidents that seem to happen when you're around."

Campos was dressed in a dark three-piece suit, intending to go to his office once the job was done. He did not expect the job to take long and did not bother to change clothes. The only addition to his everyday workday outfit was the pair of latex gloves. He had done all of the planning required yesterday.

One of the simpler jobs really.

The house had numerous entrances, but all of them were locked, well-lighted and visible from busy city streets. None of that mattered because he had a key. Mannie had given it to him along with his instructions.

"There's a live-in maid, but she's off on Thursday. Nobody else except the woman this particular person is interested in. There's a 'panic button' type of alarm by the front door and in the master bedroom, but nowhere else. I need the key back when you're done."

He said, "Got it, I'll --," but Mannie clearly had something to add.

"I know you're good at what you do. The person who wants this done? She doesn't like mistakes … Believes in zero defects.… Get it right the first time. That kind of stuff. You understand what I'm saying?"

This is not like Mannie. Usually just gives me a steely gaze and says something like, "We're counting on you." This woman must be something special, even in Mannie's subterranean world.

He shrugged. "No problem. Just make sure the money gets transferred. You know the drill."

He went down the alley alongside the house and let himself in one of the side entrances, finding himself on a landing about halfway down a narrow and badly lit staircase that apparently ran from the top floor to the bottom floor. It reminded him of an extra long escalator in a hotel or airport terminal.

Better and better! Tailor made for one of those unfortunate household accidents ...

The interior door from the landing into the house was unlocked and he found himself in a library with floor-to-ceiling bookshelves and a definite air of neglect. He could hear the sounds of a radio or TV from somewhere above him, so he moved carefully up an interior stairway toward the voices. This staircase was carpeted and the wall were lined with oil paintings, each with a discreet light mounted above it. They were all seascapes.

He found the woman on the top floor, in the dressing area outside the main bedroom. She was standing with her back to him watching a TV news report, something about refugees in Eastern Europe. She was fully dressed, but in slippers and with a robe thrown around her shoulders.

The sound of the TV covered up his approach until he was reaching out for her. Something – a sound or a reflection from the TV – made her whirl around. The first flash of fear lasted only a second, replaced by anger.

"Who are you? What are you doing in my –"

Later, he wondered about his reaction, how violent it was despite the objectivity that he prided himself on. But her sense of entitlement annoyed him; her presumption that he didn't belong; that she *deserved* to be safe because it was *her house!* It made him respond carelessly, *unprofessionally.*

He grabbed her arm, hard, and pulled her toward the door that was barely visible in the dark paneling on the far wall. She fought, dragging her feet and hitting at him. He hit her once, a hard slap with his open palm against the side of her head that knocked her to her knees and seemed to dislodge her hair, unraveling whatever was holding it in place. So he shifted his grip from her arm to her hair and dragged her through the doorway onto the landing. Once there, he stood her up and gave her a hard push, sending her somersaulting down the stairs. She tumbled to a stop just across the next landing, up against the inside wall with her feet above her head.

He walked slowly down and looked at her. She was whimpering, pulling with one arm on the side railing. He helped her get to her feet, amused by the way she held on to him with both hands, as though he was a rescuer. He pried her fingers loose from his arm and gave another hard shove.

This time, she fell more loosely, as though gravity had become weaker. When he reached her this time, she was absolutely still. He gathered her one more time in his arms. She felt more substantial, surprisingly heavy, and the term "dead weight" became more meaningful to him. He dragged her upright and let her topple forward, but she just puddled at his feet as if her skeletal structure had dissolved. He dragged her up once more, holding her under her arms and against him in an obscene embrace. He had to pivot his entire body and awkwardly pitch her forward. It was like throwing a very heavy and floppy sack of grain.

This time, she made it almost to the bottom in a series of soft "thumps," coming to rest face up with her head at an unnatural angle against the side wall. He checked for a pulse and – when he knew that he would not find any – he walked back up to the level where he had entered and let himself out into the alley.

Recon

Ali Hakan liked San Francisco and wished that he had discovered the city sooner. His opinion was an informed one, as he had direct experience with a dozen or more of the world's major cities, particularly in Europe, Asia and the Middle East. He was finishing a short assignment in Manila when the woman he knew only as 'Emily' called him.

"Do you have an American passport? I'm going to need someone I can trust in San Francisco, probably for at least a few months."

He responded instantly. He was a free lancer with a good reputation and a number of clients that valued both the quality of his services and his availability. But the woman paid well and – unlike many of his other clients -- listened to him when he offered suggestions about the best way to accomplish her objectives. He had proved himself as a shrewd tactician and – twice in the last few years – had improved on her original plan.

Those advantages just barely outweighed his distaste about working for a woman, an understandable bias given his upbringing. Ali was an Iraqi, a deserter from Saddam Hussein's elite Revolutionary Guard unit who signed up with the Desert Storm allies to take Kuwait back from Saddam and, ten years later, with the American CIA to consult regarding targets and tactics for small assassination teams in Afghanistan and Iraq. He quit when the Americans became enamored with drones in place of professional warriors with sharp blades and flexible loyalties.

"I can be there within twenty-four hours."

"Good. Once you're there, buy a reliable and ordinary-looking car. Find a place to live somewhere inside the city and wait to hear from me. And once you're settled, get us a couple of high-quality handguns. One for each of us. And half-a-dozen disposable cell phones."

The rents in San Francisco were ridiculous. Money was not a problem, but Ali could not help resenting the fact that he had to pay three thousand dollars a month for a studio apartment in a not-very-nice part of town. He told the landlord that he was driving for Uber and would be keeping irregular hours.

He was ready when she called and picked her up twenty minutes after she called. He'd purchased a three-year-old Honda Civic for cash and had been assured by a reliable source that two semi-automatic pistols would be delivered within two days.

Only in America, he thought. *Cars and guns available to all. And women in charge!*

They didn't talk, other than her giving him directions as to where she wanted to go. The first stop was a small and very ordinary house in the Noe Valley neighborhood. As far as he could tell, it was home to a Korean family with several children. She did not get out of the car, seemingly content to just look at the structure with a blank expression. He had no way of knowing that just the sight of the house had stirred up memories that she thought were buried so deep that retrieval was impossible.

It hasn't changed, except to get older. Probably has the same carpeting and ugly wallpaper. A good place to escape from.

After five minutes, she told Ali, "Go." And she knew that she would never go back. *They talk of 'closure.' Maybe there's something to it after all.* As if to confirm the thought, an image of Gary's possessions being consumed in the flames of the funeral pyre flashed in her head.

The next destination was just off of Laguna Street in the Lower Haight, a narrow three-story Victorian that looked like something out of the nineteenth century. It was a classic example of what the tourist books called 'San Francisco's painted ladies.' There was a parking space immediately in front of it, but she directed Ali to a space further down the block and across the street. Once again, she stayed in the car and watched. But this time, Ali sensed that this was a stakeout, not just a drive-by to check out an address.

After twenty minutes, she asked Ali a strange question. "What kind of a person would live in a house like that ... so vertical, painted that brightly, looking like a child's dollhouse?"

He thought about his studio apartment and rent bill. "Someone that can afford the price," seemed to him to be an appropriate response. But she wasn't listening. They left thirty minutes later. On the way back to her new home, she asked him to drive up Hyde Street. They made one more stop, at the top of Hyde near the entrance to what the tourist brochures called 'the crookedest street in the world.' This time, she got out of the car and told him to pick her up in thirty minutes.

She sat at the bus stop across the street from the house and studied the blank front, with its ridiculous looking pillars. Then she walked alongside the house on the steep downhill street and looked at – but did not go into – the dead-end alley on the other side of the house. Then she returned to the bench and thought about it.

The house angered her. *Basically a huge ugly box. Built by and lived in by people with more money than taste. Now something to be preserved just because it has survived when it didn't deserve to. It sits there, completely indifferent to what it contains or to the fact that people have been killed – and still are being killed – because of what has happened within those walls.*

Gary was stupid, leaving all that evidence behind. So smug and sure that his work would never be discovered. Then Chao Zhu commissions me to buy the house 'for family reasons.' Even though no Chinese person has ever owned or – so far as my research has taken me – even worked on or visited the damn property! And some rich ex-con wants to buy it and live in it for god-knows what reason.

But the final touch, the truly supreme irony, is that Natalie Weiss – the mayor's adopted daughter – is the strongest voice for preserving the house for the sake of 'posterity.' Why? How can a woman that lives in that silly Victorian throwback think something like this is worth saving?

Complications and coincidence all over the place, like one of those multigenerational Victorian novels.

Ali stopped in the bus zone just then and she got in the passenger side. As he pulled back into the traffic, she asked another and even stranger question.

"Ali, you were once a Muslim. Maybe still are. You believed in what you called 'fate,' didn't you?"

His first reaction was, *the woman is completely unpredictable!* But then he was jarred even more. *She says 'once a Muslim.' Am I still?* But his answer to her question was quite serious.

"It is one of the six basic beliefs." And he recited, "Whatever Allah wills happens, and whatever Allah does not will does not happen. If something happens to a person, it could not have missed him, and if something does not happen to him, it could not have happened to him."

She looked closely at him, reminded again that people were complicated creatures, especially those that she seemed to come into contact with.

First Gary, then me. We came through so much. Made so many sacrifices ... changes. Then I'm back here, as though I had never left. And cleaning up what Gary left behind. As if all that we ... I ... have done was somebody else's master plan. And, whoever that somebody else is, is laughing at me.

For the first time in a long time, she was depressed.

Emily's depression was still with her the next morning. Ali's words concerning 'fate' would not go away.

I coulda been somebody!

The irony was exquisite, given that she was looking out at the San Francisco Bay waterfront but did not recognize that her thought was an exact quote from Marlon Brando's famous line in the film 'On the Waterfront.'

It was just as well that she missed the connection. Brando's character went on to a brutal self-diagnosis – *I was a bum* – that Emily could not possibly have applied to herself, believing as she did that her imaginary shortfalls were traceable entirely to others, beginning with her parents and continuing today through the pettiness of those around her. The idea that it might be something called 'fate' was unthinkable to her.

Even the disfiguration of her eyes. The doctor had blamed the hyperthyroidism on a 'rogue gene,' a term that, to her, described a deliberate attack rather than an accident of fate.

The view from her penthouse was familiar to her, even though she'd been away from San Francisco for almost two decades. She left intending never to return, but visiting the house in Noe Valley brought it all back again. It was the place where she had last seen her mother, twenty years ago, leaving the house on her way to her husband's memorial service. In Emily's imagination, she was grieving in the manner of one who has lost a once-close college friend; a person to be mourned because they were important to her at some point in a long-ago past. She clung to her daughter in a way that left it unclear whether it was for her benefit or that of her daughter.

They never did accept that I didn't care about their whining; that their feeble attempts at shaming me into being a child to show off to their rich friends only made them even more pathetic than they were. The jerk should have used his time to take swimming lessons! And he could have left more money behind than he did ...

Her father left a small insurance policy but almost a half-million dollars of assets that his mother liquidated. Emily used what she thought of as 'her fair share' to fund her first criminal enterprise, a distribution network that sold pot and some of the more common opiates to affluent students at private schools. She was lucky in that she quintupled her investment and got out of dealing before the cops or – the far more important threat, the local street gangs -- learned about her growing business. Operating purely on instinct, she bet all of her accumulated profits on a single shipment of cocaine out of Mexico. It worked, and she left the U.S. with three hundred thousand dollars squirreled away in Asian bank accounts.

In the years between early Bangkok and today, she built The Petrel Foundation into her personal investment vehicle. It was named after her father's ill-starred boat, the only remnant of which was a four-foot section of a polished teak plank bearing its name, salvaged from the wrecked boat after being retrieved from the Bay. That piece of wood was buried along with her past, not far from where she stood.

The old man would be mortified. He raved about the petrel. How the noble bird was always in the air, far from land, soaring – never "flying," always "soaring" – in strong winds over stormy seas. Never mentioned that the boat named after the damn bird never went anywhere except to sail around Alcatraz on the occasional Saturday morning. Now it's the name of an enterprise that he would have despised.

However, neither the Petrel Foundation nor Emily Connors was sufficiently visible to elicit disapproval or any other emotion. They operated and flourished in the dark, obscure agents of dubious legality and even more obscure causes.

For the moment, that was the problem, the cause of her *"I coulda been somebody"* lament. The key to her success – invisibility – was also what kept her from the recognition that she felt entitled to; the *respect* that she demanded from those around her.

Legal Update

For Emily, the phone call early the next morning seemed to confirm her suspicions about her second-class status.

"I'm afraid we may have run into a bit of a problem."

The man's a complete asshole. He talks like what he is – a New York lawyer in a three-piece suit who doesn't want his client to get alarmed because he can't do what he's being paid $700-an-hour to do. He isn't "afraid," and he knows damn well there's a "problem," and it's more than "a bit."

But Emily stayed in the role she had assigned herself for the purposes of this transaction, that of a genteel, extremely proper and obsessively private woman trying to do good but stay anonymous, a motivation that could be read as either praiseworthy modesty or insecurity.

"That's disturbing. Do we need to increase the amount we're offering?"

She could almost hear the sigh of relief from the New York lawyer. *Nothing like having a client that doesn't care about the cost!*

"Maybe later, but that's not the immediate problem."

She waited. *So just say it, asshole! What is the immediate problem? Or are you stalling because you haven't met your billable hours quota yet this week?*

"As you know, we submitted your offer last week. As you directed, it went directly to the Mayor's office and included a two-week deadline for responding, as well as our acceptance of the city's requirements for seismic testing and subsequent upgrades."

"And they haven't responded?" she asked, even though she knew the answer.

"Not a word, other than a letter acknowledging receipt of the offer. They've held a public hearing. That's all."

Again, a long pause. *Asshole wants me to express disappointment or concern, so that he can show me how far above and beyond the call of duty his underpaid associates just out of law school went on my behalf.*

"Is there anything we can do?"

"Not officially." The smugness was as obvious as if he'd been standing in front of her waiting for her to show disappointment so that he could reveal the full extent of his powers.

"And unofficially?"

"I have some contacts in City Hall. I can't tell you who they are, but I asked them to find out what's going on."

"And? What is going on?"

"There are three different problems."

She felt like screaming at him. *Spit it out, asshole! Just tell me what they are!*

"First, nothing happens quickly for decisions like this. Delay is normal."

She couldn't help it. It was not a scream, but the combination of impatience and scorn came through quite clearly.

"I don't need an over-priced lawyer to tell me that! Do you have *anything* to say that I don't already know?" She wanted to add, "asshole," but refrained.

The verbal whiplash seemed to help. He began speaking, less sure of himself, but faster.

"Yes. Well. Our second problem ... I was able to find out that the Mayor is looking at two other options, and that's one of the reasons that she hasn't responded to us. She's considering keeping the house and using the property as part of her so-called 'affordable housing' package, or perhaps as a neighborhood office of some sort. And even if she goes ahead with an outright sale, we've got another bidder, somebody or something called the MK Foundation."

"Can't we just outbid them? Doesn't the city have to take the highest bid?"

"It's not that simple. Nothing is in that precious city! You run into something called 'the highest and best use' clause. Basically, it means that the mayor has to be able to say with a straight face that her decision is the best possible one in the circum –"

"Doesn't thirty million dollars qualify as good enough?"

"Not if you've got multiple bidders. What I'm afraid of is that it will be hard for you to stay anonymous. Selling a city-owned asset to an unknown buyer will be hard for her to justify, especially with an election year coming up and assuming that the MK Foundation has a pretty public face to go with it. We may have to disclose who the buyer is."

Ain't gonna happen.

"What do we know about this MK Foundation?"

"I've got my associates digging into that. Should have that for you tomorrow."

"Once you do that, see if they can be bought off. Pay them something to drop out of the bidding."

She smiled at the silence that ensued and entertained herself by imagining the look of disapproval that her caller was probably directing at the telephone receiver.

"Uh …. We can't do that. There's various laws … regulations of all sorts. I'm afraid that you … We …"

She cut off the stammering, knowing that his mind was already sorting through various quasi-legal options to do exactly what she had suggested.

Doesn't matter. There's someone more qualified than this asshole to do what I want!

"You said there were 'three problems.' Have we covered them?"

He recovered quickly, obviously relieved to be on safer ground. "The other issue is that we may not even get a chance to make another offer. It turns out that the house is now classified as 'city-owned real estate' and falls under the jurisdiction of the Department of City-Owned Real Estate. And the head of that department wants to keep it under city ownership."

The Department of City-Owned Real Estate! Now, there's a handy coincidence. The department that happens to employ Donna Yang. I wonder if Chao Zhu knew about that when we met in Macao?

"Can't the Mayor just tell him or her to do what he's told?"

"Not in your City by the Bay." It was a verbal sneer, expressed in tones that made the man's disdain for San

Francisco as obvious as the monologue of a right-wing talk show host. "In this case, the department head effectively has veto power over the use – or sale – of any the city's properties. And this guy wants to keep your Russian Hill house in the portfolio."

So. Only one person to persuade. Not the entire political infrastructure of San Francisco. And we don't need asshole lawyers from New York for that kind of persuasion.

"What's the name of this person? Maybe I can bring some local pressure to bear."

"Good luck. His name is Alban … Edward Alban … and I don't think he's what you'd call persuadable."

We'll see about that. And she ended the call.

She sat staring at the phone for thirty seconds, then reached into her desk drawer, selected one of the half-dozen cell phones scattered there and dialed. It was answered promptly.

"This is Mannie." The voice was neutral, no hint of the usual faint curiosity that normal people exhibit on answering the phone. This was somewhat surprising, given the often lethal nature of the transactions that this number was dedicated to.

She did not bother to identify herself, nor was it necessary. Civility was not an important part of their infrequent conversations. "You do a lot of contracts with the city. Do you have any in's at something called the Department of City Owned Real Estate?"

Mannie's hesitation was just long enough to remind Emily that Mannie not only knew quite a lot about the Department, but was profiting from its corruption. *City housing. Vacant buildings. Ideal for temporary housing for illegals on their way through. Pop up drug labs. Rent controlled apartments for residents who know who to ask. Quick sale and below-market prices for Chinese or Russian flight capital wanting trophy properties, with a nice little 'commission' for someone who facilitates the sale.*

"Yeah. I know that bunch."

"The name Edward Alban just came up. Do you know him?"

Mannie's contempt was thick. "He's the department manager. A very macho Latino high up in the city's civil service. Thinks he's a major player. Fact is, he's a poster boy for affirmative action. Supplements his salary with bribes and kickbacks."

"Is he one of yours?"

"I take a percentage. He skims, but so far it's tolerable."

She thought about how to phrase her question in a way that Mannie wouldn't see through. "What if we asked him for a favor? Something that fell within his day job?"

"I guarantee his first question will be 'What's in for me?'"

Not much difference between him and the New York lawyers, except they send impressive-looking invoices on embossed stationery.

"What's in for him? He gets to keep his kneecaps intact!" As she heard the barely subdued outrage in her own voice, she recognized that it was a reaction to her phone call with the lawyer, a release of pent up irritation because of having to be polite to an asshole.

Mannie's response was five or six seconds delayed, a pause that she knew to be a sign that he was going to disagree with her.

"This guy? Alban? He doesn't respond well to threats. Sees it as an affront to his manhood. It's a cultural thing. But wave some money at him and –"

"OK, so wave money," she broke in. She went on to tell him what she wanted from Alban.

She heard the amusement in Mannie's voice when he said, "I'll talk to him today and get back to you."

Should I tell him about my contract with Chao Zhu to counsel Donna Yang? Not a chance. In fact, I think some misdirection is called for.

"And find out who's his successor at the Department of whatever. We may need a Plan B."

But what he said next made her realize that Mannie failed to understand Chao Zhu's larger agenda and, because of that, was probably not going to be around very long himself.

"As far as Alban's successor, it's a woman named Donna Yang. She's Chinese and afraid of her own shadow. Won't be a problem. She'll do whatever she's told to do."

She sat thinking about the way coincidences were piling up and how they could be used.

Time to meet Donna.

Donna Yang

Emily had chosen to meet at the bleachers at the Aquatic Park, a place that appealed to her. *Probably because I used to do drug deals here.* Part of the appeal was the openness, a space so public that both parties could feel free from overt threats. The feeling tended to encourage a surprising degree of candor that could sometimes be useful for a person in Emily's line of work. The other factor was Emily's belief that she had an advantage if her companion found himself or herself sitting side-by-side on a cold concrete bench rather than eye-to-eye across a mahogany tabletop.

Donna Yang was not what Emily expected, even with the benefits of the dossier she had compiled before the meeting. She knew that Yang was the thirty-year-old only daughter of an utterly ordinary Chinatown couple that had been in the U.S. for thirty years. She was unmarried, living at home and apparently without any close friends. Her only non-work habit was going to movies. To Emily, her appearance was identical to every other young Chinese woman she had passed on the street in the last few days. She had worked at the Department of City Owned Real Estate for eight years, her only job after graduating from the business school at San Francisco State. Her main responsibility was personnel, although – unofficially -- she was next-in-line to the Department Head, Edward Alban.

What was *not* in the dossier, but known to Emily through her meeting with Chao Zhu, was that Yang was the architect and primary overseer of a sophisticated criminal operation, a patchwork of scams, larcenies and minor corruptions that in their totality cost the City of San Francisco millions of dollars in diverted revenues. She was also highly ambitious and impatient, a combination that Chao Zhu feared for his niece and had commissioned Emily to counsel her about.

Sitting in Macao, his voice contained both admiration and irritation. "She is as American as she is Chinese. She has no patience and does not understand the need to flatter those above her. She does not respect her elders and she underestimates her opponents, especially if they are not Chinese. I think she is dangerous, both to herself and to our larger interests."

Emily's response was instant and indignant. "I am not a teacher. Nor a therapist. My methods are –"

He broke in sharply, waving his hand dismissively. "I know your methods, and I expect you to use them on her behalf. It is time for her to learn how to move to the next level, a level that requires more than bookkeeping and personnel techniques. She needs someone like you. If she happens to learn something from watching you work, it's – how do the Americans say it – *frosting on the cake.*"

The woman that sat down alongside her on the concrete bench looked like a shopkeeper on her lunch hour. She was plain in every way – her face, rimless glasses, hairstyle, clothing, even her posture, hunched forward with her feet just barely touching the ground. Everything about her said, *here is a person of little consequence, content with what she has and with little prospect of change.* For Emily, because she knew differently, it made Donna Yang an intriguing person.

Yang spoke first, looking out at a pair of swimmers traversing the gray and choppy waters of the marina. "My grandfather said that I can learn from you. That I should listen and watch."

Emily said nothing, letting the silence build. It was a tactic that she liked to use with new clients.

When the woman didn't go on, Emily turned sideways to look directly at her and said, "He expects much of you."

"My grandfather is an old fool who has lived too long in the same place. He does not like change."

This surprised Emily. *He said she was impatient, that she didn't respect her elders. But I think he missed something even more important: this woman is unafraid, maybe even reckless, the kind of person who will be dangerous for those around her. I think she is a little bit like me.*

"I shall not attempt to *advise* you, Ms. Yang, even if I think you are doing something stupid. I am someone that will consider what you ask of me and say either 'yes' or 'no'. So, what is it that you would like me to do?"

She was pleased to see the flash of uncertainty in her eyes, quickly suppressed. *That is good. If she is unsure, it means that she can learn.*

"I have two problems. Chao Zhu recommended that I solicit your advice as to the best solution."

Emily simply stared at her and waited.

"There is a man ... my boss –"

"Edward Alban. I know of him. He is in your way."

Yang leaned away from Emily, as if to see her more fully. The look of uncertainty was gone, replaced by a look of outright curiosity, even appraisal. Emily smiled.

"He is not Chinese," said Yang.

When she did not go on, Emily realized that those four words – for Yang – encompassed all of Alban's many and diverse faults. She also knew that, someday, probably not so far in the future, Yang would say the same thing about her and would seek a similar solution.

Yang went on quickly, as though sensing that her reply revealed too much. "He takes too much for himself. And he has no vision about what is possible. Everything that happens is because of what I have done, but he thinks he is responsible. Worst of all, he is afraid. Of change. Of other men."

"What is it you want me to do?" It was the question Emily always asked the client at this point in the conversation, not because she needed any direction or clarity, but because she wanted to see if they would actually say the words.

It is as if they believe that they are somehow not responsible if they only use gestures, hints or euphemisms. That the ambiguity makes them superior to me, the person they employ to do the thing they cannot say aloud.

This woman was different. She said, "I want you to kill him, of course."

"An accident, I presume?"

"That would be best. A murder or suicide could call attention to his job, which would not be good for our business."

The pair of swimmers had reached the other side of the marina and had started the return lap. *I wonder how they can stand the boredom and the fifty-five degree water, what such people are like when they emerge from the water and go back to their lives? What they would think if they knew the two women watching them were casually striking agreements to kill someone?*

Emily stood up, but Yang did not move. Emily remembered her words. *I have two problems.*

"What is the other problem where you need my help?"

Again, that flash of uncertainty. Emily sat back down and watched her closely.

"I want to change our business model. When Alban is … gone."

The euphemism confirmed the woman's uncertainty and, for the first time, Emily became aware of the differences between them. Not just age and race, but the vast totality of their experiences. It caused a ripple of sadness to run through her, a sensation that she was unused to.

As if she understood the effect of what she had said, Yang went on hurriedly. "A lot of what we do is tied to local gangs – drug houses, pop-up prostitution sites, that sort of stuff. They pay us to provide the property, but they keep all the proceeds. That was OK at the very beginning, when we were starting out. But then they strong-armed Alban, demanded a percentage of everything we were making. He caved in. So we do all the work and get maybe ten percent of the take."

"And you want to change that." It was not a question.

"Yes, but Alban manages all of the contacts with the local bosses. I never see any part of that. I need you to find out who's who and help me figure out the best way to change the financial arrangements."

Emily did not respond immediately, thinking back to her days of managing a Bangkok sex marketplace. *Financial arrangements! That's what the new landlord wanted: a change in the financial arrangements. What he got was a machete imbedded in his skull and a ten-foot drop into a canal choked with sewage.*

She came back to the present. "Can you give me a name? Anybody particular that he dealt with?"

"All I know is that he talked a lot with someone he called 'Mannie.'"

Emily tried not to laugh.

The Last Brookings

Emily's next stop was a forty minute drive across the Golden Gate Bridge and she spent the entire time brooding. It was triggered by her ongoing irritation at Chao Zhu's insistence on her role as Donna Yang's 'coach' but then it morphed into self-doubt about her intended destination.

Ali focused on his driving but was fully aware of Emily's mood. He remained silent, leaving her to her internal monologue.

Why are you doing this? Is there something about being back in San Francisco that makes you stupid?

Emily was unused to such internal doubts and her first instinct was to dismiss them. *It's not stupidity. The house is a danger to me and I need to know as much as I can about the house.*

But some doubts persisted, and she had learned to pay attention to those that resisted her usual positive thinking. *Donna Yang is part of the job you signed on for in Macao. It's not going to work, but that's because of Chao Zhu's sentimentalism. Not my fault. But this fixation on the Brookings house? That's dangerous and maybe even stupid. You're acting on your own and – worse than that – perhaps acting against the interests of your client. That's bad for business. And it could get you killed.*

There's too much coincidence. Chao Zhu wants me to buy the Brookings House for him. Is it really coincidence or does he know about Gary and what he left behind in San Francisco? Why is he so interested in this particular building?

She was jarred out her unproductive thought pattern by Ali, speaking in almost apologetic tones.

"We're here."

Google made the last surviving member of the Brookings clan easy to find. And a few extra minutes on the internet enabled Emily to verify that the woman's financial assets were quite limited.

The tone of the interview was set from the first.

"Ms. Brookings, I'm –"

"It's *Mrs.* Brookings, damn it! Save the politically correct stuff for the simpering sisterhood out there!" She made a grand sweeping gesture with her arm, apparently to encompass any female outside of the room where the two of them sat.

Rose Brookings was a diminutive figure. The reality that she was eighty-five-years old did not stop her from dressing in a fire-red pants suit or talking very loudly. She had lacquered hair piled on top of her head, and the sports section of the San Francisco Chronicle open on her lap. Not at all what Emily expected, and the disconnect jarred her into a sudden thought.

I guess there are a lot of ways one can get older, maybe not all of them bad. Assuming one survives to experience the alternatives.

She started again, with a strong emphasis on the first word. "*Mrs.* Brookings –"

"What's wrong with your eyes?"

An instant surge of anger rippled through Emily and she barely stopped herself from slapping the woman. Then she realized that no one had ever asked her that question. They looked away, turned fidgety or became conspicuously polite, but they never asked 'What's wrong with your eyes?'

Maybe you become honest when you get old? Or maybe just cruel?

"It's a common side effect of hyperthyroidism. But I can see just fine. Mrs. Brookings, my name is –"

"Lee Wilson," the woman interrupted once more. "And you're a free-lance writer, wanting to interview me. About my house. We covered all that stuff on the phone. Welcome to the elephant's graveyard." This time, the sweeping gesture included the immediate surroundings.

Those surroundings reminded Emily of a Grand Hyatt hotel. The soaring atrium, central fountain, abundant shrubbery that created secluded conversational areas, and – very discreet, at the fringes of their view – uniformed staff awaiting a signal. The nearest one was watching them closely and – Emily thought – nervously.

I wonder which one of us is making him nervous?

The woman also was watching her closely, apparently able to track her thoughts. "They call it 'luxury living for discerning seniors,' but the official label is a 'continuing care residence.' I like to think of it as a cruise ship that never puts in to port. A very exclusive cruise ship."

A million five up front and five thousand a month. For that, you could buy a very nice round-the-world cruise. I guess that includes burial at sea, which can't be too far off for these people.

'These people' were the dozen or so residents scattered around the vast room. All but two of them were female and each of those was dressed as though a semi-formal lawn party was about to start on the manicured lawn on the other side of the French doors. Rose looked like the youngest of the lot.

"Mrs. Brookings, thank you for seeing me. I hope that –"

"We're the presentable ones. The ones that aren't quite ready for the Alzheimer's unit next door."

Four tries, four interruptions. This may take a while.

"As I was saying, I'd like to ask you about your house on Russian Hill. Where you lived before you came here. And about your husband."

Rose sat back against the cushions and pulled her feet under her. "That was a long time ago. 1995. Do you know I was the first resident of this place? Donald would have been mortified at the price. But he was dead."

She giggled. "Dead. Now that's a very real form of mortification, isn't it?"

It took another ten minutes of helter-skelter conversation before Emily could get her focused on the questions she needed to ask.

She asked, "How long did you live in the house?"

"Twenty-nine years. From the day I married until the day Donald was killed."

"Did it feel funny? Just the two of you in all that space?"

"His mother was with us until she died. Too long, in my opinion. But he wanted it that way. No servants, no company. We just closed off most of the rooms on the two bottom levels. And it was the same with his father and grandfather. Hated everyone. Misers to the core, every one of them. But they had a thing about that house, the male Brookings did."

"Sounds a bit like an obsession to me," Emily suggested. "Like maybe the house had some secret attached to it."

Rose snorted. "The Brookings Curse. That's what the newspapers called it. About every ten years, some bright-eyed young thing fresh out of journalism school would come around and ask about it. Once, a TV station wanted to film it. But it was all nonsense. It was just a big old drafty house with a lot of coincidences."

Emily switched gears. "Your husband was murdered. Was that a coincidence?"

She didn't answer the question, just looked at Emily with a funny smile. "You want mysteries? Figure out why and how his father was killed. That's a much more interesting puzzle than my miserable husband."

Was killed? "Your father-in-law – Orville Brookings – committed suicide in a Chinese house of prostitution. Where's the mystery ... unless for a psychiatrist?"

"Orville lived with us for two years after Donald and I married. He was in the house when we moved in. And he hated – absolutely hated – the Chinese. Excuse the expression, but he wouldn't be caught dead in a Chinese whorehouse."

"Do you know why he had this thing about the Chinese?"

"He thought they killed his father. Donald's grandfather."

A boating 'accident.'

Not for the first time, Emily wondered what Chao Zhu had left out of his narrative at their meeting in Macao.

"What about your husband? You have any idea why he was murdered?"

"Because nobody liked the son-of-a-bitch. He was a crook, and not a very good one. He had lots of enemies."

"I read about it. They called it a home invasion robbery."

"I was at one of my book clubs, so Donald was home alone. They tied him up and beat him quite severely. The police called it torture. Then they shot him. And they took nothing. Some robbery!"

She sounds disappointed. Because he was dead, or because the thieves didn't steal anything?

"Did you know the man they arrested?"

"No. And they didn't even convict him. At least, not for Donald's murder. They showed me his picture over and over. He was Chinese and I think they all look like a gardener my mother had when I was growing up."

"Your husband was quite wealthy, wasn't he?"

"That's what he liked people to think. In fact, he had burned through the little bit of money that his father had left him and was seriously in debt. I had to sell the house to get the money to move into this place. Lucky for me, the market was good. Took less than a month. The buyers were young, very modern. Not the right people at all for a house like that."

"Why do you say that?"

"Well, they didn't last very long, did they?"

Natalie watched the two women from the other side of the vast room, struck by the contrast between them. *Young vs. old, flamboyant vs. stylish, talkative vs. quiet, tall vs. short ... clearly some kind of interview.*

She was here on a mission, checking out one of her many undone items on her project to complete her 'history of the Brookings house' for her preservation project. Rose Brookings would be the only 'first person' source available to her. When she asked at the desk, she was told, "Rose has a visitor at the moment, but you should wait. She always wants to talk to people." When she signed the guest book at the reception desk, she noted that the current visitor was a woman named Lee Wilson.

She could see the exact instant that the younger woman lost interest in the conversation, and it was only another few seconds before she stood up abruptly and held out her hand. The disappointment of her elderly companion was equally evident. Natalie started toward the corner of the vast lobby where they sat. Midway there, she came face-to-face with the other woman who was walking purposefully toward the front entrance. When she looked up to see Emily approaching, she was visibly startled and almost stumbled.

Natalie's first reaction was, *her eyes, how unfortunate.* The woman kept on and did not look back. But she was walking faster and a certain rigidity in her posture triggered Natalie's next impression, a few steps after they passed one another.

She knows me, but I have no idea who she is. And I don't think she is pleased to see me. She doesn't like me!

Unfolding Plans

Emily was shaken by the encounter with Natalie. It was a feeling that she was unfamiliar with and one that she definitely did not like.

She kept walking, never looking back until she was in the car with Ali. Her first reaction was simple anger at herself. *So much for long distance surveillance! You knew she is close to everything about the house, so why are you surprised that you both show to interview the old woman?*

So what did I learn? Or, more importantly, what will Ms. Natalie Weiss take away from her visit with the widow? Not much, I think. The Brookings are – were -- a sorry lot who didn't get much out of life. Misers, loners and hard-luck people who deserved what they got. Best of all, they didn't know much or maybe even care very much about the house they lived in.

So let's find out.

"Ali, how good are you at breaking and entering? Without anyone knowing you were ever there?"

His hesitation was just barely perceptible. I have lots of experience. The 'without anyone knowing' part depends on how I get in and how much stuff I take away."

Emily smiled. "I'll give you a key that should work unless they've changed the locks. And you don't have to steal anything once you're there. I just need some photographs of a laundry room."

"Sounds easy."

"And I want you to do it tonight."

Once Ali was briefed, Emily allowed herself to think once more about her face-to-face encounter with the woman in the lobby. It was easy for her to recall every image from the moment she looked up to see her ten feet away to the time when she saw the by now familiar combination of shock and then pity in her expression as they passed.

I wonder what my expression revealed? Natalie Weiss up close is quite beautiful. Very natural, self-confident.

Probably a good athlete. I also think she's smart, and therefore dangerous.

She finally allowed the real question, the one that had been lurking just below the surface of her consciousness, to appear in its full, unadorned form.

Does Natalie need to go?

She met Manfred Gruber on an isolated park bench at the Yerba Buena Center. Some big tech convention was in town and there were swarms of men and women crossing the green in front of them, going in all directions. They all seemed to be about twenty-five years old, wore badges on lanyards around their necks, and carried a bright green plastic bag with a string of Chinese characters on it. It reminded Emily of a scene in a dystopian sci-fi movie whose name she couldn't remember.

"So you do actually exist," said Gruber. He turned sideways on the bench and studied Emily closely. He did not bother to disguise his disappointment. "I was expecting something ... different ..."

"You've seen too many James Bond movies. Appearances mean nothing in this business." *But the fact that you do not believe that means that you can be deceived and manipulated.*

Donna Yang wants me to kill you, although she may not know that yet herself. But Chao Zhu thinks she is rash and that I should teach her patience, or at least a useful degree of craftiness. So you shall come later on my to do list.

She said, "I thought we should meet to review our projects."

Gruber thought and then said, "Projects, huh? Such a nice word! Like Green, Alban & Kline?"

Sounds like a big-city law firm when he says it like that. "Yes, those. And that was nice work with Katherine Green. Was that you or one of your people?"

Mannie smiled politely. *Does the bitch think that she can flatter me? Christ! What's wrong with her eyes?*

"A contractor. What I call my 'accident specialist'."

"Have you thought about having that same contractor deal with Alban? He needs to be an accident as well."

"Maybe. But I want to try the hearts and minds approach first. As you said, 'Wave some money at him.' I'm seeing him this afternoon. Same with Kline."

Three hours later, Mannie was sitting in his car working on the daily Sudoko puzzle. He was parked and waiting outside Edward Alban's front door in the Outer Richmond district of the city. He figured to try the bribery strategy that Emily Connors had suggested, but he wasn't optimistic about the outcome. He wasn't making much progress on the puzzle and was glad for the interruption when Alban showed up. He almost missed him, given that he was expecting some drab-looking civil servant instead of the brightly-garbed bicyclist that was walking up the front steps before Mannie registered his presence.

He let Alban park and lock his bike before calling to him and pushing open the passenger side door. He was amused to note the stiff-legged walk – the specialized biking shoes weren't very friendly for everyday purposes – and the aggressive way that he stood with his arms crossed, making the point that he didn't have to get in the car if he didn't want to.

The schlump thinks he knows how the game is played. Worse, he thinks he gets to make up the rules as we go.

Mannie waited patiently. Unlike most of his associates in his line of business, he did not have the kind of overblown ego that required a fear-based deference. On the contrary, he always felt some form of pity for those individuals that viewed themselves as his "partner," when in fact they were merely road kill waiting to happen. In his mind, he sorted them into Yiddish categories -- putz, schlump, shlemiel or schmuck. Alban was a schlump – a pathetic human being characterized by greed and arrogance. Unfortunately for his erstwhile partners, Mannie's labeling did not translate into compassion, as Alban was about to discover.

He waited until the man got in and sat down. He looked ridiculous trying to maintain his aloof airs while sitting there in his spandex tights and form-fitting neon uniform, and both of them knew it. He got in the car, but left the door open and kept one foot on the pavement, making the point that this was to be a short visit, that he was his own person.

"What do you want?"

"Hello, Edward. How was the ride home?"

Alban glared at him, but couldn't maintain it for more than a few seconds. It was hard to seem intimidating dressed as he was.

He said it again, but this time with a tinge of real curiosity, "What do you want?"

"A favor for one of my best clients. They want to buy the Katherine Green house on Russian Hill from the city, better known as the Brookings House. My sources tell me that you are opposing such an initiative. We want you to change your mind."

Alban leaned back in the seat and unstrapped his helmet to run his fingers through his thick black hair. He sat thinking, rotating the helmet in his hands and looking off into the distance.

Mannie recognized the body language. *He's going to negotiate. Calculating what opening figure to quote.*

But he was wrong.

Alban said, "I won't do that." And he got out of the car and slammed the door shut.

Mannie got out his side and leaned over the roof of the car. Alban was already halfway up the sidewalk to his house.

"Edward. C'mon! We need to talk about this."

"No, we don't." But he stopped and waited for Mannie to approach him. "This is not open to negotiation."

"A two percent commission – that's in the neighborhood of eighty thou – if you steer the sale to my client. And the Mayor thinks you're a hero."

"No. It stays with the city, in my department."

Mannie moved closer and gripped Alban's forearm tightly enough to hurt. "No? You mean, as in 'I refuse?' As in, 'I think we should reconsider placing our business with someone else?' As in, 'I think I have a choice?' As in, 'fuck you?' Is that what you're trying to say, Edward?"

"Just 'no.'" With that, he yanked his arm free and turned away. "And stop trying to threaten me! You have as much to lose as I do if our arrangement breaks up."

"Edward!"

But Alban was up the porch and pulling out his keys, paying no attention to Mannie in the middle of the sidewalk.

Mannie just watched him, unoffended and faintly pleased that his gambit had failed. *I was wrong. He's not a schlump, he's a putz – a fool, harmful to himself and everyone around him. Time for Plan B.*

Mannie settled back into the driver's seat and thought for thirty seconds. *Lots of moving parts. It's time to start narrowing the options.* He started dialing.

"The MK Foundation."

"Martin Kline, please."

"This is Martin Kline. Who is this?"

"Call me an anonymous donor. I'd like to make a five-hundred thousand dollar donation to the MK Foundation."

There was the slightest hesitation before Kline replied in a tone of very faint amusement, "Fine. I'll look forward to your check. Or will it be cash, since you wish to remain anonymous?"

Well. This is not going to go very far. Not my day for bribing people!

"You don't believe that I'm serious, do you?"

"Actually, I do. But I'm waiting for ... I love this bit ... the *quid pro quo*. Or should I say *the other shoe?*"

"We'd like your Foundation to drop out of the bidding for the Brookings House."

"I'll have to discuss it with the Board."

"You *are* the Board, Mr. Kline."

"I'll be happy to accept your donation, but I will not drop out of the bidding. In fact, you've made me think that the Brookings House is perhaps more valuable than my original estimates."

Kline's tone as much as what he was saying confirmed for Mannie that this was going nowhere. *I told Connors that I'd try the hearts and mind approach. It didn't work for Alban and it sure as hell isn't working for this guy. Time for the old-fashioned stuff.*

"There are rumors that the house has a curse on it. Ownership – or even bidding – might be dangerous."

"That's an interesting phrasing. Some might read it as a threat."

"You're young, Mr. Kline. Doing good work. It would be a shame if that were to end. Goodbye."

Mannie's next call was to his accountant.

"Good evening Paul. This is Mannie."

"So what's up, partner?"

Partner? Campos is getting way too familiar. Pretty soon, he'll want more money. Probably beginning to think he's indispensable, that he can blow the whistle on us if things don't go his way. Serves me right for trying to develop some home-grown talent rather than sticking with the pros.

"Remember the guy, Alban, that we talked about?"

"Yeah. You said to wait. But I'm ready whenever you say 'go.' I've already scoped out the man and I know how I'm going to do it. I plan …"

"Whoa! I don't need details, especially on the phone. Just do it within the next three days. And remember what happens if you screw it up."

A silence followed and Mannie knew that Campos was framing some smart-ass, tough-guy rejoinder. He didn't give him the chance.

"And I have another job for you. One that will require some imagination on your part. I know you like that."

"Who's the subject?"

When Mannie told him, Paul recognized the name immediately. This would be by far his biggest job.

"And Paul …"

"Yes?"

"An accident is good. That's your specialty. If that can't be arranged, then make it look like a holdup gone wrong. One of those random urban tragedies. What it *can't* look like is a targeted killing."

"Understood. I promise you it will be the lead story on the six o'clock news within the next three days."

He ended the call, but his caller ID popped up on Mannie's screen only twenty seconds later.

"Something else?"

"For this Kline dude, would suicide be OK?" Campos sounded eager and it was clear that he was excited by the idea.

"Absolutely. But it has to be crystal clear. Not one of those amateur jobs that makes the cops wonder."

"I got it. Watch the news."

Mannie's final phone call was on the special cell phone, the one that only called a single number.

Emily answered on the first ring. "What do you have?"

"It's mixed news, but mostly what I expected. Our city real estate person is insistent on his own way. Not tempted at all by a two percent commission. He's got some big ideas about what he can make from the property if it stays under his control. And I talked to our other bidder on the property as well. He was not receptive to our monetary offer and, if anything, is more determined than ever. Approaching him was a mistake. Based on my conversations with both of them, I've commissioned my usual vendor to arrange to take them out of the picture."

The pause was long enough to tell Mannie that his proposal was being processed; long enough to make him wonder if he'd screwed up. But her response was straightforward.

"Sounds good to me. Let me know if anything changes."

Murder by Accident

"You want me, the best and most feared homicide detective on the west coast, to go investigate the death of an old woman who fell down the stairs? Me? The man who is currently working six – no, seven – open cases?"

Mayo Marsh was trying very hard to simultaneously look offended and to sound like a man with a valid grievance. But he knew his boss well enough to know that such stagecraft would have zero impact. Hector Ramirez was as immune to such appeals as a lottery winner with a lot of indigent in-laws.

"No, Mayo. What I want you to do is to go along with Detective Morrison here and give her the benefit of your vast experience and superior knowledge. It's her case, not yours. You should view yourself as, let's say, a consultant."

The woman standing near the window looked at Mayo without any expression. She was short and stocky, wearing a pinstriped pants suit that made her look more like a banker than a policewoman. To Mayo, also also looked incredibly young.

"Consultant, huh? Lemme see. That means I can give her advice, but can't tell her what to do?"

Hector smiled. "See? How all that experience gives you an immediate and penetrating grasp of the situation?"

"Hector, this is not –"

"Mayo." The single word was in the register that the veterans called 'the voice.' It was understood that whatever followed would be the end of the discussion.

"Mayo. You're retiring in the near future, taking with you all the informants, history, gossip and – god help us – real skill that you've accumulated in the last couple of centuries on the job. We need to find a way to transfer some of that vast reservoir of knowledge to those poor souls who are continuing on. Like Detective Morrison here. So until we master the Vulcan mind meld, I'd like you to *assist* her on this case."

Mayo buttoned his sport coat, stood almost erect and made an attempt to click his heels together. Hector ignored him and waved at the two of them to get out of his office. He was almost through the door when Hector stopped him.

"Oh. And I think you'll be interested in this case. It's like finding a time machine."

What the hell does that mean?

Once in the hallway, he turned and started to say, "Look, Detective Morrison –"

"It's Vic – short for Victoria – and it's his idea, not mine." It came through quite clearly that she was as worried about the alliance as he was.

The name triggered his memory. *Aha! She's the one that got Bolton transferred out of Homicide. Kicked sideways into Vice, on a desk.*

It wasn't clear exactly what had happened, but the speculation occupied a lot of water cooler time and emotional energy within the Division. The only thing known for sure was that she'd been assigned to Bolton as his rookie partner. Given that he was the most sexist, foul-mouthed and laziest detective in the unit, it was guaranteed to be a rocky relationship, but everyone assumed that the rookie would put up with it as the price of admission into the closely-knit and male community.

The shouting matches were impossible to hide, remarkable for their frequency, intensity, and – surprisingly – for the way they left Bolton open-mouthed and eviscerated. Gradually, the underdog became admired. Then, one day, Bolton was gone; transferred without comment. It was unsettling to the veteran detectives. Not because they liked Bolton, but because they worried about a brave new world where a rookie female cop could seemingly snap her fingers and overturn the existing order.

Mayo became aware that she was staring at him and that he hadn't responded to her introduction. And he was certain that she was reading his mind. She immediately confirmed it.

"Bolton was a Neanderthal. Worse than that, he was corrupt. I told Hector that I wouldn't work with him and that if he stayed in the Division, I was going to Internal Affairs."

He looked more closely and saw that she was not as young as he had first thought. There were wrinkles at the corners of her mouth and eyes. And those eyes somehow conveyed the impression that they had seen more than they wanted to, like a bartender dealing with a drunk who wants to talk. It was the characteristic look of most cops.

A couple of ways to go here. But I don't have the time or stomach for diplomacy.

"Should I worry?" he asked. "About Internal Affairs? Assuming you disapprove of me ... or my methods?"

She smiled sadly and he felt a twinge of remorse. "From what I hear, the distance between you and Bolton is measured in light years. I think I can learn a lot from you and I'd like to have the chance."

"We'll see." And he headed for the stairs. "Tell me about the old woman who fell down the stairs. And oh, yeah. What the hell is a Vulcan mind meld?"

The trip to Russian Hill was dedicated to Vic providing a detailed and almost reverential description of the Star Trek series, including a biography of Mr. Spock and his various abilities, including tapping into the thoughts of other entities. By the time she was done, Mayo had the growing feeling that Spock – other than being a male -- was what she aspired to be.

When they pulled up in front of the house, he realized that he'd been there before, and he finally caught on to "the time machine" reference that Hector had thrown at him as he was leaving his office.

"Be careful. This place is rumored to be haunted," he warned Vic as they approached the front door. When she looked at him with a barely concealed skepticism, he added, "It was built just a few days after the 1906 earthquake. And then half the family was killed by the flu right after they moved in. And then it was the site of a couple of mysterious deaths. Owners, I think. Then, mid- nineties maybe, the owners disappeared. No trace."

That's the brief version. Twenty years ago and I was the rookie on the case. But I remember Donald Brookings ...

and his killer, Warren Wah. I did some of the legwork on it. Then there were the Greens. Couple of older hippies. The theory was they went off somewhere to a commune. Left all their material possessions behind. That was a long time ago. I wonder if they ever turned up?

"And now the current owner dies tragically?" Vic said. "Maybe there's something to those rumors."

She took out a key to unlock the door. Something bothered him about that and he finally diagnosed the reason. "No crime scene tape?"

"Nope. Two reasons. First, Bolton convinced our superiors that it's not a crime scene. Just one of those unfortunate accidents that befall frail old people living alone when they should have self-committed themselves to a zonked-out wheelchair existence in one of those warehouses mislabeled as a 'skilled nursing facility.'"

He looked at her closely. "Sounds to me like you have a grudge."

"A long and sordid story. About sibling rivalries and aging parents. You don't want to know."

"What's the second thing?"

She looked at him blankly, so he prompted her. "You said there were two reasons for not having crime scene tape …"

"Oh yeah. I've already been over the scene. Done what I could. And it's not like there's a lot of traffic in and out. Not much chance of contamination."

"And? You find anything to indicate … what do the newspapers call it … foul play?"

For the first time, she looked unsure of herself. "Yeah, well. That's why I asked Hector if I could borrow you for a bit. I'm already known as the bitch who got Bolton canned and I don't want to make it worse by looking like Nancy Drew on steroids."

The insecurity becomes her. Much more human. And that's hard to do for a cop, especially when you're on the job.

The unbidden thought jarred Mayo, first because it made him aware that she was a woman and, second, it brought to the surface the question that he persistently refused to answer. *What are you going to be like when you stop being a cop? Is there a real person in there somewhere?* He wondered if the two thoughts were connected in some way.

He coughed and pushed the door open to cover up his confusion. "I gather something's bothering you. Show me what it is."

She led the way into the entry. "We've come in the main entrance, but we're on the third floor. There's one more above us and two below us." She headed for the wide and carpeted stairway going up to the next level, talking the entire time.

"She was up here, apparently watching TV. Dressed in slacks, blouse and slippers, with a housecoat on. No sign that she was expecting anyone.

"And this is how she left the room."

Vic went over to an almost invisible door in the wall and went through it with Mayo trailing. He found himself on the top landing of a very long, uncarpeted, steep and narrow stairway.   It was lit only by a dim bulb at each of the four landings and by natural light from a series of small windows spaced along the length of the staircase.

"This is where she fell. We know that because one of her slippers was found where you're standing and there's some blood traces on two or three of the stairs immediately below us. This stairway connects all four levels of the house. As you can see, there's a landing at each level with an entry into the main house. It was designed for the servants, so they could move from floor to floor without disturbing the occupants."

She could see that Mayo was bothered, and she thought she knew why. "That's my first problem with the slip and fall scenario. Why would she even use this stairway? It's faster, safer and more convenient to use the main staircase in the house."

Mayo ran his fingertips along the top of the railing. "Lots of dust. Doesn't seem to be a high traffic area."

"Like I said, that's my problem number one. Why is she even out here?"

She had his attention now, and her voice picked up, louder and more assured. "Problem number two." She pointed down the staircase. "She was found at the very bottom of the stairs, crumpled up against the door into the garage."

Mayo looked down the long passage, calculating distances and velocities.

"How wide are those landings between here and the bottom?"

"Eight feet two inches."

Mayo walked down to the next landing and stood thinking.

"Doesn't seem very plausible, does it?" she said. "That an adult woman, conscious and trying to arrest her fall, would go all the way to the bottom?"

"Did you –"

"I tried it a dozen times. Pushed a full-size body from the top. Never got past the second landing."

Mayo grinned at the unbidden image, picturing Morrison repeatedly throwing a body down the stairs and then dragging it back to the top to do it again. "Who in the hell volunteered for that? Or did you borrow a stiff from the morgue?"

"In a past lifetime, I went through EMT training. We practiced CPR and other rescue techniques on life-size manikins. I borrowed a couple from the fire department."

"Was Bolton with you?"

Her voice turned cold. "Bolton said – and I quote – 'The bitch fell. Stop wasting my time.' He spent the time in a bar down the street."

"What did the coroner say about cause of death?"

"Multiple bruises, contusions and fractures. Including the spine and neck. Totally consistent with falling down the stairs. His only minor puzzle was that a patch of her hair was pulled loose from her scalp."

Mayo came back to the top landing. "Is there a problem number three?"

She went back into the room, closing the door behind her. "I found her other slipper here, near the TV. Question: Why would she take off one slipper, but leave the other one on while she walked into a stairway that she shouldn't have been using in the first place?

"Oh, and I found some strands of hair – with small bits of scalp still attached – there, about halfway to the door."

By now, Mayo was running through his own internal checklist. "Any witnesses?"

"None very useful. It was several hours before she was found by the maid. No one saw her or anyone else during the entire day except for a ten year old who saw what she called 'an average looking white guy' walk into the alley early that morning. No chance of an ID, but she did say that he had on a dark suit with a vest. And the alley goes nowhere but to the side entrances to this house."

"Who wears a vest these days? She have any enemies?"

"The woman apparently lived her entire life without offending anyone except her ex-husband, and he has ironclad alibis."

"Who inherits? The house alone is worth tens of millions."

"Everything goes to charity – opera, symphony, etc. -- except the house. That is willed to the City of San Francisco 'for use as the City sees fit.' The will was redone a month ago."

Mayo stood thinking. *Damn Bolton! He can be an asshole and a drunk if he wants to, but to screw up a murder investigation .... No, to not even open a murder investigation, to sweep it under the rug ... He should be thrown off the force, not transferred!*

"Uh, Mayo ..."

"I'll talk to Hector. Get a proper forensics team out here. Treat this like what it is – murder. You did well, Vic. Too bad we saddled you with a loser like Bolton."

"What now?"

"Now? First, we go to Starbucks and get some coffee. I'm buying because you earned it. And then we can talk about the far more interesting part of this."

"And that is?"

"How to find the son-of-a-bitch that did this and put him away.

The Mayor's Options

Janet Li was a complex woman. Not very surprising, given that she was the two-term mayor of one of the least governable American cities, a Chinese-American unmarried woman who had grown up in dire poverty and had been one of the most highly-decorated veterans of the San Francisco police force. She spoke four languages, had a doctorate in public policy from Georgetown University and was outspoken to the point of recklessness about the rampant stupidity of her fellow politicians at local, state and national levels.

She had significant advantages in the political arena. She was smart without seeming to be so, and she liked it that way. She was ordinary looking; showing a slightly dumpy frame in clothes that seemed to be just a little bit last year. Women did not find her threatening and men tended not to see her if more than a few people were in the room. But, at the end of the day, she almost always got what she wanted.

Her enemies – and they were many – liked to portray her as "the dragon lady," conjuring lurid images of the comic strip character from *Terry and the Pirate*s and implying that her power was exercised in a scheming, deceitful, domineering manner. Some of them liked to insinuate that she was a lesbian, but – in San Francisco – such an accusation strengthened rather than weakened her popularity.

In fact, she liked men. She liked their simplicity and transparency; the lack of any agenda except the one that they were pressing at the moment. It made most of them predictable and therefore controllable, leaving a very small number of them of greater interest.

I can deal with the people. It's the goddamn departments that make this such a miserable job. Like fighting against feather pillows. And supposedly they work for me.

To her, the issue was crystal clear. *The woman gave us a house worth maybe thirty million dollars. We can sell it and use the money to do some good. Or we can use it to house some community agency. Flip a coin, for god's sake! But, no!*

We'll spend months, maybe years, in bureaucratic squabbling about what to do!

She ticked them off in her mind. The Housing Department, the Russian Hill Neighborhood Association, City Planning, Environmental, Historical Preservation, Traffic, Economic Development, Real Estate, Public Works ... even Parks and Recreation. They all wanted a say in the decision, but not a one of them was willing to say what they wanted. The only agency that had put forward a specific proposal was the Controller.

"We've got a major deficit. Thirty million bucks is manna from heaven. Sell the house to the highest bidder and use the money for your homeless initiative, or public health, or education."

That's Option A. And I've got two eager buyers competing for the deal.

The Petrel Foundation – whatever that was -- was offering thirty million, agreeing to manage an earthquake retrofit and to use the house purely as a headquarters for the foundation. Even better, the MK Foundation also was proposing to buy the house, do the earthquake retrofit and use the building as the foundation offices and as a residence for the owner. However, unlike Petrel, the MK Foundation's mission involved providing services for ex-felons; parolees and probationers that were transitioning from prison back into the community. For obvious if not honorable reasons, she knew that the Neighborhood Association would favor Petrel over MK.

Unless Petrel is a front for a Russian oligarch or the daughter of a corrupt Chinese government official. And I'll bet it is.

Option B was to retain ownership and modify the house to accommodate her own Affordable Housing Mandate, a campaign promise that had become a cornerstone of her administration. She and most of her staff preferred this alternative, but it had at least two serious drawbacks. First, it would stimulate a furor of departmental infighting and alienate the Neighborhood Association, making her reelection campaign far more contentious than she liked. Second, the strongest and most visible advocate of the Affordable Housing option was Natalie Weiss, her daughter. She would have to be very careful to minimize "conflict of interest" controversies.

I've got about three weeks before I need to make a clear public commitment to one of the alternatives. But why wait? I'm not going to know any more then than I do now.

She didn't know it, but the woman entering her office was about to give her another option. It was her long time aide Mallory. Mallory and Janet Li's daughter were the only two people in the world that she trusted absolutely.

"You want the good or the bad news first?" As usual, Mallory didn't waste time with small talk.

"The bad, of course. It makes the good news so much better when it comes."

Mallory sat down in the chair in front of the desk. Between the two of them, they called it 'the petitioner's chair' because most of its occupants wanted something from the Mayor. She referred to the single sheet of paper she was carrying.

"OK. Our dedicated civil servant, our albatross from prior administrations, our most esteemed incompetent that we cannot fire, Mr. Edward Alban, does not want us to sell the Brookings house."

Li winced. "When you say, 'does not want us to sell,' do you mean –"

"That he will use every considerable means at his disposal to make it impossible. We've been through this before."

Li had no trouble remembering. *My first month in office, determined to make good on all those fiery campaign promises about lean but not-so-mean government. Tried to sign a sweetheart lease to use one of our many decrepit piers as a site for a business incubator. He had us knee deep in environmental impact reports, rezoning amendments, neighborhood petitions, and even ancient maritime laws. That pier still sits there today, rotting away. If Alban had his way, he'd have us nationalize every structure within the city limits and then declare it unfit for any conceivable use!*

"You said something about 'good news'?"

Mallory sat straighter and leaned forward slightly. Li knew that she was going into sales mode.

"The San Francisco Guest House." Mallory made motions with her hands in the air, as though sketching one of the seven wonders of the world.

Li said nothing, waiting for more. Mallory, on the other hand, had the look of a saleswoman who had just delivered her best pitch ever. She said nothing, just sat there looking expectantly at her, so finally Li said, "I give up. It's a hotel? I think there's a chain, isn't there? Guest House Hotels?"

Mallory looked pained, obviously disappointed in the Mayor.

She said, "Think Blair House."

"You mean the place in DC where the first family puts up dignitaries that don't have quite enough status to stay in the White House Green Room?"

"It's the Blue Room, not green. And the Blair House is famous. Abraham Lincoln –"

Li cut her off. "You want me to use this Russian Hill house as the San Francisco equivalent of the Blair House?"

Mallory leaned forward. "I think you should consider the idea. And it would be more than a guest residence. We could set up our Mayor's Office of Protocol in the space as well. There's plenty of room for one or two staffers and the Neighborhood Association will probably go for the idea."

Li swiveled around in her chair and stared out the window. Mallory knew her well enough to remain silent.

"OK. Sounds interesting. And it's ready to go, isn't it?"

"All furnished, sitting empty. If we own it, we eventually have to do an earthquake retrofit, but it can be used in the meantime. And somebody gave me an idea for a trial run, a good way to see if the idea makes sense. We've got the Chinese trade delegation coming next week. Let's put them up in the house and see how it works."

Wheels began to turn in Li's imagination and Mallory knew her well enough to sit quietly. But she could not see into her thoughts.

Chao Zhu arrives tomorrow. The Green Fence deal is about 98% done; the only thing left is the Gruber question. If that deal gets done, there'd be enough distraction to cover any number of initiatives for the next month or so.

"The delegation arrives here *just before* our announcement of the new Green Fence plant, right?"

Mallory nodded, "Assuming it's a done deal."

The mayor went into silent mode once more, then asked, "Who gave you the idea for our version of Blair House?"

"One of your more important constituents from Chinatown, the head of the Merchant's Association."

Li merely nodded. *And a cousin of our chief negotiator on the other side. Chao Zhu, the man with multiple agendas. Why would he care about a house?*

Mallory stood up and headed for the door. She was almost there, when Li stopped her. "Mallory. This is a real possibility. But I want to keep the other options on the table for a while."

What the hell kind of game is Zhu playing?

Death of a Bureaucrat

Edward Alban was an ordinary man who did not deserve what was about to happen to him. His flaws were ordinary, quintessentially human foibles, unremarkable except for the greed that made him an accomplice to graft and corruption.

It is probably the case that the same would serve as an epitaph for most murder victims, often dying for trivial reasons or because they became inconvenient to someone who did not abide by the same morality that keeps us from killing one another.

He lived in the Outer Richmond District of the city, only a short walk from the edge of the Pacific Ocean but on the other side of the city from his office. Ordinarily, the logistics involved in getting to work would subject him to a grinding start-stop commute through heavy traffic with serious parking fees at the end of it. But Edward was a biker, one of the increasing number of fanatical San Franciscans who despised cars and their drivers.

He left his house every weekday in pre-dawn darkness dressed in form-fitting neon-colored clothing, resembling a speed skater or a luge captain at the winter Olympics, with the additional touch of florescent panels in front and back. His fellow biker commuters teased him. After all, it was an easy ride, about three miles on city streets, with lots of red lights to slow him down. Most of them commuted in "casual Friday" outfits, on fat-tired bikes with a backpack for their laptops and essentials.

But the brightly colored tight fitting special purpose clothing was important to him in ways that he could not explain to them. And perhaps did not fully understand himself. Edward had grown up in a small Mexican village in the Sonoran Desert. Until he was ten, he dressed every day in coarse cotton garments; drab, ill-fitting and itchy. He looked like every other boy in his village. But now when he looked at himself in the mirror with the gold and silver synthetic cloth with all those medallions and brand names, he felt special.

This same feeling of specialness required him to change his name from Eduardo Albanado to Edward Alban and he truly believed that those few omitted syllables and his sense of his own uniqueness were in some way responsible for his successful career in the Department of City Owned Real Estate.

The first part of his daily ride was ideal. He crossed two city streets and entered Golden Gate Park very near its westernmost point. The next two mile stretch through the park was on lightly traveled roads and bike paths through meadows and groves of giant trees. The John Kennedy Parkway twisted through the Park and was friendlier to cyclists than to cars. At that early hour, it was their domain. Perhaps because of that, Edward did not notice the truck parked just inside the Park for the last three days. It was easy to overlook since it was one of the standard white pickups with the Park logo painted on its side. There was nothing about it that indicated that it had been 'borrowed' from the park's motor pool just an hour ago and was intended for lethal purposes.

The driver sitting in the darkened truck appreciated Edward's colorful clothing and florescent panels. It made him easy to see in the darkness and distinguished him from the occasional other cyclist. He had no particular feelings about Edward and knew nothing about him other than that someone found him to be inconvenient. After three days, however, he began to become irritated with Edward. Somehow, he managed to pass his truck at the precise time when another car or cyclist was in the vicinity. He felt silly stealing the truck and then returning it before the work crews began to arrive. Mannie's union contacts made the theft a low-risk venture, but it was getting tiresome.

The terms had seemed liberal when he took the job. Mannie told him, "I told my friend that you were the best man for the job. You have a week. If the job isn't done within that time frame, two things will happen. First, you will not be paid. Second, I will tell my friend that you failed."

It was the second consequence that worried him. In his world, failure was not an option. One simply did not "disappoint" the kind of friends that the caller referred to. And the job paid well and promised to be simple. But now three of the seven days had passed. He began to worry and to brainstorm other ways to solve the problem. But then, on the fourth morning, all the necessary components fell into alignment. The fog was particularly dense, reducing visibility to a minimum and making the road slick. Best of all, Alban was the lone cyclist in the first stretch into the Park and no other cars were around.

As soon as Alban passed him, the driver started the truck and pulled into the roadway about fifty yards behind the still accelerating bicycle. He judged his speed carefully, so that he came alongside Alban when the bike was at full speed down the first slightly downhill stretch of the Kennedy Parkway. They were at about thirty miles an hour when the driver carefully and gently nudged Alban's rear wheel with his right front fender.

A fast-moving bicycle is a remarkably stable device. But a very slight bump from a four-thousand pound vehicle changes that dramatically. To the driver of the truck, it seemed that both the bike and rider were suddenly airborne, cartwheeling side-by-side through the beams of his headlights, and then tumbling to an abrupt stop still in the lane of traffic. He stopped the truck just short of where Alban lay sprawled on the roadway and got out quickly.

Alban was conscious and trying to push himself into a sitting position. Most of his left side, from shoulder to knee, was bleeding, easy to see because his long bouncing skid on asphalt had torn away his prized brightly colored fabric. His left arm seemed to have another joint just below the elbow, where bone was protruding. When the man got to his side, Edward was mumbling and looking at his arm with a puzzled expression. When the man reached down to move him, he looked up and said "Who … what –"

There was no time. The man dragged the uncomprehending Alban a couple of feet and positioned him carefully. Then he unsnapped and removed the helmet, and slammed the unprotected back of Alban's head against the pavement as hard as he could, twice.

He held his fingertips on the carotid artery, feeling for a pulse that he didn't want to find. He had a reputation for thoroughness, but he could see headlights approaching from around the curve. Cursing, he replaced the helmet, gripped it tightly in both hands, and made a quick wrenching motion. He thought he heard a faint 'snap,' but couldn't be sure.

No time. That's got to be enough. He got back in the truck and sped away just as headlights crested the hill behind him.

An Unfortunate Accident

So today I'm a traffic cop.

Mayo's involvement was purely chance. He heard the call on the police radio at the same time he saw the flashing lights ahead of him. *Bicyclist down. Hit and run. Kennedy Parkway.*

They'd closed the Parkway for a two-hundred yard stretch. The body was still there, covered with a blue tarp. The nearby bike was being photographed. Mayo found what looked like the man in charge, a uniformed sergeant that looked vaguely familiar. To his surprise, the guy seemed pleased to see him.

"I'm Robinson. You the guy from CIU?"

Why would they call the Criminal Investigation Unit for a traffic accident?

"Yeah, name's Marsh. But I'm not responding to a call. I just happened to be on the Parkway when I heard the call. I'm not the one you want."

Robinson ignored the attempt to get away. "I know you. You worked those North Beach carjackings."

A major meth lab operating out of a rundown two-story Victorian. Would have gone on a lot longer except one of the lesser mutts got in the habit of walking out the front door, waving a gun to flag down the first car going by. Said he needed to get home to Oakland and didn't want to ride the train. Three times a winner. On the fourth try, the driver tried to take off and the perp emptied the magazine into him. Found the meth operation while knocking on doors looking for witnesses. Couldn't find the shooter, but his coworkers did. Slit his throat and tossed him in the Bay.

"That was in the dim, dark past. So why did you call in CIU? This looks like your classic 'slip and fall' case, except it involves a bike rather than a stepladder. Reckless rider goes too fast, loses control, breaks neck."

"Maybe," said Robinson in a voice that clearly conveyed his disbelief. "But there's a couple of troublesome facts. At the very least, it's a hit and run."

He paused and then added, "Or something worse."

Mayo looked at him, at first annoyed by Robinson's transparent attempt to suck him in, and then by his realization that it had worked. He was curious.

He turned away from Robinson and walked over to the tarp. He pulled it away in one swift tug and stood looking at the body for a full minute.

"Broken neck?"

Robinson nodded. "Yes, but that's not the only fatal injury." He knelt and pointed to the head, still encased in its protective helmet.

Mayo got down on his knees and looked at the wound on the back of the head. He grasped the helmet with both hands and tested its range of motion. Then he stood and looked back up the Parkway.

He pointed to some chalk marks about forty feet away. "Those are bloodstains, yes? So that's where he first hit the pavement ... and skidded or bounced to where we see him?"

Again, Robinson nodded, looking at Mayo with a pleased expression.

Mayo was talking to himself by now. "Flat pavement, no curb, no prominent rocks or any other objects. Helmet projects out about three inches at the back of his head. Seems kinda unlikely that his head could hit the pavement hard enough to cause that kind of injury."

Robinson said, "Seems curious that the wound is covered up by the helmet, too."

Mayo knelt again, verifying what Robinson and said. "Maybe the helmet shifted while he was tumbling down the road ..."

Robinson nodded. "Could be, I suppose. But then there's this."

Robinson lifted the biker's head and pointed to a small dark pool on the pavement where the head was resting. "There's one more bloodstain other than those skidmarks. And it's not just drainage. There are hairs and bits of scalp imbedded. This is where the head injury was incurred. With his helmet firmly in place. *After* he'd skidded to a complete stop."

"You a traffic cop, Robinson?" It was not a hostile question.

"At the moment. But I'm trying for Homicide."

"That's a tough jump to make."

Robinson nodded.

"Give me a call. Maybe I can help."

Mayo looked at the road in both directions from where they were standing. "Who was first on the scene?"

"We got a 911 call from a motorist passing by, but he didn't ID himself and he didn't hang around. We're trying to trace the call back. All he said was that there was a cyclist down and that it looked serious."

Robinson pulled the blue tarp back over what was left of Edward Alban. " One more thing."

He walked the few steps to where the bike lay. It looked to Mayo like something built purely for speed – skinny tires, no fenders, fancy shifting mechanism. Aside from the front wheel being folded in half, it seemed undamaged.

Mayo's last bike ride was when he was fifteen years old, but he had vivid memories of careening downhill, catching a patch of loose dirt, and finding himself flying over handlebars.

"Can that happen if you lose control at high speed?" He pointed at the folded tire.

"Sometimes. Those wheels are really flimsy. But why did he lose control?"

As if to answer his own question, Robinson pointed to the rear tire, to a white smear along the outside circumference, maybe ten to twelve inches long.

"I'll bet that's paint from a vehicle. I think he got bumped."

"That makes it a hit-and-run."

Robinson just looked at him, finally saying simply, "Or?"

Mayo thought about it. *He's right. The paint on the tire could be an accident, but the caved-in skull? That's murder.*

The Preservationist

"Dead? He can't be! I just saw him."

Damn! You sound like an idiot! It only takes an instant to be dead and you saw the man two days ago. But he seemed fine. Kind of an ass, but that's not correlated with life span. What the hell?

Natalie Weiss smiled crookedly at the clerk, unsure of the protocol at this point. *Was he a close friend? Should I be sympathetic?*

"Bike accident," said the clerk, sounding as casual about the tragedy as the local traffic reporter commenting on a delay on the Golden Gate Bridge. "Happened yesterday. Early morning. On his way to the office."

"That's awful. He seemed to be a nice man." *That's not true, but what else should one say in this case?*

The clerk looked at her in such a way that Natalie was instantly sure that the man's death was not all that disturbing, and that whatever he was, it was not 'a nice man.' It caused her thoughts to veer off. *I wonder what they would say about me if I got hit by that proverbial bus?*

"Um. I was wondering …" She was unusually hesitant, totally unsure of how to proceed. "I had an appointment this morning and --"

The clerk was already shuffling through papers on her desk. "I can't help you. And there's no one else who can right now. Mr. Alban has – had – a number of projects that he was evaluating and it's going to take a while before the rest of his group can get up to speed."

Natalie stood helplessly, staring at the clerk and feeling anger seeping in. *Three weeks of ass-kissing to get to this point with these obstinate bureaucrats and their incomprehensible rules and petty little jurisdictional limits. And the man dies just when we get to the 'go' point! Now what? Start over with another one like him?*

She closed her eyes and took a deep breath, letting the anger go. *Nice work Natalie! Getting mad at the guy because he died and missed your appointment!*

The thought triggered an instant depression, and she knew the reason. *I had the same reaction when Brad walked out on me. He didn't die, but taking up with the bimbo was about the same. I invested six years in the marriage and he walked away from it like it was one of his 'portfolio companies' that had underperformed.*

She was dismayed when she reflected back on her innocence, thinking that her marriage was rock solid; that their status as 'a beautiful couple' was somehow compensating for the erosion of passion and the sameness that had slowly taken over. The idea of 'starting over' with another man was depressing. And so she had focused instead on her career, if her interminable battle with the labyrinth of city bureaucracies could be termed a career.

If one enters into a moratorium on dating, it helps to be in San Francisco, a city where sexual identity so often is completely independent of one's physical appearance. Between the gays, lesbians, trans-genders and bisexuals, it was relatively easy to maintain a cool neutrality that effectively cut short the kinds of advances that a woman such as Natalie would attract. If it weren't for Janet continually prodding her to 'find somebody that appreciates you' – by which she meant marrying somebody who was both smart and a Democrat – she would be content to stay on the sidelines.

Her mother never quite came out and said it, but the irony was that Natalie would make a great trophy wife, at least visually. She was beautiful, with jet-black long hair, startling green eyes and a large mouth that always seemed to be on the verge of a grin, set off by a faint two-inch scar on her left cheekbone. She was tall, just under six feet, with broad shoulders and long arms. She'd played volleyball for four years at Santa Clara University on a team that was ranked fourth in the country, where she became noted for her competitive intensity. The scar was the result of a diving save that wiped out a television cameraman who was ten feet away from the end line. Her team was up by fifteen at the time.

That same intensity was amplified by the Jesuit education, the result being a passion for social justice that led to a law degree with a specialty in city planning and – starting five years ago – her job with the San Francisco Historical Society. And much of her time and emotional energy was taken up with people like the inconveniently deceased Edward Alban.

She turned back to the clerk. "Who's going to be handling the work that Mr. Alban was doing?"

"It'll probably be his assistant, Donna Yang. But it'll _"

"I know, I know. It'll take a while to get up to speed."

She turned away to leave, bumping into the person behind her, a Chinese man in a suit. He smiled and bowed slightly, gesturing for her to go ahead. She heard him say to the clerk, "My name is Warren Wah. I'm looking for Ms. Yang."

Lucky man. He made an appointment with one of the live bureaucrats.

Biography of a Philanthropist

Martin was sitting in Starbucks feeling sorry for himself.

One more time ... Remind me why I'm doing this?

The depressing thought was so routine that it no longer required an answer. It had become his silent mantra, triggered by his frequent encounters with people who were suspicious of his attempts to help them. The question reminded him that he could quit at any time, and it was that option that made the transparent hypocrisy that was so much a part of his world tolerable, even amusing.

Maybe they'd be more receptive if I dressed more like one of them? Or, even better, if I had a string of letters after my name. Maybe Ph.D. or OBE?

He thought of the meeting he'd just left at the SFPD and laughed at his pretensions. *These guys are cops. No way I'll impress them with degrees or fancy honorific credentials. They know me. Grew up with some of them. Half of them hate me and the other half doesn't like what I'm trying to do. Once Mayo's gone, I'll be back to square one.*

The thought of Mayo brought a slight surge of guilt. *Somebody I need to do a better job of keeping up with.*

He and Mayo shared an interesting history. He was a street-smart fourteen-year old in the Tenderloin at the same time that Mayo was a beat cop. He could remember their first encounter, word-for-word.

"You go to school, Martin?"

"Every day." That was the last true thing he said during that first meeting.

"You got parents?"

"Sure." *Not for three years now. They were passed-out drunk when the fire started on the ground floor. At first, the arson guy thought the building was uninhabited. When they found the bodies, they knew they had squatters, but they never did know who they were.*

"Got a place to live? Somewhere indoors?"

"Most of the time. City shelters sometimes." *Nope. The shelters were deadly for a kid all alone. And the social workers prowled those places. Better to stay in the rough.*

"Staying out of trouble?"

"Absolutely." *Depends on your definition of trouble, doesn't it? Haven't been caught. Haven't hurt anybody that I know of. Don't count shoplifting, panhandling, scamming the tourists ...*

Mayo smiled, part of their game. "Ever lie to a cop?"

"No sir. That would be wrong."

Mayo looked around to make sure no one was watching. Then he handed him a ten-dollar bill. "Here. Just in case your family allowance is a little short this week."

Martin took the money, a violation of his personal code.

But this cop is different.

"Officer, I –"

"Call me Mayo. Like the clinic in Minnesota. Or the salad dressing. Mayo."

Might as well be named something weird; nothing else is predictable about the man.

"Mayo, sure." He turned to leave, but was stopped by an unlikely thought. *I think this may actually be a good time to be a snitch.*

"Uh, there was a girl that was ... beat up ... last night. On Mission."

"Yeah. I know. That's part of my territory. Name's Letitia. She's at SF General. Deserves better than she got." He stood quietly, watching with his gentle eyes.

Martin went on, his voice more sure of itself now. "There's a kid, maybe sixteen years old. Called Tubby, but he's real skinny. Pretty deep into meth. Matching dragons tattooed on his forearms. Hangs out against the wall at St. Anthony's. He has a thing about Letitia .... Thinks she's property of some kind. Just for him."

"I'll be sure to look him up. Sounds interesting. Thanks."

They maintained their wary relationship during their shared time, first in the Tenderloin and then the Mission, spanning the years when Mayo went from rookie cop walking a beat up to his transfer into Homicide and while Martin was ricocheting from foster home to street and back again. They continued their super-cool, elliptical conversations about the neighborhood and Martin's precarious social existence, always with a running subtext that took on a 'big-brother' flavor in both their views. It broke into the open only once, just before Mayo transferred into Homicide.

Three neighborhood teens were murdered savagely during a one-week period. It was quickly dubbed 'the Mission Murders.' And it changed both of them.

Mayo stopped him on the street. "You knew them. All three of them."

The terse phrase had none of the usual bantering tone. It was accusative, for reasons Martin could not fathom.

"We were all at Mission High, Mayo. Everybody knew everybody. Almost."

Mayo looked at him with an unreadable expression, just staring.

"Mayo. I didn't run in their circle. We weren't even on the same social planet. They were a clique … jocks who clowned around a lot. Kids with real parents who lived better than most of the rest of us."

"It could have been you. You spend most of your time in some of those alleys where we found them."

Something in his voice tipped him off. *The doofus is worried about me!*

He tried for a flip tone. "Mayo! C'mon! It's some nut case. Picking victims at random!" *But it's not. Those three were connected in a dozen ways. And they were killed because of one of those connections.*

"Maybe, maybe not. But you fit the profile." He made a sweeping gesture with his arm, including the street in both directions. "And how many others like you do you see out there … ones that could be a random selection?"

It was obviously a rhetorical question. Both of them were well aware that the streets were virtually deserted after dark these days, emptied by the same kind of fear that causes swimmers to visualize great white sharks lurking beneath them. The few that had to be out and on foot walked fast and stayed near the curb, away from the entries into those ominous dark alleys.

Mayo testified as a character witness in Martin's trial, a few weeks after his eighteenth birthday. His testimony was far more important to the two of them than it was to the jury.

It was a brief trial. Martin was convicted of manslaughter and sentenced to ten years in Folsom prison. The twenty-year-old second baseman of a visiting major league team got into a bar fight and died from a head injury. Martin was identified as his assailant based on testimony provided by two other bar patrons. The DA raced through the case, highly motivated by city officials concerned about the opinions of major league baseball and the Chamber of Commerce. It was a legal blitzkrieg carried out against an orphaned street kid and a first-year public defender.

Martin was out in five years, bearing a carefully tended grudge and a graduate degree in sociology. He got out early because his rookie public defender was now a partner in a very aggressive public interest law firm. Together, they filed a suit against the City of San Francisco. Their case was almost laughably easy. She quickly established that the DA had suppressed evidence and that the two prosecution witnesses were not even in the bar at the time of the fight. The City paid Martin five million dollars. "About a million dollars a year sounds right for Mr. Kline," was the judge's final pronouncement.

Over the next ten years, Martin parlayed the five million into a hundred million by picking winners in the startup-crazed technology industry. He found himself to be thirty-three years old, rich, good-looking and absolutely clueless about what to do next.

He was sitting in Starbucks in the financial district in the middle of a Tuesday morning, watching the flow of people; people with places to go and important things to do; people that had somebody to be with.   It was an unusual feeling and he didn't like it, this feeling sorry for oneself.

A man pulled out the chair opposite him and sat down.

Martin looked up. "I know you."

"Sergei Prokov.   The yard at Folsom.   Eleven years ago."

They called him 'the Russian hacker,' but he was Jewish and Israeli. Always scribbling in a notebook. Stuff looked like gibberish. Kept to himself, but everybody had a story about him. How he destroyed a global bank, or shut off the electricity to Chicago for four hours, or downloaded all of the nuclear codes from the Pentagon. He just smiled and kept scribbling.

"That was a long time ago. How you been?"

No answer. He just sat looking at Martin, the way a hitchhiker might check out the driver before he got in the car.

"Coffee, Sergei? I'll buy."

"I have a new idea, but I need money to make it work."

Same social skills as in the yard. But he did have a rep as a mad scientist type ...

"Why me?"

"You invest money in new ideas. And you were like me."

Martin raised his eyebrow.

"You didn't belong in that place."

They talked for three hours.   'The new idea' was incomprehensible to Martin, the verbal equivalent of the gibberish scrawled in those prison yard notebooks. And Sergei knew nothing about the business side of things -- budgets, strategic plans or marketing. In that sense, they were perfect complements for one another. After he got home, Martin used Google to do some historical research on Sergei Prokov. All the coverage was twelve years old, concerning how a "young computer genius" had defeated every firewall ever devised. As far as Martin could tell from the newspaper articles, Sergei's only crime was to encourage cyber-terrorism by posting his considerable accomplishments on the internet.

The next morning, he and Sergei formed a company. Six years later, they sold it to Cisco for four billion dollars.

Martin realized that his coffee had gotten cold. *I haven't thought about Mayo or Sergei for a while. Time to fix that.*

Martin met Sergei at the Cantor Museum on the Stanford campus. The small restaurant on the outside patio overlooked half an acre dotted with Rodin sculptures. Martin got there early and spent an hour in the Museum and strolling among the sculptures. He spotted Sergei half-a-block away, coming from the center of campus, walking fast with his head down. It was easy for Martin to see him as a threadbare graduate student worried about a Ph.D. dissertation that wasn't quite coming together.

They ordered lunch, an act that took perhaps ten seconds. One of the many things they had in common was their indifference to cuisine. It was a handy trait in Folsom Prison, but it persisted even when they found themselves living in San Francisco – one of the world's great cities for gourmet dining – and still ordering grilled cheese sandwiches while the investment bankers around them agonized over ornate wine lists and ten-page menus with far more adjectives than nouns.

"So, Sergei, you wanted to meet at Stanford. You've finally decided to return to pursue your degree?"

They both smiled at that. As far as Martin knew, Sergei's previous college experience had been a single year in the advanced mathematics program in an Israeli university. He dropped out when they insisted that he take some token courses outside of the mathematics department.

"I've got a dozen universities that will give me an honorary doctorate if I endow enough buildings … why go to class?"

He's serious! Sergei doesn't know what irony is, let along practice it.

Sergei was all business. "Thanks for coming down. Why here? I'm spending some time with a computer science guy who's got a couple of doctoral students working on encryption algorithms that I think have some possibilities. I'm trying to help them."

He wound up in Folsom because of that same curiosity. "Uh, Sergei. Please tell me that you're not –"

"Relax, Martin." Sergei held up both hands, palms outward. "I'm actually working as a consultant for NSA these days. I get to play as much as I like as long as I tell them what I'm learning about places and people and computer systems that are supposed to be invisible.

Sergei made another jump. "He didn't finish school either."

Martin said, "He?"

Sergei gestured to the sculpture gardens spread out before them. "Rodin. Quit school at age fourteen. And the idiots at the Ecole des Beaux Arts in Paris wouldn't accept him. Found his sculptures to be unpromising."

"I have a favor to ask," Martin said in a slightly embarrassed tone.

The man is consulting with NSA, working at the outer edges of information science. And I'm about to ask him to do something about as challenging as finding an unlisted number!

"Sure. Tell me about it."

"Two things, actually. Maybe three. First, I need to know everything there is to know about a particular building in San Francisco. Related to that, the complete history of a man named Hiram Brookings and his descendants, particularly the circumstances surrounding the deaths of his son, grandson and great-grandson. Finally, whatever you can find out about a foundation called the Petrel Foundation."

Sergei stared unblinkingly at him during this recitation. He took no notes and asked no questions. When Martin was finished, he nodded and said, "Sounds straightforward. Mostly local stuff. Probably some city or county data bases that have to be gotten around. I'll need the address of whatever building it is that you're curious about. Anything else?"

Martin hesitated. *I could ask for a deep dive into the personal history of a woman named Natalie Weiss. Why not? These days, everybody 'Googles' everybody. All I'd be doing is enlisting an uber-Google type to do the search for me.*

Instead he shook his head. *Am I afraid that I would find out something that would diminish her? Do I need her to be mysterious?*

"No. That's it. And thanks, Sergei."

A Storefront on Mission

Martin went from Stanford to a rundown storefront on Mission Street in the city. At one time, it had been a bookstore and some of the walls were still lined with floor-to-ceiling shelves. The internet, Amazon and the changing demographics of the Mission District finally overcame the bank account and the sheer stubbornness of the owner, who one day just walked away from the mortgage and his commitment to the concept of neighborhood preservation. Somehow, the building wound up being owned by the City of San Francisco and the MK Foundation had signed a one-year lease, conditional on using the space to help ex-prisoners with their transition to civilian life.

The fancy word was "recidivism," referring to the depressing rate at which ex-cons failed that transition and wound up back behind bars. The reality was that the con went from a highly structured institutionalized existence where everything was provided and choices were non-existent into a world where nothing was assured and the rules for existence were bewildering. All the infrastructure of modern life had to be reconstructed, usually from scratch - housing, employment, transportation, communication – in a zero-tolerance environment.

Martin would never forget his encounter with one of his early clients, a forty-year old who'd been incarcerated since he was fifteen years old.

"Lemme think about this. They spend a hundred thousand dollars a year to keep me in prison. Then they give me two hundred dollars and wish me luck on my own. I'm unemployed, cold, homeless, sick, starving and broke. And they call that 'free.'"

The next day, he bought a toy gun and made a halfhearted attempt to hold up a Bank of America branch. He got a paper bag filled with cash from the teller, but stopped to talk to the rent-a-cop outside the door until the SFPD showed up.

Martin's first hire for his drop-in center was a parolee from Folsom Prison, an ex-social worker who had embezzled money from Medicare. Martin got him relicensed and paid him to hang out at the storefront on Mission from nine to six, six days a week. He knew every social service agency in the city and had the tenacity of rainwater running downhill.

The furnishings were simple: some couches, stuffed chairs, big-screen TV, a pool table and ping pong table. There was a gallon-sized coffee urn and a refrigerator stocked with soft drinks and bottled water. The only requirements to get in the door were to have been in prison and to check in with Bartholomew, an ex-lifer and Martin's second hire. When he was paroled last year as a result of the Federal court's mandate to California to reduce its overcrowded prisons, Bartholomew's only possessions were a bible, the clothes on his back and an aura that radiated the kind of aware stillness that a Zen master would seek.

For Martin, walking down Mission Street was to revisit his childhood. It was a city within a city, a neighborhood with a distinctive feel and culture. It started out as a working-class stronghold and slowly shifted into a mixed-used district, the center of Latino culture in San Francisco and a breeding ground for countercultures. The late 1990's and the dotcom boom brought the techies, and the Mission was slowly but surely being gentrified, invaded by an army of geeks bearing laptops and seeking suitably hip housing near their startup companies or, if those companies were thirty miles away in Silicon Valley, near a bus stop where the Google or Facebook buses with their leather seats and 24/7 connectivity made continuous loops.

And I'm partly to blame. The Chronicle's headlines were explicit: "Ex-Felons Among the Billionaires." All it lacked was an exclamation point. Neither he nor Sergei gave interviews, and Cisco certainly did not welcome widespread publicity about its acquisition strategies, so the feature writer had to make do with the little bit of information that was in the public domain. It ended up with Martin and Sergei sounding like a blend of Bill Gates, Steve Jobs and Horatio Alger. The writer got carried away. She used the line "It's as if Butch Cassidy and Sundance didn't die in Bolivia, but came home and started a hedge fund."

Sergei called him, clearly upset. "Can't we sue them?"

"That'll make it much worse, trust me. Just ignore them and they'll move on. They've got the attention span of a brain-damaged gnat."

The real problem is the implication that if ex-felons can get rich quick, then surely some maladjusted sophomore halfway through an engineering degree should be able to drop out of school and code his way to fortune. Go to San Francisco! Join a startup! Hell! Start a startup!

They're too young to remember the 2000 internet bubble and too soused in technology to see the alternatives. And the so-called realists – the bankers, VCs and aging veterans – are as caught up in the fever as the kids. It's too bad that we have to destroy whole neighborhoods in the process.

A cluster of eight or ten swept past him as to prove the point, half of them with their eyes down and looking at their smart phones. All but one of them wore blue jeans. The men all seemed to have three-day-old beards and the three women were talking loudly and waving their arms.

The voice came from behind him, somehow in perfect sync with his thoughts. "I will send a plague of frogs on your whole country. The Nile will teem with frogs. They will come up into your palace and your bedroom and onto your bed, into the houses of your officials and on your people. The frogs will come up on you and your people and all your officials."

Martin did not turn around, but raised his hand to acknowledge the voice.

"Good morning, Bartholomew. Or should I call you Moses? That is Exodus you're quoting from, isn't it?"

The man was sitting in the doorway of the storefront with his green plastic chair tipped back against the frame. He was coal black and quite large, wide as well as tall. To Martin, he looked ageless, but he knew him to be seventy-four years old. The last fifty-two of those years had been spent in Folsom Prison.

"Chapter 8, Verse 2. The second plague. Still several to go before we kill the livestock and the first-born children …"

All the lifers had hobbies. Bartholomew memorized the Old Testament. "Because," he said, "the stories are easier to relate to than all that Jesus stuff in the New Testament."

And I am totally dependent on him.

"What's up? I get the impression that you're a sort of acting doorman?"

"Hey, Mr. K. You know me. Anybody can go in. It's the outgoing that I'm the sort-of doorman for."

When Martin raised his eyebrow, Bartholomew inclined his head toward the interior of the building and went on. "It's L. Donald; he's got some ketamine on board and is slightly psychotic. Figure we'll keep him in a safe place till he comes down a bit."

"Who else is around?"

"The usuals, maybe eight or nine. And one newbie."

"From Folsom? San Quentin?"

"Nope. Pelican Bay. Hard time. Name's Warren Wah." He said the name in a way that hinted that Martin should know it.

"A problem?"

Bartholomew's hesitation before answering was unusual, and a clear tipoff that there might, in fact, be a problem. "I think he wants to be straight, but … He's got some friends from his past life that might make that difficult."

He's a good kid; he just fell into bad company. How many times have I heard that phrase? At my own trial, for starters.

Martin walked a few steps away to the bus stop and sat on the bench. He used his cell phone to Google "Warren Wah" and was surprised at the number of hits. It took only a few seconds of scanning before all of the memories came flooding back.

The nineties. Scandal involving the Mayor's office. One of his aides doing deals with vendors for outsourced public services – garbage, towing, vehicle maintenance, building inspections, etc.   Warren Wah was a Chinese-American gofer that seemed to have a hand in most of the deals. A criminal 'rags to riches' story ... a legbreaker who worked his way up the hierarchy. Busted on suspicion of murder charges and the state cops wanted to use him as an informant to get at the crooked politicians. But he never rolled over. Spent the last six years at Pelican Bay, one of the so-called "supermax" prisons for the truly serious prisoners.

He went back to Bartholomew who stood up as he approached, clearly with something he wanted to say.

"Mr. K, this one's different. He don't need us. He's connected. Got money, a place to stay. And he ain't lookin' for any of that peer group social bullshit. The man's here for a reason --"

"Stop fretting about it. I'll talk to him, Bartholomew."

"That's good. Because he asked specially for you."

Warren Wah

Warren Wah watched the two of them talking, knowing that Bartholomew didn't like him and would try to protect Kline. He was there because of his uncle. That was ironic, because he did not like his uncle very much. He knew that Chao Zhu resented him because he was not 'pure' Chinese, but the product of a love affair between an American gangster and his sister-in-law. And that distaste was sharpened by the fact that Chao did not place much value on the outlying branches of his family. At least when compared to the ferocity with which he advanced the fortunes of his direct descendants.

But he was so steeped in paternalism that he made sure that Warren was taken in by the Chinatown powers, that he had a home and was made a part of Chao's extensive network in Northern California crime circles. When Warren displayed not only loyalty, but a real talent for the selective application of a calculated violence, he moved up in the ranks.

He was one of two men that entered the Donald Brookings' home on Russian Hill in 1995. The other was Xi, the grandson of Chao Zhu. It was a masterpiece of ironic theatre. The irony was that the break-in and murder had been planned for ninety years, an honor killing that was the exclusive assignment of Chao Zhu's direct descendants, a rite of passage as duty-bound as any bar mitzvah, but it was executed as sloppily as though it was a spur-of-the-moment 'smash and grab' operation. Xi beat the man senseless and then shot him with a gun that was registered to him. When the cops traced it, Chao told Warren to take the fall.

"Xi is stupid. But he is my grandson. Do this for me, and I will take care of you."

He ended up serving sixteen years, the last six of them in Pelican Bay. Chao was waiting for him at the entrance gates the day he was released and drove him the 363 winding miles to San Francisco on U.S. Highway One.

It was a strange journey, an extended conversation between an impoverished middle-aged half-breed without a past and a wealthy dying old man with interests on four continents, an aristocrat who traced his past back hundreds of years to Chinese royalty.

When Chao let him out of the car in San Francisco, he said, "I want you to talk to four individuals for me. I need to know what you think of them."

One of the names on the list was Martin Kline.

Martin checked him out from the doorway. Warren Wah looked more like a suburban husband with overdue bills than he did an alleged murderer and a graduate of one of the most notorious supermax prisons. He was sitting on one of the couches watching three or four of the other men playing an enthusiastic game of eight-ball. He looked like a spectator who had some side bets riding and was not optimistic about the outcome.

More Chinese than Caucasian. Manchurian maybe. No obvious tattoos showing and none of the overdeveloped musculature you get with a lot of the long timers. Dressed like a middle manager on casual Friday. If it weren't for the eyes, he'd look like your everyday civilian.

He stood between him and the pool game. "Warren, I'm Martin Kline. Bartholomew told me you were here and wanted to see me."

The man looked up at Martin and his outstretched hand and held his gaze just long enough to establish that he was choosing to respond, that any conversation that took place was at his discretion. Martin had seen the look many times. It was a trait of imprisoned alpha males, a way to preserve and signal status when confined in an institution that dedicates itself to reducing all of its inhabitants to classlessness.

"Bartholomew. Huh. He a lifer?" He did not offer to shake hands.

"Folsom. Fifty-two years."

"Must be tough." And Martin knew that he was referring to life in the real world, not the half-century behind walls.

"The man's pretty adaptable. More than most."

Curious how one automatically falls into the old speech patterns. Pretty soon I'll put my hands in my pockets and lean back against the wall. If there was a wall.

Wah stood up. "Your man said the coffee's pretty good. Want some?"

"Sure."

They walked to the back of the space. Martin took down two large mugs with logos from the San Francisco Maritime and filled them from the urn. He handed one to Wah and took his own mug over to a nearby table with a chess set and a laptop computer on its discolored and scratched-up surface. They both sat down and sipped their coffee.

Wah nodded at the half-dozen individuals grouped around the pool table. "Quite a collection. Are there more like them?"

"We're not real big on metrics. Eventually, most of the local parolees stop in here. Some stay, some leave. We help if we can."

"Your money, is it? That does all this good for us poor folk? The MK Foundation ... Martin Kline?"

"Actually, the 'MK' stands for Maximilian Kolbe."

Wah looked blank and then his tone hinted at a very faint irritation. "Mr. Kline, I've been locked up for sixteen years. I'm not familiar with your generation of philanthropists –"

"You should know this particular one. Maximilian Kolbe is the patron saint of drug addicts and prisoners, a Franciscan friar who volunteered to die in place of a stranger at Auschwitz. And did."

Martin sat up straight and pushed his mug away. "What is it you wanted to see me about, Mr. Wah?" He tried for as neutral a tone as he could muster, but didn't think that he achieved it.

The man seemed not to have heard him. He surprised Martin by asking, "Do you remember a parolee out of Club Fed at Lompoc? His name was James Lee, but most everybody called him 'the doctor.'"

Hard to forget. Maybe a year ago. White guy in his sixties. About as different from Warren Wah as one could be.

Came out of the federal detention facility for white collar criminals. Three years for insider trading in biomedical stocks. His wife had a hard time while he was inside. He didn't need us, but liked to hang out. One of our success stories, but not one I can talk about.

He answered casually, watching Wah closely. "Yeah, I knew him. A very gentle fellow. I heard that he died. Just a couple months back."

There was the slightest flicker of something – sadness, maybe anger – across Wah's face, so fleeting that Martin distrusted his perceptions.

Wah stood up and leaned forward over the table until he was about six inches away. He spoke very softly, but Martin knew that this was why he had come, to tell him whatever he was about to say.

And it had nothing to do with James Lee.

"You've got what's called a diversified real estate portfolio, don't you? A storefront in the Mission, a house in the Presidio, and now you're trying to buy a historic property on Russian Hill. Seems like one property too many for someone as busy as you are, helping us newly-released and disoriented prisoners make their way back into the civilian world."

Well. That was polite. If it wasn't for those eyes and the nose-to-nose distance, one might think of it as well-intentioned advice rather than a serious threat. But why? And who is it that is sending the message? Probably the same guy that wanted to make a five-hundred thousand dollar donation ... his idea of a one-two punch, I guess.

Martin sorted through his options, finally settling on the one that had the best chance of offending Warren Wah.

"If you're hungry, we've got some vouchers for meals at Saint Anthony's dining room. If it's counseling you're looking for, you'll have to come back at –"

Wah's expression did not change. He stood erect, nodded at Bartholomew who had moved within a few feet of the two of them, and stared at Martin long and hard. Then he simply turned around and walked out the door.

Bartholomew watched him go. "He's trouble, Mr. Kline."

Yes, he is. For more than one reason. I need to know more about this damn house!

Meeting the Mayor

It was Martin's first visit to the Civic Center Parking Garage since the mugging incident. This time, he found a parking space immediately, in a well-lighted space near the exit stairway. He decided to treat it as a favorable omen.

Two hours later, Martin no longer believed in omens of any sort and certainly not favorable ones. He had visited five city departments, each of which had some input into real estate issues in city neighborhoods. By his calculation, he had achieved seventeen minutes of face time with two actual officials. They were uniformly polite, sufficiently so to convince him that – to them -- he was nothing but a nuisance who could vote.

The best is the enemy of the good. Whoever said that must have worked in San Francisco! These people would not commit to anything until – What was it the last woman said? – "Until I know that it's the absolutely best use of our resources." And knowing that will require more studies and public hearings. Everything but an actual decision!

He stood looking at the Directory, trying to decide whether to spend more time on cold calls on indifferent bureaucrats or to go home to his cat. He didn't notice the woman who'd been watching him for the last couple of minutes until she nudged him with her elbow and said, "How about a coffee? I owe you one."

"Natalie. How nice to see you again."

It was a conventional, knee-jerk response, but even as he was saying the words, he realized that he meant it. She was a very pleasant surprise.

He pointed and smiled. "Nice purse. Looks new."

"Last year's model, but it does have built-in anti-mugging software."

He looked slightly confused, so she said, "It was a joke. I thought it was pretty snappy repartee."

Martin laughed at himself. "Sorry. I've listened to so many crackpot presentations for new technologies that I can no longer distinguish between sarcasm and realism."

She pointed at the Directory. "So you're taking your campaign on the road?"

"Campaign?"

"The building you're trying to buy."

He took her arm and steered her away from the directory with its depressing list of inaccessible officials. "Let's get that coffee. I feel like one of those Middle East refugees. In a strange land where I don't speak the language and they really don't want me around but can't say that openly."

"You poor fellow." She changed course as they crossed the lobby, heading for the stairway. "C'mon. I'll introduce you to someone who actually likes refugees."

"Mummy the mayor?"

"Yep."

He followed her meekly through three security checkpoints. She clearly knew everybody from the security guards through the Chief of Staff who turned out to be a formidable woman named Mallory. She nodded them into the Mayor's office after a ten second phone call.

Janet Li stood up when they came in. She walked around her desk and held her hand out.

Natalie started, "Janet, this is –"

"Mr. Martin Kline. I know. I've wanted to meet you for a long time."

The Mayor smiled when both Natalie and Martin looked confused. "First, Mayo Marsh has told me about you. He likes you and that's good enough for me. Second, I was running for local office when the court ordered the City of San Francisco to pay you five million dollars. I thought it should have been more. Third, you and your foundation are making my life difficult with your proposal for the Russian Hill property."

She cocked her index finger at Natalie. "And you are not helping!"

Martin was impressed. *Looks tough enough to be a match for Natalie. Be interesting to see where this goes. And they don't need you to referee. Get out of their way and let it run.*

Natalie tried again. "Janet, Mr. Kline and I –"

"Are on opposite sides of a hot potato that's on my desk at the moment. So I'm pleased to finally meet Mr. Kline but I can't talk about it right now. I'm working on the final stages of a billion dollar deal."

She grinned, "I've always wanted to say that line."

She got between the two of them, talking the entire time and putting a hand on each of their arms and steering them toward the door that was opened by a smiling Chief of Staff at the exact moment they reached it.

"So pleased that you stopped in, Mr. Kline. I really did look forward to meeting you. My door is always open. Bye, Natalie."

They stood in the anteroom and looked at each other. They broke out laughing simultaneously.

"Well. That was interesting," Natalie said almost to herself.

"Yes, it was. Do you realize that neither of us said a word during that entire encounter? I think we're out of our league when it comes to lobbying skills."

She laid her hand on his arm. "Let's get that coffee."

Martin looked at his watch. "I'm overdue for an appointment with –"

Her grip tightened on his forearm. "I don't care how you finish that sentence. I introduced you to the Mayor, so you owe me. And it seems we have a lot to talk about."

He bowed slightly and gestured with his free hand toward the door onto the Plaza.

The cat's appointment with the vet can wait. I've got a beautiful and smart woman who wants to talk with me. And she's buying the coffee.

After half-an-hour, he began to regret his decision to have coffee with Natalie rather than take the cat to the vet.

She is in fact both beautiful and smart. She is also excessively curious about things that I do not wish to talk about.

The questions began as soon as they sat down with their coffee.

"OK. Let's start with an easy one. I hear you're rich. They say you're a billionaire?"

So she's interested enough to have done some basic research.

"Actually, it's only seven hundred million. Taxes, you know."

She shrugged, as though whether he was only a multi-millionaire rather than a billionaire was not very important to her. He liked that.

Then she asked, "Who's this Mayo that Janet mentioned?"

Not so easy, really. Keep it simple.

"He's a long time city cop. Close to retirement. My guess is that he and Janet – your mother – worked together when she was in SFPD."

"And he knows you how?"

He tried to waffle. "It's a long story. Not very interesting really."

She leaned back and crossed her arms, signaling an infinite degree of patience.

Martin sighed. "He walked a beat in the Mission – what they called 'Community Policing' – when I was growing up there. This is like thirty years ago."

When he stopped with an expression that translated as "OK, I answered your question," she frowned at him. Her next question came out of the blue.

"Have you tried on-line dating?"

Wow! This is one of those questions where any answer may be wrong.

"Uh, no. But what does that have to do with anything that –"

"In on-line dating, there's a mutual agreement – usually implicit, but quite well understood by both parties – that personal questions are OK, even useful. It's also understood that exaggerations, omissions and even outright lies may be forgivable in early stages, but that it is *not* OK to not answer the question in some form."

"We aren't engaged in on-line dating, are we?"

She looked at him closely, as if debating with herself about what to say. "What we are engaged in predates computers and the internet by thousands of years."

The words hung in the air between them.

It was his turn for an internal debate. *There's a line in the sand if there ever was one. Answer the damn question or go home and take the cat to the vet. Continue this slow dance with this smart, beautiful woman or wonder forever where this would have gone. Take a risk or stay lonely.*

She said simply, "Mayo?"

He began talking, listening to himself and realizing as he went that he was telling stories that he needed to hear; stories that did not yet have an ending; stories that he wanted this woman to interpret for him.

"I was an orphan in the Mission District. A series of foster parents that didn't really care very much. Ignorant, smartass, tough kid. A juvenile delinquent who could have gone either way. Mayo was a force for good ... nudged me away from the hard core stuff."

"Sounds like a father figure maybe?"

He thought about that, finally shrugged. "Ask the therapist that I've never had. But I think that's too dramatic. Mayo and I just got along. He didn't give me advice or counseling. Just was there. More like a big brother, if anything."

We each needed something from the other. In my case, it was an adult that cared. For Mayo? Maybe somebody on the street that was actually glad to see him coming.

"A big brother ... For thirty years?"

"I haven't seen him much in the last twenty or so years. Just the occasional 'keep in touch' visit since the trial."

"Trial?"

Martin winced. *You said the magic word. You must want to talk about it.*

"I was arrested and convicted on a manslaughter charge. Mayo was a character witness on my behalf."

"So you've been in prison?"

"Five years in Folsom."

That's interesting. She didn't ask, "What did you do? Who did you kill?"

His name was Charles Cobb. Made a big deal about having the same name and being from the same state as Ty Cobb. A twenty-year-old kid with a major-league arm and a 350 batting average. Also a mean drunk who thought his million dollar bonus entitled him to paw women in bars. Even then, with all that, he didn't deserve to die.

"Was that hard? The five years in Folsom?"

Christ! Now I understand why it's OK to lie during on-line dating!

"Yes and no. 'Yes' because I was eighteen when I went in and Folsom is a tough place for an eighteen year old. 'No' because I learned a lot of useful stuff, mostly about people and myself. In some ways, it was like joining the army. See the world and grow up at the same time."

He tried to look sincere, but realized that he didn't know how to do that. "Look. This is hard for me. How about one more question and then let's stop?"

"OK … for now. Janet said something about the city paying you five million dollars. What's that about?"

He grinned, thinking about Marcie.

"A happier memory to talk about, I gather?"

"Mayo and Marcie picked me up at the Folsom gate on the day I was released. The next day, she filed a lawsuit against the City of San Francisco, claiming wrongful arrest and imprisonment."

"So, who's Marcie?"

"At the time of my trial, she – Marcie Greely --was a brand new public defender and I was one of her first clients. We had a lousy case to begin with and the DA steamrollered everybody -- Marcie, the witnesses, the judge and jury. Made a testosterone-fueled bar fight into a something that sounded like a hate crime. Marcie didn't even realize how many corners he'd cut until she got a couple of years under her belt. She was mad as hell and spent the time until my release building her case. The DA resigned 'to spend more time with his family' and the City wrote me a big check."

"Marcie sounds like a person I'd like to meet. In my line, I could use –"

He cut her off, more abruptly than he intended. "She died of pancreatic cancer three years ago."

He stared at her as if daring her to offer the standard expressions of shock or sympathy.

OK girl, you started this line of questioning. Now get yourself out of it. But who was to know that it had so many dark alleys? Time for a softball question.

"So. You were innocent, then. You didn't kill the guy?"

The question startled him, and he recognized the reason. *It's funny. Nobody's ever asked me that question since the lawsuit was settled. Who is this woman?*

"No. I wasn't innocent. I killed Charles Cobb."

She didn't look surprised. She leaned forward and asked, "Why would –"

He stood up. "We agreed on one more question. You've asked four more since then. Save it for our next date."

If there is one.

He felt exhausted. *This on-line dating routine is not as easy as it seems.*

Natalie & Martin

Two days had gone by since the coffee session that resurrected all those parts of his past that he had pushed down to somewhere deep in his subconscious, thinking that they were safe there.

It was six o'clock in the evening on a Saturday and Martin had just returned from his twice-weekly run to and from Sausalito. For once, fog had stayed out near the Farallons, so his two passages across the Golden Gate were spectacular, the sunset on one side and the Bay and city skyline on the other. But the bridge was clogged with tourists shooting selfies with the city as backdrop, so he stopped timing himself before he even began the return trip across the bridge.

He stopped at the midpoint of the Bridge and located the house at the peak of Russian Hill. From that far away, it did not look so outsized.

It's just a house. Why are you so fixated on having it? And don't give me that line about needing to see Alcatraz. There are hundreds ... thousands ... of houses where you can see the island.

It was all make believe. You wanted a mother and father and they were there. Now the house represents them and what you thought you had.

So what's wrong with that? Isn't that what a home is – just a house with a lot of pleasant memories? Why shouldn't you live in a place where you were happy?

As always, he finished his run on the deep sand at Baker Beach, a short distance from his four-bedroom leased house in the Presidio. It was old military housing, but the location and views were world-class and the extra bedrooms enabled him to take in the occasional client; usually a recent parolee who was trying to transition back into the civilian world.

California was court-ordered to reduce its prison population and there was a steady stream of 'early releases' coming home, including some who had been behind bars for decades.   It was a tough transition, one that the MK Foundation was created for.

When the doorbell rang, he was sitting at his kitchen table, still in his sweatsuit, drinking a beer and watching the last rays of the sun being swallowed up by the fog bank at sea. He had long ago given up on seeing 'the green flash' and no longer believed in the phenomenon.   And on a day like this with the distant fog bank and no clouds in the sky, the sunset was a non-event.

It was Natalie, carrying what looked like a thick roll of blueprints.   She smiled brightly and said, "Hi," as though her standing on his doorstep was a routine event; like the next-door neighbor dropping in to borrow a cup of sugar.

"Hi."   And then he waited, remembering how she had used her silence to lure him into telling secrets.

The silence lasted long enough that he began to feel silly, amused by his own obstinacy. *This is a game that I don't need to win.*

He gave up and stood aside.   "Come on in.   Sorry I'm not dressed for company.   Can I get you a beer?   Some wine?"

"Actually, I passed you on the Golden Gate about thirty minutes ago.   Saw you running.   Figured you were headed home.   Thought I'd drop in.   Show you these."   She indicated the rolls of paper under her arm.   Slightly yellowed architectural drawings of some kind.   The string of staccato phrases made her seem nervous.

Could be, I suppose. Seems unlikely that somebody driving on the bridge would be able to pick out a single individual from the crowds going both directions. Especially if that individual is wearing a hooded sweatshirt. In any case, she wouldn't have been able to recognize me on the bridge unless she was headed north, away from the city. And supposedly I have an unlisted address.

Maybe this is one of those times where – how did she put it – exaggerations, omissions and even outright lies are permissible?

He was acutely aware that his heart rate had stepped up and that he was nervous and unsure of himself.

The room seemed to get slightly smaller once she came in and he closed the door behind her, making him more aware of the space between them. She was dressed casually; blue jeans and a sweatshirt with a Greenpeace logo of some sort. Ragged tennis shoes.

"Nothing to drink, thanks. But I do think you should see these." She moved his beer bottle onto the counter and started to unroll the sheaf of drawings on the tabletop.

"What are they?" He stood closely behind her and looked over her shoulder. She smelled of soap and her hair was still slightly damp. *Showering while driving across the bridge, I guess.*

"The original plans for the Russian Hill property."

"That's funny. The planning office told me that they were lost long ago. I guess you have better connections than I do."

"No. Just more creativity. I found these through the Historical Society."

She was struggling to flatten the prints, but they kept curling back up. He reached around her to hold one corner down, bringing them into close contact. She pulled away sharply and her hand slipped, allowing the stubborn sheets to recoil back into their tubular shape. She swore, "the hell with this!" and turned into him, pressing him back against the counter and wrapping her arms around him.

The kiss was mutual and totally abandoned, as though it was important to shed all of the pretexts and charades; to commit without reservation to something more primitive; to make up for their prior restraint. They broke repeatedly, gasping, but always came back together, mouths locked and hands frantically exploring wherever they could reach.

The sweatshirts were easy; pulled off in a single motion and tossed aside. She wore nothing beneath hers and the sensation of skin against skin was unbearable. She arched back in his arms, holding his face between her two hands. He licked her nipples and buried his face between her breasts. Her jeans were a problem, much too tight to simply step out of. She pulled him to the couch and lay down with her feet in the air. He took one cuff in each hand and yanked the jeans off violently. She arched her back and slid her panties off, leaving her legs spread and reaching out to pull his sweatpants down to his knees. He fell on top of her.

There was no finesse or consideration of the other's needs. No concern for timing or what would happen next. One, maybe both of them, made incomprehensible sounds. It was an utterly selfish giving in to pure sensation and need, a violent, primeval coupling. It left them sprawled half on the floor, panting, afraid to look at the other.

She was first to recover. She rasped, "We frightened your cat."

Martin twisted around. His cat was crouched on the arm of the couch, looking at them with enormous round eyes, his tail twitching in short, rapid arcs. When Martin reached out to him, he leapt away, his claws scrabbling for purchase on the hardwood floor.

"Sorry," he said. "She's kind of possessive. Doesn't like me to pay attention to other women."

She giggled. "I'm just glad you don't have a Rottweiler instead of a cat. This might not have ended so well for me."

She tried to disentangle her arm from under him, causing them to slide fully onto the floor. Once there, he propped his head on his arm and looked at her. "I don't think I would have noticed. The Rottweiler, that is. That was absolute and pure selfishness."

"For both of us. Anyway, I've always thought that foreplay was overrated."

"Natalie … I … We …"

She raised her hand to his face, with her fingertips on his lips. "Relax Kline. This was not your doing … other than that part at the very end." And she started giggling again.

"So there's a master campaign plan?"

"That sounds like something sinister. Or an attempt at semi-permanent, which is sort of the same thing." Her brow furrowed. "No. This was more like a reconnaissance-in-force, something with a time horizon of about sixty minutes."

He looked at the watch still on his wrist. "Well, then its still got forty-three minutes to run, doesn't it?"

"There was some slack built into the timeline. Just in case. So ..."

He pulled himself into a sitting position, leaning back against the couch and reaching up to turn on the lamp. The cat took that as a cue to return and began nudging his left ear with her muzzle.

"How about dinner?" he asked.

"That'll take more than forty-three minutes, won't it?"

"That's one of the problems with a reconnaissance-in-force; it can become an extended engagement." After a short pause, he added, "What I'd like to do after dinner is to come back here ..." He gestured toward the doorway behind him. "There's actually a bedroom back there. We could try this again. Without a timer."

"What about the other woman?" Natalie asked, inclining her head toward the cat. It had returned to the arm of the sofa and was watching them with eyes that seemed infinitely wise.

"Her name is Charley and we have a purely platonic relationship. She'll understand."

Cold Feet

She's seen too many gangster movies!

It was the first time that Emily had a foreboding that her involvement with Donna Yang might come to a bad end. In the time since their first meeting at the Aquatic Park bleachers, she had learned that Yang was a meticulous organizer; a planner who had contingency plans backing up contingency plans. She was scrupulously honest, in the ironic sense that she did not skim even though it would have been easy for her to do so, given the covert and highly illegal projects she managed. When appointed Department Head in Alban's place, she moved quickly to tighten operations and move her most trusted lieutenants into key roles. Her cash flow was already showing improvement. Ironically, the Department also became more efficient for the city. The mayor even had called her to commend her for moving quickly to fix longstanding problems that Alban had ignored.

So Emily was not surprised that Yang seemed more confident, surer of herself than in their first meeting. It became apparent from the instant they sat down on the concrete bench facing the inlet.

The meeting started out well. Yang said, "I did not expect that you would ... that things would happen so quickly, but the ... unfortunate accident ... suffered by Mr. Alban has enabled me to make some long overdue changes."

Emily smiled. "As you said, he needed to go." Then she moved immediately to her agenda.

"The next phase will be more difficult. As we discussed, it is time to change your financial arrangements with Gruber and his organization." Emily spoke decisively, as though they had already agreed on this point.

Yang's expression did not change, but her body language was quite expressive of the indecision that Emily's words had induced in her. She wrung her hands together and pulled her arms tight against her torso. "He's mafia, right?"

She's afraid! Of something that doesn't exist except in her own mind. I wonder what Alban told her about the deals he was making? Must have made them sound like contracts signed in blood with hooded figures. Italians with machine guns.

"Donna, there's nothing –"

"I think that we should ask to renegotiate our percentage split. Nothing too drastic at this time."

It took Emily half-an-hour to convince Yang that her original idea was sound, that her operation should not be required to pay extortion to what she called 'the mob.' She finally agreed to let Emily set up a negotiating session. But her last words were, "I want to know what you intend to do. And I get to approve it before you do it. I don't want a blood bath over a few percentage points."

She's out of her depth on this one. There is and never has been much of 'a mob' in San Francisco. We've got Hispanic gangs and Asian gangs at the street level, but the mafia is mostly non-existent here. Mannie's about it. He's got no crime family status and the New York and Chicago and Las Vegas made guys would laugh at the idea. I know; I've dealt with the real ones. The closest thing this city's got to a crime family is in Chinatown – and that's Yang's own people!

She watched Yang thread her way out of the bleachers, a nondescript figure with her head down, walking with quick small steps. Perhaps the very ordinariness of that image, so at odds with the nature of her ambitions, was what caused the vague misgiving that Emily felt come across her like a shadow on a cloudless day; the sense that this woman, in this city, was somehow deadly for Emily and all of her ambitions.

Picnic With a View

Martin was headed out the door when the phone rang. It was nine in the morning. The fog was still offshore and looking like it would stay there.

"How about a walk?"

"Good morning Natalie. A walk sounds good, especially since my only alternative is hanging out at City Hall and waiting for an audience with the assistant to the aide to the deputy to the department head. I can run after we get back."

"You may change your mind about running. I'll pick you up in thirty minutes. Wear good shoes."

The so-called 'walk' turned out to be a six-hour hike in the Marin Headlands. She had the curious habit of treating every uphill stretch as a time trial, something to be covered at a fast and unvarying pace. Martin's calves were burning by the time they reached what she labeled 'the halfway point,' which was the westernmost point in the Headlands, the Point Bonitas lighthouse. And during that time, she kept up a running monologue about the history, geology and environmental importance of the Marin Headlands.

"Um, it's two hours back to the car. Maybe we should _"

"You tired?" she asked innocently. "C'mon. It's time for lunch."

He followed her meekly back to a picnic table at Battery Wallace with its spectacular views of the Golden Gate. The first item out of the small backpack she was carrying was a checkered tablecloth, followed by sandwiches and two kinds of pasta in plastic containers.

"Any milkshakes in that pack?"

"I thought about wine, but it's dehydrating. You'll have to make do with water."

She's beautiful. Hair in a messy ponytail, slightly sweating. Great color. The most alive person I've ever seen.

"So how did you get to be an orphan? A nice girl like you …"

Natalie looked closely at Martin, wondering if this was his way of opening up some of his own closed-off spaces or just the kind of light conversation suitable for a daylight outing. *He looks innocent enough, but he's good at that. And things have progressed to a point that such invasive questions are not unreasonable.*

For his part, Martin was deeply serious. The question was a calculated one, both in its timing and phrasing. He'd even factored in the setting, figuring that the casual and public atmosphere would keep all of his – and her -- options open if the going got difficult.

She sighed deeply. *You've done this before. Which one of the many versions shall I use – the 'poor me' or the 'no big deal' story line, maybe the 'I really don't want to talk about that' version? C'mon, Natalie, get over yourself! He's an orphan too. And we've spent some quality time in bed together, really close in all respects. And maybe it's just that – just a question.*

Martin watched her eyes and knew that she was thinking about how to respond. "Forget it, Natalie. I don't need to know."

"It's not about *your* needs," she said. And then she shook her head and said, "I became an orphan like any other kid. Involuntarily and unprepared." *But he didn't. He got to practice being an orphan before it became an official fact.*

"Two stages. My father died in an accident when I was eight years old. Eleven months later, my mother died of ovarian cancer."

"No relatives to take you in?"

"None that would. I spent six months in a foster home – it was OK, but –"

"Then Janet Li came along."

He asked, almost inaudibly, "Why did she pick you?"

Each of them understood the enormous significance of that question among all the others. The flip side of the *other* loaded question, the one that couldn't be asked out loud: "Why did your parents leave you?" For an orphan, knowing the answer to those two questions would explain everything about you, both the good and the bad, your place in the world, why you deserved everything that had happened to you up to that point and everything that was to follow.

Natalie chewed on her lower lip, thinking about how to respond to a question that as much about him as her. *Easier for me to answer than him. My parents loved me and never rejected me; they just were taken away. His were there and they may even have loved him, but they didn't care enough to try harder.*

Her eyes glistened and both of them understood why.

"Janet was Superwoman. A recent Ph.D., Chinese-American woman, a street cop with multiple citations who was moving up fast through the – mostly male and Caucasian– ranks of the SFPD. She wanted kids, but not a husband. She told me once that a woman without children is incomplete in some important way … 'stunted' was her word."

She didn't answer the question. But that's OK.

As if he had spoken out loud, she said, "Why did she pick me? I don't know. I've never asked… and I don't think I ever will."

His next question was such a natural one at the time that it came out without thinking. "How come you're not married?"

She looked at him closely, giving him the feeling that she was evaluating him on some obscure dimension that was important to her, that his question had triggered some critical doubt that could be resolved if only she looked closely enough.

She responded with a question. "Do you remember what I said about the protocol of online dating?"

He smiled. "How exaggerations and even small lies are expected, and tolerated?"

She was deadly serious. "Yes. Well, we – at least I – have passed that point in this relationship. Especially with that kind of question."

"Fine with me. I never felt very comfortable with the prior rules. Felt too much like an audition. In fact, I sort of assumed we set them aside when you seduced me."

That brought an outright grin. "More like rape than seduction."

Her seriousness came back. "I *was* married. You know that, I presume?"

She went on before he could respond. "We were a mismatch from the start, but it took me six years to see it. I think I was relieved when he took up with the other women. As much my fault as his."

He was thinking what to say, how to tell her how surprisingly little her prior life mattered to him, that she was so perfect, so *complete*, that what she might have once been was irrelevant. But she broke into his thoughts.

"And you. Why are you not married?"

Try the easy way out. "Out of circulation, in Folsom. Then handicapped by my ex-felon status. Then I got too busy making money, having fun. Then I was rich and a little bit exotic. Made me feel like women viewed me like a target, maybe a trophy to display."

"Sounds lonely."

A seagull glided in to a graceful landing at the far end of their table and they both watched the bird as it seemed to consider the three feet of space between it and the grapes they had been picking at. Martin picked up one of them and rolled it toward the bird. It stopped midway between them and the bird. The gull, who was watching them closely, became quite still.

"There were a couple of what might be called 'relationships.' *Laura and Stacey.* Started out with some passion and hopefulness, but … Good people, but they either expected too much or too little of me. I couldn't tell which it was. In the long run, I didn't fit their image of what they wanted me to be. Mostly because of the money, I think."

"You grew up on the street, or in prison, or in not-so-fostering foster homes. That can't have helped with learning to trust. And being rich makes it even harder, I think."

As if responding to the word 'trust,' the seagull hopped once, snatched the grape and flew off, only to circle back and take up his position at the end of the table once more. Martin took another grape and placed it on the palm of Natalie's hand lying open on the tabletop. The bird was quite still, eying the grape with his head cocked to one side.

Martin looked at Natalie, wondering where this oblique form of conversation therapy would lead them.

He said lightly, "Trust? Didn't somebody define it as 'the virtue peculiar to those about to be betrayed?'"

"Ambrose Bierce, in *The Devil's Dictionary*. But he was talking about *fidelity*, not trust. Not quite the same. And you're evading the question. Maybe you don't trust me enough to answer truthfully?" Her tone was playful, but her expression was one of the utmost seriousness.

Later, Martin still could not figure why he responded as he did. "I met a guy the other day; a con who dropped in on the Mission Avenue storefront. Murdered a man - maybe a few more - for no reason that he would talk about and did sixteen years of hard time, a lot of it in solitary confinement. Makes my time in Folsom look like reform school in comparison. Very impressive fellow, in his way. I looked up his story. An orphan – like you and me – dropped out of school and took up with Chinese gangs – he's half Chinese and grew up in Chinatown. Worked his way up to chief hit man –"

Natalie's tone was sharper, but he noted that she was careful to keep the hand holding the grape motionless. "Martin, what's all this got to do –"

He held up his hand, slowly so as not to alarm the gull who seemed to have one eye on the grape and the other eye on them. "Despite all that really shitty stuff, or maybe because of it, he was a totally *self-contained* individual – that's the best depiction I can come up with. He didn't *need* anybody's respect; he was completely at home with who he was."

"Sounds like you envy him."

"A little bit, for sure. At least until he threatened me with bodily harm. But it made me try some research. Nothing fancy, just googled the word 'survivor.' As usual with Google, lots of irrelevant crap. I wound up reading about what the shrinks call 'resilience.' It seems that *resilient* people – i.e., survivors – share three characteristics. They are realistic about their current circumstances, optimistic about their future, and they are very good at forming strong relationships."

Now it was her turn to look inward. *She's wondering about herself and how she stacks up on those three.*

The gull made up his mind, as if Martin's speech had convinced him. He took two quick hops, picked the grape cleanly from Natalie's palm, and swooped away.

Natalie looked at him and smiled in a way that made her look incredibly wise. She said, "Now, *that's* trust."

Mayo & Martin

Martin was meeting Mayo at their regular place, a bar in the Mission District that had so far survived the gentrification movement. It had memories for both of them, since it was the scene of the bar fight that landed Martin in Folsom.

"You're invited to my retirement party."

Martin smiled. "I heard about it. The rumor is that the Mayor's hosting it and that half the department will be there. I expect there'll be a lot of speeches. People will say nice things about you ... which will be hard for both them and you."

"That's why you need to come. Keep me from getting a swelled head."

"I'm not exactly friends with your crowd. A lot of them don't like what I do."

"Just don't get into a discussion about the merits of capital punishment. C'mon, you don't have anything better to do."

"Can I bring a date?"

Mayo leaned back and looked at Martin as if he was a near stranger who had asked him for a loan. "You mean, like a girl?"

"At our age, we call them 'women.' And she's the Mayor's adopted daughter."

Mayo was startled, but didn't show it. *Natalie! Now there's a pairing that should generate some sparks! I wonder what Janet thinks about the prospects?* But he merely smiled at Martin and said, "Bring anyone you like. Just so they don't make a speech."

It was settled, and Mayo went for two more beers. When he came back to the booth, Martin asked him the question.

"You going to miss it?" Both of them knew what 'it' represented.

Mayo leaned back and laced his hands together behind his head, looking at Martin as though considering whether or not to answer the question.

'There's no easy way to answer that. I'll surely *not* miss all the departmental politics – the ass-kissing and CYA maneuvering that goes on. That's like a daily root canal. But the rest of it ..."

His voice trailed off. Martin waited.

"The problem is, I don't know what I'm going to do."

"Golf, fishing, grandkids, travel, water colors ..." Martin reeled them off with a faint smile.

Mayo hadn't been listening, still talking to himself for the most part. "You never get used to it, you know?"

"Dead people?"

"That. And the idea that there's some bastard out there that killed them. That took away absolutely everything they had or could be. Usually for some reason that's important only to them. I can't accept that they get to be free."

Martin said, "Mayo, half the murder cases in San Francisco go unsolved."

"So you see my problem," said Mayo with a very sad smile.

"Your clearance rate is higher than anybody in the Division –"

Mayo was shaking his head. "Meaning that I let fewer get away than most."

This is hopeless. Let's try a diversionary tactic. "So what are the cases that really bother you right now?"

"All of the old, cold cases that I worked on. Like my first year in Homicide ... in the nineties. That includes the so-called Mission Murders and the society dude ... Brookings, I think. Then there's the two new ones on my plate. And they worry me."

"Because?"

"We catch most of the murderers because they're either unlucky or stupid, sometimes both at the same time. But every now and then we find one with brains. They're the worst because they plan it, and they plan it so that they won't get caught. The Green and Alban cases are like that. So were the kids in the Mission."

Martin sat bolt upright, so abruptly that Mayo looked at him sharply.

"Green and Alban? First, I know those names. And second, why is Homicide interested? I thought they were accidents."

Mayo studied him closely. "Remember: I said some of these guys have brains. Officially, for the moment, we've classified both Green and Alban as 'accidental deaths,' but I think they were murdered. And just why do you know those two names?"

"I had an appointment set with Alban, for the day just before he died. To talk about the Brookings House. And Green was the owner of the Brookings House when she fell down her own stairs, which I am trying to buy on behalf of the MK Foundation. And you're worried about a twenty-five-year-old killing of a man named Brookings. Kinda coincidental, huh?"

Mayo and Martin looked at one another.

The signboard in the lobby of the Four Seasons Hotel read simply "Marsh Party" and directed them to a ballroom on the second floor. They heard the sounds of too many people in too small a space talking too loudly when they were halfway up the escalator.

Natalie said, "Not your usual civil servant sendoff, I think."

Her view was confirmed when they pushed open the doors into the ballroom. The noise was almost a physical force, surging out of the room. The greeters, one on each side of the door, were the Mayor and the Police Chief.

"So nice to see you again, Mr. Kline," chirped Janet Li. "And I see you're still keeping bad company."

Natalie made a face and said "Hello, Janet" in a way that conveyed she was too mature to engage in such bantering. Martin was busy watching the two of them together, still struck by the comfort level between the two women and the way they played off of one another.

Li went on, "I'm stuck by the door for a while. Good for my coming reelection campaign. I'm sure you'll find lots of people you know. I'll find you later, after the speeches." It wasn't clear if she was speaking to him or to Natalie, and Martin suspected that's the way she intended it.

The room was vast and he guessed that there were somewhere between two and three hundred guests milling around, most of them males. There were bars set up in three of the four corners and perhaps ten tables with chairs scattered around. A small stage with a podium and microphone was against the far wall and a very large screen behind it was running a slideshow. The photos featured Mayo as a child, at the Academy, walking a beat, receiving a decoration of some sort ... the entire life cycle of a distinguished retiree. While he watched, a shot of Mayo and a uniformed female officer – the Mayor long before she became Mayor – scrolled past.

Nobody seemed to be paying much attention to the screen. They were all engaged in talking within the clusters that filled the room, apparently with everybody talking at once and waving their arms. It was still early, but the alcohol was clearly fueling the animation. Mayo was nowhere in sight.

A woman named Mallory latched onto Natalie and pulled her a few feet away for a whispered conversation. Martin headed for the nearest bar and wormed his way through the three-deep bulwark of thirsty cops to order two glasses of wine and work his way back to Natalie. He found her with Mayo and Janet Li. Mayo seemed to be doing most of the talking.

"Martin. You asked 'Can I bring a date?' I felt sorry for you, and then you show up with the second most beautiful woman in San Francisco."

Both Natalie and Janet smiled at Mayo's compliment. Janet also elbowed Mayo quite sharply, a move that acknowledged his diplomacy in her favor and somehow made Martin wonder about the exact relationship between the two of them. *Two divorced cops sharing a thirty-year stretch in city office. Could be something there ...*

None of the three noticed the man and woman in the far corner of the room who were watching the three of them with great intensity.

Martin turned to talk to Natalie but was stopped cold by her expression. She was standing with her hand to her mouth, her eyes wide.   A picture of surprise and – more than that – shock. He followed her eyes. She was looking at the screen. It was showing a faded newspaper clipping alongside a color photograph of a bright yellow dress. The caption – just barely legible – read 'Clue to Triple Homicide.'

"Natalie, what's wrong—"

She gripped his forearm so tightly that it hurt. "That dress. It's mine."

Ten minutes later, the four of them – Martin, Natalie, Mayo and Janet – were in a small conference room down the hall from the ballroom. Even there, the crowd noise filtered through the closed door. Mayo had a laptop computer open on the table with the screen showing the slide with the yellow dress. Natalie had magnified the section of the screen with the news clipping and was reading the text.

She sat back and started talking.   "I was …" she paused, clearly counting to herself, "eight years old. It must have been 1995." She shuddered. "The year those three boys were killed. I remember how everybody was talking about them. I wore it maybe twice. My best girl friend – Suzie – and I dressed up. I was Princess Diana."

"Are you sure it's the same dress?" Mayo asked.

"Absolutely. The color, the material, everything about it." She pointed to the screen. "Look at the belt. I remember punching extra holes in it because my waist was so small. It was my favorite one."

"Where did it come from?"

"My mother." Natalie glanced at Janet as if to apologize. "My real mother."

"It was hers?" Mayo asked the question gently and Martin wondered if Natalie appreciated the importance of her answer.

"No. It's not the kind of thing she would ever wear. She brought it home for me and we kept it for my playacting with my friends. She got the dresses at the Salvation Army resale shop; she volunteered there on weekends. We had a cardboard box in the garage labeled 'dresses for Natalie'."

Mayo's voice got even softer. "Natalie, this is important. Did you ever wear the dress outside the house?"

Her reply was instant. "No. We never even left my room. Suzie and I – we both knew we were little girls playing at being grown ups. It was just for us."

Janet asked, "What happened to the dress?"

"I don't know. It went back in the box along with several others. It was about then that my father died and we moved. A lot of stuff got sold or given away. I know that I never saw it again until that photo showed up on the screen."

Martin watched Mayo, seeing the ambivalence flaring with each question and answer. On the one hand, hoping that the cold cases that were haunting him would be solved and, on the other hand, fearing that Natalie had in some mysterious way been involved in their deaths.

Martin found it painful to watch Mayo's expression as his last and best clue came to a dead end. *I think that the idea of retirement will become more real now. And I'm not sure that's a good thing.*

Incident on the Bridge

Campos answered on the first ring. As soon as Mannie started to say, "I want –", Campos broke in. "Not another purse snatching, I hope. Did you get what you wanted from Weiss's handbag?"

"Not your concern." *But yes, I did. The MacBook Air had all of her notes, emails and downloaded material from the web. She's not very far away from the complete story on the house. She's more dangerous than any of the others. And I can't touch her! At least, that's what the woman says she wants. But maybe she doesn't always get what she wants.*

He raised his voice. "You're overdue on the Kline project." He hung up without waiting for a reply.

"Fuck you!" said Campos to the dead phone.

Might as well be running on an indoor track. The early morning fog obliterated everything except the next fifty feet of glistening pavement and the shrouded lights of the oncoming traffic. The skyline, Alcatraz, Bay Bridge and the usual sights that made running across the Golden Gate bridge an aesthetic experience were all left to the imagination. Even the vertical steel cables seemed to end, unsupported, twenty feet above the roadbed.

Martin glanced at his watch at the instant he reached the midpoint. *Four minutes ahead of my best time. Must be the view that slows me down.*

Ahead of him, a figure pushed himself away from the guardrail and stood with his legs spread and arms out, a clear signal to stop. Martin pulled up six feet short of him, expecting some sort of appeal for charity. He even felt inclined toward such a gesture, probably because of his certainty that he was about to set a new personal record. And he always carried some money with him in case of unforeseen events.

Two equally startling things occurred to him at the same instant. *It's the purse snatcher from the Civic Center garage! And he's got the same damned gun!*

There were no other pedestrians in either direction. Not surprising given the fog, early hour and cold air. A steady stream of cars was racing past them only twenty feet away, but there was no chance that they would pay any attention to him. Commuting across the Golden Gate on a foggy morning was an attention-consuming task.

OK. You're on your own. Stall. Keep him talking. We've done this before.

"I have a good watch." He extended his arm to reveal it. "Probably bring a thousand bucks at a decent pawn shop. I carry maybe fifty bucks in cash. That's about it. We get to an ATM, I can get you an instant five hundred."

"I hear you're a billionaire. Is that the best you can do?"

Martin shrugged and looked away as though thinking about the question. A figure was coming from the San Francisco side behind the gunman, but he stopped well back, still indistinct in the grayness, and gripped the vertical bars of the safety railing, looking outward into the fog as if expecting it to part and show him the world-class view that he had been told of.

The man with the gun saw the figure as well. He moved another foot closer to Martin, bringing the gun to bear on the Nike emblem on his shirt, right over his heart.

"Forget the stupid watch. I want you to jump. Right now."

The absurdity of it almost made him laugh. "You want me to jump? Off the Golden Gate Bridge? Now?"

I guess that's one way to stall. Ask a lot of stupid questions.

Even as he was talking, he realized the man was deadly serious. The calculations followed automatically. *Two hundred twenty six feet above the water. A few survive the jump. And a few of them even make it to shore. Not a good option.*

"Either that or I shoot you." The gun was jumping around and the man's left hand – the one without the gun – was twitching erratically. "You choose which option you like. I'll give you five seconds to think about it."

Martin turned toward the railing as if to comply. *Get him a couple of feet closer and I might have a chance.* But even as he turned, he could see the man make up his mind. He raised the gun. *He isn't even going to honor the five seconds he promised!* When Martin turned to his left, he saw why. The blurry figure had given up on the view and was walking purposively toward them.

He lunged toward the gun, two quick steps and then a headlong dive. But it was too far and even as he was launching himself, he watched the man extend his arm and the muzzle track his movement. The shot was incredibly loud. His momentum carried him forward, careening head-down into the gunman. They toppled to the pavement together, Martin on top. He scrambled up, expecting pain or weakness, some effects of a close range gunshot. Then raw instinctual fear took over and he started running, a mindless sprint for the San Francisco anchorage.

He did not look back.

Thirty-five minutes later, he was back. But this time, he was sitting in an unmarked police car in the curbside lane. Several black and white SFPD cars sat behind them with flashing lights. The fog was still in, but from his passenger-side window, Martin could easily see the sprawled body, lying face up with his left arm protruding into the roadway.

Mayo got in the driver's side, still listening to his cell phone. When the call ended, he turned to Martin. "Name's Paul Campos. Very dead. Apparently a CPA. No record, not even a parking violation."

A uniformed cop tapped on the window and Mayo lowered it for a brief conversation that Martin couldn't hear over the steady drone of traffic headed in and out of the city.

"The gun is unregistered ... to him or anyone else. And he was wearing a three-piece suit. Like he just stopped off on his way to the office, to kill you. An errand before going to work."

Martin was still not quite back to the real world, not quite keeping up with Mayo's rapid fire recitation. "How could he miss me? He was six feet away."

Mayo looked at him closely. "He didn't miss you. The gun hasn't been fired."

"But I heard the shot."

"Yes, you would have."

"Well then –"

"Campos died from a bullet to the head, hit just above the left eye with a massive exit wound. The bullet probably went into the water, but we're going to close the bridge and check the roadway just in case. Commuters will be mad as hell."

Martin sat straighter. "The other pedestrian."

"Has to be him. What can you tell me about him."

"Basically nothing. Not tall, not short. Wearing some kind of dark-colored knee-length coat, probably a raincoat."

"Old or young? White or black? Thin or fat? Anything?"

Martin shook his head. "Sorry. He never got close enough. It was foggy and ... Hell, Mayo! The whole affair lasted about ten seconds. And all I could see was that damn gun!"

"It's OK. We'll go over all this again later, when some of the adrenalin has cleared your system.

"We've blocked off the pedestrian walkways at both ends, and we're asking everyone that we corral if they saw anything, but a fast walker could have cleared the bridge before we got there. Or he could have had an accomplice with a car. I don't think we're going to catch this guy quickly."

"I won't feel so bad if you don't catch him."

Mayo looked at Martin, clearly thinking about what to say.

"What? He saved my life, for god's sake!"

"Maybe."

"Mayo! The man – this guy, Campos? -- he was going to kill me. He told me 'Jump or I shoot you!'"

"Yeah, and maybe, just maybe, our mystery shooter had the same idea. He might have been shooting at you and happened to hit Campos. You said you were all tangled up together and the guy was – what – fifteen feet away?"

That stopped Martin cold. *I was still six feet away when I heard the shot. Campos and I were more or less in line. He can't have missed me by more than a few inches.*

Mayo switched gears. "Martin, you said you knew this guy. Campos."

"That's a little overstated. I didn't know his name or anything about him. But I did have an encounter with him a few days ago." Martin told him about the purse-snatching incident.

"So he could have shot you then? And didn't? All he wanted was Natalie's bag?"

But Martin was thinking about something else.

"I got a call late yesterday. No idea who it was, but he offered me a half-million dollar donation for the foundation. When I objected to his conditions, he made a not-so-veiled threat."

"Was it Campos? The caller."

Martin thought about it. "No. A deeper voice, maybe an accent even."

"What were the conditions you objected to?"

"You'll like this, Mayo." Martin smiled, the first time today. "He wanted me to cease and desist in my efforts to buy the Brookings House."

What he did not tell Mayo was that Warren Wah had also made a not-so-veiled threat at about the same time, that visit at the Mission storefront. *He's fresh out of Pelican Bay, and they'll put him back in for sure if I tell that story. Too soon to blow the whistle on that one.*

An hour later, Mayo was back in his office. Detective Victoria Morrison was sitting on the other side of his desk. She had a small black notebook flipped open and was referring to it as she talked.

"No luck on the bridge. Maybe half-a-dozen pedestrians going north and about the same south. None of them saw or heard anything. And they're all tourists from out-of-town. We're checking, but I'll bet my pension that's all they are."

Mayo asked, "Cameras? The bridge is covered the whole way, isn't it?"

"I'm off to view what they've got when we finish. But the damn fog will probably make them pretty useless."

"What about Campos? Anything coming in yet?"

She looked at some scribbled notes. "Unmarried, lived alone, neighbors expressing shock and saying the usual stuff about 'how normal he seemed.' So far, he looks like your everyday citizen, other than he seems to enjoy killing people."

"Or snatching purses."

Morrison waved that off. "C'mon, Mayo. We both know that mugging bit at the Civic Center is connected with what he tried this morning with Kline. Both he and Weiss are connected by the Brookings House; they both want it. And Kline got a call to warn him off buying the house. You've got coincidences stacked on top of coincidences ..."

She broke off because it was apparent Mayo had stopped listening. He was staring off into space with an unfocused stare.

"Mayo! Goddammit! I'm –"

"How are you doing on the Stephanie Green case?"

"Green? What's that got to do with –" she started, but stopped abruptly. "The house. She was the owner of the Brookings House."

"And," Mayo asked gently, "what do Green's murder and Kline's attempted murder have in common?"

She thought for a few seconds. "OK. Both were early morning. A homicidal attack meant to seem non-homicidal, an accident for Green and suicide for Kline ... a male assailant ... wearing a three piece suit."

Mayo stood up and pulled on his coat. He pointed at Morrison. "Get somebody really good in Forensics to see if they can find any links between Campos and the Green murder ... fingerprints, fibers, the usual stuff. See where Campos was when she supposedly fell down those stairs.   Maybe even DNA, who knows these days?"

"And where are you going?"

"There was a fatal bike accident not very long ago, except it may not have been an accident.   A civil servant named Alban.   Early morning and a witness saw what he thought was a man in a suit leaving the scene.   Driving a pickup with a city logo."

"That's flimsy as hell, Mayo."

"Yeah, maybe.   But how many people do you know that wear three-piece suits any more?   Especially if they drive a pickup.'

He's right.   I don't know anybody.   Even the bankers have gone tieless.

"And the other thing, Morrison?   Alban's main work project at the time of his death was to figure out what to do with the Brookings House."

Mayo sat back down at his desk, looking at the wall and thinking about his first days in the Homicide Division. *That goddamned house!   It was 1995 and I was working sixteen-hour days on the Mission murders.   But there were other things going on ... the Donald Brookings thing, a home invasion gig.   We know who did it but couldn't get the DA to go with it.   And after that, the new owners of the house disappeared.   Nothing we could find.   Wrote 'em off as a couple of counterculture eccentrics.   John and Moira ... Malloy, I think.*

Morrison was almost out the door when he stopped her. "And since you've got so little to do, pull some files for me.   A murder case – Donald Brookings, from 1995.   You know the address.   And a mysterious disappearance investigation that same year, a couple named Malloy.   You know –"

Morrison said, "I know the address.   Christ!   This is beginning to resemble a horror movie ... the case of the evil house!"

White Collar Crime

Martin spent the rest of the morning at Mayo's office answering questions and filling out statements. Bartholomew called him on his cell just as he was leaving the station.

"Warren Wah is here again. Says he wants to talk to you about James Lee."

I should have Bartholomew ask him if he was out walking on the Golden Gate Bridge this morning. Instead, he merely said, "OK, I'll stop by. Ask him to wait for me."

By now, the fog had receded to about a mile offshore and the city streets were in bright sunshine. Martin decided to walk and, while he was at it, try to make some sense out of what had happened. Starting with Warren Wah wanting to talk about James Lee.

It was six months ago. Martin was at the Mission Avenue storefront when James Lee came in and walked back to the alcove where Martin was sitting and talking with Bartholomew. He stopped short of them and stood waiting. Martin had come to learn that Lee was big on deference. That was part – but only part -- of the reason that the other clients, mostly jail-hardened and mistrustful cons, not only accepted him, but welcomed him into their cliques.

Martin gestured to him. "James, come and join us. You can help us decide on what color we should paint this place."

Bartholomew stood up and waved at James to take his place. "Man wants pastel colored walls. Says he read a book where it's proven to be a 'cool' color, good for making people feel calm. Me? I like dark. Can't have a pool table in a place painted *pastel*. You went to college. Know how to talk to white folk. See if you can make the man see some sense."

James moved to the sofa. "I agree with you, Bartholomew. I spent three years in small rectangular rooms, every one of them painted pastel. I think the Federal penal system people read the same book as your boss. I'd gladly go with something more gothic."

Bartholomew walked past Lee, headed for the front desk, and the two of them executed a very amateurish 'high five' as they passed one another.

James sat down and immediately began fidgeting with the sharp crease in his khaki trousers. For the first time in the few weeks he'd been around, Martin saw him to be nervous.

"You know about me?" Lee kept looking down, making the question seem less important than it was.

Such a dangerous question in this place. Everybody's got a story about everybody else and they often don't overlap a whole lot. But most of these guys will go a long way to establish their version. Call it street cred, or rep. But it's important to them. James is different. Doesn't seem to care very much.

"Hard not to. You're one of our more exotic clients. You've got a Ph.D. in some kind of hyphenated science. Bio something or other. Started an investment company with that as a specialty. Got in trouble with the SEC. Went to Club Fed for three years."

Safe enough, I think.

James smiled. "Very correct, and tactful to boot. They showed graphs to the jury, showing how I was always buying shares just before the prices went up. Selling ahead of the sharp declines. Said it happened too regularly to be legitimate. Had to be insider information. Found themselves an 'informant' that traded me for immunity. "

"Was it? Insider trading?" Martin asked, trying to sound like the answer wouldn't matter very much.

A clear breach of protocol to ask that. But he was remembering how startled he was when Natalie asked him, "Did you kill the man?"

An even sadder smile, and then James asked, "Do you know anything about DNA and nucleic acids?"

"No."

"Neither do jurors, or 99% of investors. I do."

James stopped fidgeting with the crease in his trousers and looked directly at Martin. "You know that I'm dying?"

The man doesn't waste time. Gets right to the core of things.

"I heard pancreatic cancer." *Another reason the hard guys cut him some slack.*

"Another couple of months. With painkillers all the way."

A hard conversation. But he's leading up to something.

"James, if there's anything I can do …"

"Actually, there is. I'd like you to lend me half a million dollars."

Well, there's one from out of the blue. Funny how sensible it sounds when one has a few hundred million to spare.

"Lend?"

"I need it for maybe thirty days. It's at risk, but not so much. Basically, it involves a Stage III drug trial in a very obscure little company that's about to go public."

"Don't the terms of your parole prohibit you from engaging in investment activities?"

James smiled. "If I get caught – which I won't – how will they punish me?"

"OK."

That stopped the smile. "You mean you'll do it? Lend me half-a-million."

"Yep."

"Without knowing why I need the money?"

"Yep. I presume it's a good cause."

"My wife had a stroke three months ago. A bad one. And there's likely to be some ongoing impairment. She's going to need long term care, in a good place. I need to set it up. So that when I'm not around …"

"I'd call that a good cause."

A silence settled between the two of them as if to seal the agreements reached, both the explicit and the unspoken ones.

Martin cleared his throat. "Cash?"

"That would be best."

"It will take a few days. Thursday OK?"

I saw him two more times after that. To give him the money and when he came to pay it back.

Warren Wah was waiting for Martin, sitting on the same couch and with the same expression as his last visit.

Before Martin could speak, Wah asked, "Have you heard of a woman named Mei Ling?"

"Don't think so."

"That's her Chinese name. For most people, she was Mrs. James Lee."

So that's where this is going.

Martin's expression did not change, and his voice was carefully neutral. "I knew he was married, but never knew her name. I liked James. We had some time together in here. People felt comfortable with him. I was sorry when he died."

Wah nodded in a way that acknowledged the tribute and retreated into himself, perhaps to intentionally create a moment of silence to honor Lee.

"She's my aunt. Mei Ling. More than that, actually. I grew up in her home. Before she married Lee."

"I hope she's well."

"Mixed news on that front. Physically, she's severely disabled. Needs twenty-four hour care. But the mind? That's as sharp as ever. Plays a mean game of mahjong. Does the crossword every day. The nurse reads the clues to her and she dictates the answers."

"I'm glad for that. Hope I do as well when it's my turn."

Wah nodded absentmindedly. "She's in a good place, close to her kids and friends. One of those upscale CCR's – 'continuing care residences.' A million dollars paid in advance and cash set aside for the monthly dues."

Martin said nothing, thinking about James Lee and their strange conversation.

Wah looked off into the corner of the room. "Funny thing is, James was broke when he came out of Lompoc. But you probably know that."

"I got to know him a little bit. He was a smart guy, with friends that trusted him, I think."

"I heard that one of those friends fronted him half a million bucks without asking any questions."

Martin said, "That's a lot of money. Must have been a really good friend."

Wah nodded. "I saw him two days before he died. I was a day out of Pelican Bay and he was my first stop. The cancer was pretty bad and he was swallowing painkillers like M&M's. He was floating in and out of consciousness, didn't make a lot of sense sometimes. 'I ran out of time,' he said. Talked a lot about 'being a hundred thousand short'. Said the man didn't care, told him to make sure Mei Ling had what she needed."

Lee was waiting for me, sitting there at that same table with a Nordstrom's shopping bag with bundles of hundred-dollar bills, hunched over as if to contain the pain. 'Got most of it,' he said. 'The rest will take a little longer.' I said something about nucleic acids and he smiled and said, 'We made almost three-hundred percent on our investment. But the CCR took more than I planned on.'

Wah stood up and turned to leave. "Friends are good. Everybody needs one at some time or another."

The Brookings History

"So you're a preservationist. Makes me think of a withered disapproving old woman with her hair in a bun and a shrill voice."

Martin figured it was a safe-enough insult, given that Natalie was so obviously *not* remotely like his caricature. The contrast was particularly easy to see because she was standing nude in the middle of his bedroom looking for the various articles of her clothing that they had tossed aside so vigorously thirty minutes earlier.

She looked at him. "And you're a billionaire. Makes me think of an overweight, balding Republican who plays golf with a caddie and worries about whether anybody likes him for any reason except his money."

He leaned back against the headboard of the seriously rumpled bed and held up his hands in mock surrender. He started to say, "It's only –"

"I know, I know. It's only seven-hundred million. The fact is that you don't even know how much money you've got."

"I make it a point not to know. It helps to make me feel less guilty."

She wasn't paying any attention, focused on getting her blouse turned right side out. He enjoyed watching her as she moved around the room gathering up the other pieces of clothing, absolutely unselfconscious, perhaps even legitimately unaware of the intense pleasure he derived from simply watching her.

When she sat down on the bed to put on her socks, he stroked the curve of her back as she leaned forward. "I'm serious. What does a preservationist do?"

She looked at her watch, then scrambled on to the foot of the bed, sitting with her feet under her, looking like a college coed at a slumber party.

"It's more about 'why' than 'what'."

"OK. Why?"

She took a deep breath. "Do you remember your parents?"

Hell of a question to ask an orphan!

She went on before he recovered enough to answer the question. "Not just remember them, but understand them. Who they were? What they wanted? What they were really *like.*"

The words came at him like thrown rocks, threatening parts of his existence that he'd thought were shielded, if not forgotten. *She's an orphan too. But she's let herself think about it. Maybe even deal with it.*

Natalie saw the confusion, and understood it.

"Martin, if we don't understand and confront where we come from, especially as an individual but also as a community, with all the warts and ugliness and horrors … It's like trying to describe Germany without talking about Hitler, Mozart without knowing about his father, seeing the coliseum but not visualizing the gladiators –"

She stopped, seeing his slow grin.

"Sorry," she said. "I tend to get carried away."

"You make it quite vivid. So that's what a preservationist does? Confront us with our past?"

Natalie saw the deflection, the uncertainty that she had created. *He's not quite ready to talk about orphans yet, I think. But we'll get there.*

She said, "It's pretty mundane, actually."

"Preservation … Is that why you want the city to keep the Brookings house?"

"The house is important. When it was built in 1906, the houses on Russian Hill were modest, generally wooden and much smaller structures dating back to Gold Rush days. The widow Brookings purchased three of them, demolished what was left of them after the Great Earthquake, and built her new house on their remains."

"It's an ugly house. Not an attribute that should be preserved?"

She shrugged. "It's about much more than architecture. Most of my time is spent on digging out the old stories. We need to reconstruct Hiram Brookings, not his house."

"Is he worth it?"

"Not for me to judge. But he's certainly interesting. He came here in the initial wave of Gold Rush hopefuls, in 1849 or 1850, at the peak of the craziness. He was like thousands of others, envisioning instant riches. Unlike those others, he did in fact strike it rich, but not by finding gold. After almost starving to death in the Gold Country, he stumbled into the venture that would make him one of the first millionaires in California. He began with a leaky boat that he found abandoned in Yerba Buena Cove and started a shipping line that transported both cargo and passengers among the several ports along California's coast. By the end of the nineteenth century, he was firmly established, if not admired. He died at age seventy-six with more money – adjusted for inflation – than you have. Along with Stanford and Huntington, he built a good part of the transportation infrastructure for California."

Martin couldn't help it. He said, "And yet he built an ugly house, notable only for its age and size. A house that you won't let me buy and fix up properly."

"That's like saying the Taj Mahal is 'only a tomb' so let's convert it into a tourist hotel." She smiled sweetly at him. "And his widow built the house, not him."

I don't think I want to get into a public debate with this woman! "So what else do we know about the man?"

"His early life and his business career are pretty well documented and not all that interesting. But there are two major mysteries.

"First, there's the three month gap between him leaving the gold fields in 1857 and starting his shipping company. We know he was destitute, sunk so low as to be living with Chinese miners, when he gave up on prospecting. Three months later, he's running two expensive boats back and forth along the California coast. All we know about Hiram during that time was that he built a very modest house near the waterfront of Monterey. He did most of the work himself. Hired laborers for the heavy work. He and his son ran their steamer operations out of the house."

"So maybe he had a silent partner?"

"Not that any of the amateur historians have found. Like his successful peers in those rough days, his methods of dealing with competition were as brutal as they were effective. But the popular theory – which I subscribe to – is that there's a major criminal act somewhere in there, something more dramatic and one-time than the kind of predatory competition that Stanford and his colleagues used to amass their wealth."

"San Francisco had a lot of rascals who made – and lost – a lot of money in that era, didn't it?"

"Sure, and they were very prominent in the news of the time. And Hiram Brookings was one of them. Not of the same scale as Leland Stanford, Huntington or Crocker, but nevertheless one of those builders of modern California whose amorality was approximately matched by his success."

"And the second mystery?"

She hesitated only slightly. "People say there's a curse."

When Martin rolled his eyes, she went on quickly. "I know. You're wondering when I'm going to pull out the buried treasure rumors. But there's enough to it to keep the conspiracy nuts fully employed.

"Hiram married at age thirty and had a son. Despite his growing wealth, he stayed in Monterey and kept mostly to himself. His wife died in 1904 and he remarried a widow, a much younger woman with three female children. He moved from Monterey to San Francisco in early 1906 because of her insistence. She's the one who built what we now call 'the Brookings House.'

"Our so-called curse? It begins with the first version of the house being destroyed in the earthquake while it was still under construction. And Hiram was killed during the quake. Probably the single most prominent fatality in the city. The fire engulfed the original house and the latticework of new construction as though it was a stack of kerosene-soaked kindling waiting for the torch. They found Hiram's badly burned body beneath a pile of collapsed timbers.

"His widow mourned briefly and then set out to rebuild her house. Her first step was to demolish what was left of the original work and have all of the debris carted away.

Along with most of what had been the pre-earthquake San Francisco, tons of fire-blackened debris were carted down the hill and dumped into Yerba Buena harbor, helping to create the landfill that would enable what is now the Marina District.

"She commissioned a new house on top of the wreckage and she, along with her three daughters and her stepson Douglas, moved in nine months after the earthquake. Douglas Brookings soon complained that the damn house was too vertical, with too many stairs between the bedroom, parlor and dining room – the only parts of the house that he inhabited. He immediately contracted for the construction of what would have been one of the first residential elevators in the United States. But the digging for the elevator shaft had barely begun when all three of his new siblings were stricken by influenza and died within a two-week period. ... more fuel for the believers in a curse.

"The deaths of her children and the loss of her collection of dolls and ceramics in the earthquake seemed to derange the new Mrs. Brookings and she slipped into a state of melancholy that she never fully recovered from. It is said that the widow and Douglas considered building a new home down the hill, near the wharfs where their ships docked; but she decided against it, having just completed 'a place suitable for a woman of means.' And, the Brookings family – three generations of them -- occupied the house until 1995.

"But the real evidence for the curse is that every one of the direct male descendants of Hiram Brookings has died an unnatural death. That's his son, grandson, and great grandson. One of them while boating on the Bay, one by suicide, and the last one shot 'by assailants unknown.' The last one was in 1995."

Martin thought about it. "Good stuff for the conspiracy theorists, I suppose? The odds of that within a single family must be pretty low."

She smiled in a way that signaled the conversation was proceeding exactly as she intended. "I'm sure they are. Especially if each of the three died within a day of his sixtieth birthday."

He smiled. "Even I can calculate the odds of that happening by chance. It's precisely zero."

She waited for the next and obvious question.

"Are there any more of them – male Brookings – who are nearing a sixtieth birthday?"

"No. In fact, the Brookings line is about to end entirely. Not so surprising given that they kept producing only sons. The last surviving family member is Donald's widow, and she doesn't have long left."

Sergei Reports Back

Sergei called the next morning. It was as if he and Natalie were conspiring to educate him about the Brookings House. As usual, Sergei skipped all of the normal social preludes to a conversation.

"You were right, by the way."

Martin felt and looked puzzled, not uncommon in his conversations with Sergei.

"About the press. You said, and I quote, 'Ignore them. They have the attention span of a brain-damaged gnat.' This was back when they wanted to interview us about being ex-felon billionaires."

"I'm glad my advice worked," Martin said. "But that's not why you're calling, is it?"

"No, it isn't. Remember those questions you asked me to look into?"

The Russian Hill house, and the Brookings. "Yes. Anything turn up?"

"Got a pen and some paper handy?"

"Yep. Go."

"The easy part first. Your Russian Hill building. Most of it is in the public domain and I'm sending you the web links in your email. No reason for me to tell you things that you can read about. I must say that I'm impressed with how much emotion is involved with a *building*, for god's sake! Must be a goy thing."

And he's from Israel, where people have been killing each other over disputed real estate for two thousand years! I don't think I'll bring up that topic.

Sergei was still talking. "... not public are the documents around the construction – in 1906 – and the one-time sale of the property, in 1995 after the death of the last Brookings family member, and an 'almost' sale just last year before the owner died and left it to the city. I'll come back to that in a minute. There are also some documents in the City Planning and Department of Real Estate, but it's all mostly boilerplate, with one notable exception."

Martin made quick notes. "OK. We'll cycle back to this. What about Hiram Brookings and his descendants?"

"People are more interesting than buildings. And Hiram is more interesting than most people, even though he was a raging bigot and almost certainly more of a criminal than most of his capitalist cronies."

Martin picked up very faint undertones of outrage. *So Sergei does react to bigotry, even in historical form.*

"So, what is it that makes him particularly interesting?"

"Again, a lot of it is publicly available info, although not a lot of it is digitized. I've put together a file of documents that you can read through. You'll find it in your email inbox."

"Tell me the un-public part. For example, did you learn anything about the three months between him leaving the gold fields and starting his steamer business?"

"No. Just some imaginative and completely unfounded speculations. But there are some other things."

"How about the so-called 'Brookings Curse?'"

"My Russian peasant grandmother would have loved it! And I can see how your over-the-top conspiracy nuts would go for it. Three generations of Brookings dying within a day of their sixtieth birthday! I played around with trying to compute the likelihood of such a series of events, but there's not enough good actuarial data to get beyond two or three digits after the decimal point."

"Uh, Sergei, just calling it 'unlikely' is good enough for me. Any curious tidbits?"

"More than a few. Hiram was one of 498 unlucky San Franciscans killed in the 1906 earthquake. A wild underestimate, by the way. They omitted what were probably several hundred deaths in Chinatown. The only oddity about Hiram was that he was killed in the post-earthquake fire, not by the quake itself. According to witnesses, he refused to leave his partially completed house until it was too late."

"Sergei, how do you find this stuff? The last survivor of the 1906 earthquake must have died ten years ago."

"Actually, he died six months ago. But that particular fact comes from a University of California Ph.D.

thesis, written in 1953 and entitled 'Post-Catastrophe Mortality Causation: A Case Study of the Great San Francisco Earthquake.' Happily, it's been digitized as part of the Google project."

Well, you asked, didn't you? "What about the Brookings descendants?"

"That's where it gets a little spooky. Hiram had an only son. Douglas, age 30 at the time of the earthquake. He died in 1936. He and a fishing guide went out in a small boat, somewhere outside the Golden Gate. The weather was unsettled at the time. The capsized boat and his decomposing body were washed up three days later. Apparently a straightforward drowning."

"What about the guide?"

"His body was never found. Not unusual for those waters.

"He – Douglas – also had an only son, named Orville. He committed suicide in 1976. Found hanging in a closet of a lower-class whorehouse. He was a heroin addict, pretty heavy user. Ran up lots of debts and led a hard life. The police ran a perfunctory investigation but everything pointed to a sad and self-inflicted end to a sad life.

"Orville was also survived by an only son, Donald. He was childless and unmarried, so the last of the Hiram Brookings line. He was murdered in 1995, a fairly savage home-invasion style killing. There was a fairly extensive police investigation because Donald was suspected of chiseling on some city construction contracts – faked inspection reports, shoddy materials ... that sort of corner-cutting. The cops thought that the murder was connected with that, but couldn't prove it. They busted a guy they described as a killer-for-hire, but they couldn't make it stick. They put him away for an unrelated armed-robbery charge."

Martin looked at his notes. "Sergei, when we started, you said there were a couple of unusual things about the house itself."

"For one thing, the house and the land it sits on has been in the Brookings family for a long time, from 1905 when Hiram showed up in San Francisco until 1995, when it was sold after Donald's murder. From 1906 on, you've got an eighteen-thousand square foot house being occupied by successive families of two or three members – parents and their only son."

"OK. What else?"

"You'll have to trust me on this. I don't have any great 'smoking gun' kind of document I can pull out of a hat. It's more of an impression based on scanning dozens of ordinary looking documents ... and not finding other documents one would expect to find. And ..."

He's actually nervous. Something I've never seen before in Sergei.

"Sergei ... and...?"

When Sergei started speaking again, Martin revised his opinion. *It's not nervousness; it's embarrassment.*

"Martin, I can tell you – but no one else. If this gets out – how you found out this information – I can be back in Folsom, or worse. You can't use me or this information as your source for whatever you've got in mind."

"No problem, Sergei. I promise."

"OK. Your Department of City Owned Real Estate is as crooked as it could be. The operation is being run to generate cash for the department manager. It's very well done and can probably survive the occasional internal audit for the next year, maybe two. The abnormalities can easily be passed on as the usual inefficiencies that you find in a municipal bureaucracy. But it's a top-to-bottom criminal enterprise."

Martin filed that one away for later consideration. "Sergei, at this point, you probably know more about the property and the Brookings clan than any other living person. Tell me what stands out for you."

"Other than four generations of only sons, which doesn't sound much like a conspiracy ... OK, I'd list six factors.

"First, the fixation about keeping the house, starting with Hiram's willingness to die rather than flee the burning house and continuing through three more generations who don't seem to have any obvious reason not to sell. Second, the coincidence of the next generations of direct male descendants dying within a day of their sixtieth birthdays. Third, and related to the previous point, the questionable nature of those deaths. The fishing 'accident' and the 'suicide' could easily have been cleverly disguised homicides. My fourth and fifth factors, you already know -- about the mystery involving how Hiram got started but almost certainly involves some significant criminal act. And the corrupt city department."

When Sergei stopped, Martin knew that the final factor was the most important one, something that none of them had seen, except for Sergei.

"You said there were six factors. You've only listed five."

"Do you know that Einstein said that coincidence is God's way of staying anonymous?"

"No, I didn't know that. Was God involved with the Brookings?"

"Most definitely not, but someone was, and they wanted to stay anonymous."

"Who, Sergei? Just tell me who."

"The Chinese."

The Chinese Connection

The Chinese.

Even the way Sergei pronounced the two words gave them added significance.   But, for Martin, they were so out-of-context that he sat back and looked at Sergei, startled by the way this man who spoke only facts and data had been captured by the unfolding story of the Brookings clan.

Even though he was unseen, on the other end of the phone call, it was clear that Sergei was caught up in the story.

"Go back to the beginning.   Hiram Brookings was forced to live in the Chinese mining camp during his last year of mining.   It was the lowest form of existence there could be for a white man in those times.   He probably worked *for them* as the price of their toleration for a round-eyed white man in their midst.   Their contempt would be obvious, even if veiled.   For a man from his background and upbringing, it would be excruciating.

""We know that he hated and feared the Chinese for the next fifty years; that he did his best to minimize contact with them.   He wouldn't transport them on his boats, wouldn't haul their goods, didn't employ them in his business or household or even use the Chinese laundries that popped up all over the city.   Even when he excavated tons of dirt to build his Russian Hill house, he paid a premium for non-Chinese labor, refusing to use the 'coolies' that built so much of San Francisco during that time.   And he vigorously supported every anti-Chinese piece of local or state legislation – and there were some dandies – that came up."

"Any idea why he was so phobic?"

"None that I could find.   It was odd to some of those who knew him because he had lived with Chinese during his last year in the gold country.   That was pretty rare for those days."

Martin broke in. "But there's no evidence that his son, or even the later generations, shared that view. Yes, they were probably   anti-Chinese   --   anti-any-kind-of-immigrant –

everybody was at that time, but they interacted with them… employed them."

"You're more right than you know. For example, the fishing guide that was with Douglas on his fatal fishing trip beyond the Golden Gate… the body that never turned up … he was Chinese."

Martin stared at the screen of his phone.

"And remember Orville, the grandson of Hiram who allegedly hanged himself in a whorehouse, one that he supposedly visited frequently? It was a Chinese whorehouse, in Chinatown. There was a *very* brief investigation. I've seen transcripts of the interviews. It's pretty clear that he'd never been in the establishment until that day. And he was terrified of the Chinese, man or woman."

"And Donald, the great grandson, was murdered by –
"

Sergei interrupted, "By a person or persons unknown, according to the police report. But the homicide officer in charge of the case – whom you know – will say, off-the-record, that he knows who killed Donald."

"I know …?"

"Mayo Marsh, your friend, was the lead investigator."

"I'll talk to Mayo. But, just to save time, what will he tell me?"

"He'll tell you that they arrested a half-Chinese man, one who was known to do wet work for the Chinese mob that ran most of Chinatown's nastier operations – drugs, prostitution, extortion and so forth. He'll tell you that he could have made it stick, but the state police took over, pushed him out, and tried to get the killer to rat out those above him. In the end, he wouldn't do it but they totally contaminated Mayo's case. The suspect still got a major sentence because he made the state cops mad, but the Donald murder remains an open case."

Martin was beginning to feel exhausted by the piling up of coincidence, by Sergei's recitation of disconnected 'facts' that were demanding a narrative, a re-sorting into a coherent story where everything would fall neatly into place.

"Anything else?"

"Yes, and it falls into that 'you can't tell anyone where you got this' category that we talked about."

Martin thought back to the beginning of their conversation. "You mean the bit about the city real estate group being crooked?"

"Yes, that bit. It was pretty easy to hack into the City and County of San Francisco telephone directory. Guess what you see if you look at the list of employee names for the Department of City Owned Real Estate?"

I think I can answer this one correctly. "A lot of Chinese surnames?"

"Eighteen of the twenty employees. The two Anglo or Hispanic names are both part-time drivers, on the low end of the pay scale."

Martin had filled a page-and-a-half with notes, overlaid by arrows that looped from one part of the paper to another and punctuated with circles and exclamation marks. The magnitude of what he was looking at was just beginning to seep into his consciousness.

"Sergei, you've done a great job. Just three more questions. First, are you sure that you haven't left any tracks? Any electronic footprints that can be traced back to you?"

I started out worried about getting you busted for violating the terms of your parole and I wind up thinking I've made you a target for a very real Chinese curse!

"Don't worry about that one. It would take a computer genius to even know that I've been rummaging around in their systems and – even if they had such a genius, which they don't – they would wind up thinking they were hacked by a Southern Baptist missionary doing evangelical work in Bangladesh. Trust me: this was child's play."

"Great. Question two: Were you able to find anything out about the Petrel Foundation?"

"Nothing. In fact, there is so little information that that's suspicious all by itself. Founded and run by a woman named Emily Connors. Came here a short time ago from Singapore. She has no history that I can find and her Foundation apparently does nothing."

He sounds disappointed.

"Isn't that unusual? A blank slate like that?"

"It's so rare that I'm sure that both she and her foundation are fictitious creations. But they have been put together by somebody very smart who really – *really* – wants to stay invisible."

"Singapore. That's mostly Chinese, isn't it?"

"You're stretching now, Martin. There are approximately one-and-a-half billion Chinese in the world, so if you're looking for coincidence, you're likely to find it wherever you look. What's your third question?"

"The hit-man for the Chinese mob, the one that Mayo liked for the killing of Donald Brookings ... What was his name?"

He heard the clicking of keys, three or four seconds of rapid taps. Then Sergei was back.

"His name was Warren Wah. He just finished six years at Pelican Bay. And may or may not be an illegitimate member of a fairly extended and prominent Chinese family."

"Prominent how?"

There was a burst of more key clicking before Sergei responded. "Two particular features. The negative one is that the family is reputed to be heavily involved in Chinatown gangs. The old Tong system."

"And the other? The positive piece of their prominence?"

"They can trace their lineage back several hundred years, to royal origins."

Martin thought, *I know the answer, but I'll ask anyway.*

"Who heads the family?"

Sergei was scornful. "The eldest male member, of course. His name is Chao Zhu."

Manfred Gruber

It was inevitable that Mannie would overreach and make choices that would get him killed. He was out of his league, but didn't know it and would not have accepted that reality even if fully informed as to his inadequacies. In that respect, he was like a spoiled child who was about to get a new set of parents.

There were signs that should have tipped him off that his status was changing, that the past was no longer predictive of the future. He should have paid more attention to the original call from Emily, particularly the part about 'representing the interests of Chao Zhu.' He'd never heard the name until quite recently, and was contemptuous of anything Chinese, but he should have known that any of the clients for a contractor such as Emily would be substantial figures, potentially dangerous parties and certainly worth some due diligence on his part. It would have been easy for him to discover that Donna Yang was not only the successor to Edward Alban, but was also Zhu's prized granddaughter.

And he completely missed the significance of Warren Wah. He viewed Wah's visit to him as a form of tribute, a public display of respect from a vassal to the ruling warlord. He failed to see it as the scouting mission that it was. If he had paid more attention, then the mysterious death of Paul Campos would have -- at the very least -- seemed a troubling coincidence, the kind of unexplained event that should have raised red flags for somebody whose success – no, survival – depended on a hyper-awareness of such oddities.

In his defense, he was distracted by the Green Fence project. It was requiring most of his time and attention as the details were being negotiated. In his mind, it was looming larger and larger; the kind of deal that could make him not only respectable, but one of the real power brokers in San Francisco. The 'King of Garbage' could transform himself into the visionary who brought technology and environmentalism together. And he would make ungodly amounts of money!

So when Donna Yang called him, the combination of his racism, arrogance and focus on other matters made errors in judgment inevitable.

"This is Donna Yang."

"So?"

Even with that single spoken word, his contempt was so obvious that Yang almost ended the call on the spot, a reaction that – with hindsight -- would have been beneficial for both.

"I now am the Department Head for City Owned Real Estate … after the unfortunate death of Mr. Edward Alban."

"Congratulations. So?"

"I wish to renegotiate the terms of my department's contract with your management company."

"It's not renegotiable."

A very slight pleading note edged into her voice. "Your terms are quite unfavorable for us. We could meet … A few percentage points –"

"I said: It's not negotiable."

His raised voice stopped her.   Before she could respond, he added, "Mr. Alban also tried to renegotiate the contract. Just before he died." And he pushed the 'End Call' icon.

He sat for a moment, staring at the phone and thinking. Unfortunately for him, habit took the place of prudence and he picked up his phone and made the final mistake.

"Lennie, this is Gruber. I need you to pay a call …"

Two hours later, as Donna Yang was unlocking her car door in the car park under the freeway overpass, a pair of nondescript but large men approached her. Without saying anything, they pulled a cloth bag over her head, wrapped duct tape around her several times, pinning her arms to her sides, and tossed her in the trunk of the car that was next to hers. After a twenty-minute drive, the car stopped, she was yanked from the trunk and, for what seemed an endless time to her, beaten severely. In actuality, the calculated beating was fairly mild by Lennie's usual standards – what he thought of as his 'soft tissue special' -- and only lasted seven or eight minutes.

It left her badly bruised and terrified. They returned to her car, cut her free from the tape, and left her sprawled next to her car, still with the bag over her head.

Her first act after her release from the ER was to place a call to her grandfather.

Reflections

Chao Zhu watched the green hills and brown fields of southern China unroll forty-thousand feet below him. As always, the experience of modern flight amazed him.

No matter how often I fly, I am like a peasant standing in awe in the mud of his rice paddy, seeing for the first time a Boeing 747 – what seems to him to be a gigantic metallic bird -- hanging in the sky on its final approach.

Times have changed. Ah Yang crossed those fields below me on foot, to sit in the smelly hold of a sailing ship for weeks before arriving in San Francisco. Now I make the trip in twelve hours, traveling in a luxurious private room at six-hundred miles an hour. An eighty-million dollar palanquin – jiao – borne on the shoulders of giant engines rather than the dozen porters that would have conveyed the emperor.

And when he got there, Ah Yang dug his hard-won wealth out of the ground, using picks, shovels and his own hands. Then the stuff had to be transported, refined and weighed. It was a world of tangible things. Now we have electronic transfers, deeds, loan documents, shares of stock. But wealth still must be in motion. Left immobile, it can be appropriated, stolen or – these days -- taxed. It becomes lazy and the owners become complacent. So I must go to San Francisco to buy a house for thirty million dollars, so that the wealth is in a safer form. I must arrange for the building of a recycling plant so that wealth in the form of trash is acquired by my patrons rather than buried in landfills.

And all this fixation on acquiring and preserving wealth leads to so many complications! Accountants and lawyers with their contracts. Bankers and politicians and consultants with their Powerpoint presentations. Capitalist job creators.

And people like Emily Connors.
What shall I do with her?

The object of Chao Zhu's concern was also thinking about the past, but focused on the last few weeks rather than past centuries.

I should not have returned to San Francisco.

Regret was a new emotion for Emily, one that unsettled her and made her uncertain not only about her past decisions, but also about what to do next. She had first sensed its presence at her first meeting with Chao Zhu and it had grown with each day in the city.

The most obvious reason was her growing certainty that the secrets of the Brookings House were going to be discovered.

Amazing. Twenty years and nothing had changed. Ali had photographed the interior of the laundry room in the Brookings House. To Emily's eye, it looked exactly as Gary had remembered it. The wall on the uphill side of the room still had the sink and the same ugly white cabinets for the entire length of the wall.

But that can't last. The earthquake retrofit requirement is triggered. Once they get into the foundation, Gary's handiwork will be front page news. And yet she stayed. Then there was the reality that she had not performed on her commitments to Chao Zhu. The chances that the Petrel Foundation would be selected to buy the Brookings House were close to zero despite her efforts, including eliminating both Green and Alban. And Chao's desire for Emily to mentor Donna Yang, his granddaughter, was a miserable failure due to Yang's obstinacy and fears. Emily's involvement and advice actually led to her being beaten up by Emily's primary agent.

Daniel told me. Don't trust anybody who values family and honor more than money. Chao might put up with some business setbacks, but I don't think he'll ignore attacks on his honor.

Her personal doubts were always the strongest during those times when she was watching Natalie. At the moment, she and Ali were parked half-a-block away from the Victorian where Natalie lived. It had become part of their routine to observe her for a couple of hours several days a week. Emily stayed at a distance, but Ali was particularly good at shadowing Natalie and provided detailed descriptions of what she was doing, and with whom.

Why are you doing this?

But she knew the answer.

You can't decide which ending you want. Tell her about Gary and blow up her entire history. Make her confront her own part in what happened and deal with it, or not. Or walk away, back to where there were no regrets and leave her in her own little world, content and smug. 'Preserving' things that were best forgotten. So you spy on her, as though there will be some mystical 'sign' to tell you what to do. Some way to sort out whether what you're feeling is anger, or regret, or revenge, or something else.

It's time to go.

She was ready. She had booked flights on three different airlines to three different Asian countries, scheduled on each of the next three days. Whichever destination she elected would be the jumping-off point to a final sanctuary, still undecided but one where she would be invisible, as off-the-grid as Gary ever was.

Only one thing left to do.

An inviolable part of Emily's creed and a major reason for her anonymity was her practice of eliminating her confederates. Not the clients. They were powerful individuals, protected and capable of a swift and sure retaliation. But those that she employed and knew of her 'projects' were expendable. And Mannie was high on her list.

She smiled as she thought about all of the imbedded ironies.

Mannie's been working for me to get the Brookings property lined up. Katherine Green first, and he made the approach to Alban and – when that didn't work – he got his personal hit man to arrange an accidental death. Very nicely done, too. The Kline job didn't go well, least of all for Mannie's guy. Still don't know what happened there, but that's another reason to make Mannie a loose end to be tied up. Future clients will see it as more evidence that they need to honor their commitments to me. The only drawback is that I'll have to do it myself. Can't hardly ask Mannie to arrange his own assassination, can I?

As for getting approval from Donna Yang, well, that's not going to happen. She'll like the outcome and that's what matters. Chao Zhu told me, 'Do what you have to do.'

It wasn't until she dialed Mannie's number that she realized that she was looking forward to the job.

A Recap

Martin was sitting in his car waiting for Natalie to finish up a presentation she was making to some sort of civic group at the Cliff House. On the way to the meeting, she described them as "a bunch of rich people with more money than morals ... but they like the concept of preservation."

Martin laughed, "As long as it's their way of life you're preserving."

He could see her actually wince, as though his words had a physical sting to them.

"Sorry, that was a cheap shot."

"No," she said. "You're right. And it bothers me."

The exchange depressed both of them and they were silent for the rest of the brief trip. He dropped her at the main door and found a parking place about halfway down the hill where he could watch the strollers and surfers on Ocean Beach. But his mind was elsewhere.

She's asking people she doesn't much like to give her money. That has to be tough. And she doesn't ask me, who she knows has several hundred million that he doesn't much care about. What does that say about her view of where this is going? Good news or bad?

His cell rang before he could work out an answer.

"This is Mayo. Can I buy you a cup of coffee?"

"Sure. Officially or unofficially?"

"Some of each. But I can leave the handcuffs in the car if that will make you more comfortable."

"Can Natalie come along? She's with me now. And she's got a stake in this too."

"Sure. She's a lot better looking than you are."

"That's sexist, Mayo. Not professional at all."

"Hey! I'm retiring. I can revert to my inner self and there's nothing you or anybody else can do about it."

Thirty minutes later, they met Mayo at one of the hip new coffee shops on Mission Street, a two-story glass box with an interior that looked like a set from a sci-fi movie. They found a table on the mezzanine and Natalie immediately began bombarding Mayo with questions.

"Any luck with the dress?"

"Absolute dead end. Has been for twenty years. Last seen being worn by a killer of a young boy in an alley off of Mission Street. Time before that, by an eight-year-old girl – that we all know and love – pretending to be a grown-up."

She ignored the dig. "What about the CPA that tried to kill Martin?"

"The CPA – Paul Campos – is turning out to be an interesting story. He had a very nice practice. Tax work, bookkeeping for small companies. Some simple auditing assignments. Turns out that several of his more profitable clients are at least semi-shady. Maybe fronts for stuff that might not be all that legal. We've got something called a 'forensic accountant' looking at it."

Mayo looked at Martin closely, clearly thinking about what to say.

"But that's not what worries me about Campos."

Natalie was ahead of Martin on this one. She spoke directly to Mayo. "You think he was working for someone else, don't you?"

"Yeah, I do. I can't see any connection between him and Martin. And he does – did -- seem to have some connections to some nasty people."

Martin didn't like where this was going. "So I'm on a hit list? What about simple robbery?"

"Doesn't work for me. First, Campos made a very nice living in his day job. No need to open up a chancy sideline by holding up joggers. Second, you'd have to have a negative IQ – which he didn't -- to stage a holdup in the middle of a bridge where the nearest exit is a mile away on foot. Third, he didn't ask you for money; he just told you to jump off the bridge. He was there to get rid of you, not to rob you. And fourth -- if you need more reasons -- you'd already seen him in the Civic Center Garage. This was a continuation of whatever he was doing there."

"But that was about Natalie. I just happened along."

"I know. It makes no sense."

Martin asked the next obvious question. "What about the second guy that came out of the fog?"

"You mean the mystery guest that either tried to kill you or rescue you? Not much there. The bridge has got cameras all over the place, both for traffic and suicide prevention, but the fog made them pretty useless. Morrison spent most of a day looking at the tapes and thinks she sees our two guys – Campos and mystery man -- going onto the bridge from the south end, walking about fifty feet apart. Consistent with a tail. And she says neither of them came off the bridge on foot. From either end."

"So he hopped into a car?"

"Looks like it. Could have been there within sixty seconds or so if he had a driver waiting in the Fort Point parking lot. That's what I would have done."

Mayo abruptly shifted to a new line of questioning. "Martin, have you had anything to do with a man named Manfred Gruber? Or Gruber Waste Management Services?"

"Not that I know of. But isn't that the company that runs the garbage trucks I see all over the city? Big green logo?"

Mayo didn't answer. "How about Katherine Green?"

"Nope. I know she was the last owner of the Brookings house, but that's all. I never had anything to do with her."

"Edward Alban?"

Where is this headed?

"I had a phone conversation with him to set up a meeting. He was killed the day before my appointment with him. Other than that, he's a complete unknown."

Martin deliberately let his exasperation show itself. "Mayo. You called this meeting. Why don't you just tell me –
"

Mayo was undeterred. He asked, "How about John and Moira Malloy? Ring any bells?"

Natalie had been watching the back and forth between them, feeling like a tennis spectator watching a series of indifferent volleys being returned. When Mayo said 'Malloy,' however, he glanced at her and then focused intently on Martin.

This question is different. Mayo's been setting him up for these particular names.

Martin's reaction confirmed it for Natalie. He looked at Mayo, at first startled but quickly shifting to an accusatory stare. He did not respond, even when Mayo said again, "John and Moira Malloy?" But his sudden and complete stillness gave him away, a clear signal that those two names were not only familiar, but important to him in some highly personal context. He stood up and walked over to the window, keeping his back to the two of them.

Natalie said, "I know those names – Malloy—but I don't know why …"

"It was twenty years ago … 1995," Mayo said to Natalie. "They lived in the Brookings house for less than a year, the first non-Brookings to own the house. They were basically rich hippies. Took in some runaways, kids off the street, that sort of counterculture stuff. They disappeared without any notice, apparently to begin a new life, somewhere far away and off of the so-called grid."

He glanced at Martin, still with his back turned to them. "They took in street kids. Two or three at a time."

Martin gave no sign of having heard, but he asked without turning around, "How did you know them? The Malloys?"

Mayo said, "I didn't, until after the fact." Then he faced Natalie, who was sitting quietly watching the two of them.

"They just fell off the world. One day, they were there and the next day, they weren't. It bothered their friends enough that me and several other cops spent some time checking what we could, trying to make sure that nothing bad had happened to them. It was fishy, but everything checked out. They'd been planning their exit strategy and had everything set up for it. We went with the facts that we had at the time."

Natalie breathed, "Another episode of the Brookings curse …"

"For the conspiracy nuts, that's for sure. For the cops, it turned out to be just a more exotic story of runaways. Consenting adults. No harm, no foul."

"What's this got to do with Martin?"

Mayo didn't answer, just looked again at Martin. He had turned around and was watching them closely.

"I was one of the street kids." He came back and sat down in his original position across the table from them. "Wasn't I, Mayo?"

Mayo went on without acknowledging the question. "We know from the neighbors that there were for sure three kids there, maybe a fourth, when the Malloys took off. One of them was a teenage girl. We're pretty sure that she and one of the boys were probably into heavy drugs, both using and dealing. They pretty well stayed downstairs in the house. Trashed a couple of the bedrooms. As far as we could tell, they took off when the Malloys left town. But the other kid spent his time with the Malloys. Went to the market with Moira, helped John wash the car, that kind of stuff. For him, we got a pretty good description. And we know – neighbors again – that he came back several times looking for them."

"You knew it was me, didn't you?" said Martin. Why didn't you talk to me then?"

"Bad policing, maybe?" A slow, sad smile. "Then again, maybe I figured you didn't need any more hassle at that particular time."

But Martin had tuned out again, clearly somewhere else with his thoughts. When he started talking, Natalie knew that both she and Mayo were irrelevant; that Mayo's questioning had triggered a story that he needed to tell.

"They became the parents that I had been imagining since ... for as long as I can remember. Even when I supposedly had parents. Oh, not in any official way, and not even in their own minds. They were just nice people who liked kids and treated them like they mattered. But, to me, they were everything I never had. They talked to me like I was real, cared about me. They said 'stay as long as you like' and they meant it and I would have done it if they hadn't taken off. And the house! For a street kid, it was like a castle. And for an orphan, it – and them… Well, they were miracles. And then they were gone. No word. Nothing."

Each of the three of them sat there, carefully not looking at the other two. Thirty seconds passed before Natalie broke the silence.

"You were sixteen."

Martin smiled, but it was a very sad smile, and she could see the brightness in his eyes. "I thought I was a tough, totally self-sufficient street kid. Didn't need anything from anybody. Then I met them and it turned out that I was Peter Pan wanting a Wendy… Oliver Twist, Harry Potter … all rolled into one super-orphan bundle of mush that wanted what all those other kids had."

She said, very quietly, "Martin. They didn't desert *you.*"

"I know that, of course," he shrugged. "At least, I know that *now*. And I'm sure as hell not about to go psychoanalytical on you and muse about how it damaged me for life and how I need therapy to deal with my suppressed anger. But – then? When I was sixteen …"

He shook himself. "Do you know that I tried to find them? A couple of years ago. I saw an article in the New York Times about the impossibility of someone literally being 'off-the-grid' these days. Too many digital traces. So I asked Sergei to look. No one better than Sergei for that kind of search. He took it as a personal challenge, not just a favor for a friend. But he came up empty."

Again, a respectful silence settled over them. This time, it was Mayo that broke it. "Is that why you want to buy the Brookings house? Because of those few weeks you lived there?"

Martin stared at Mayo. *Is it? One of the problems with being rich is that one doesn't have to justify how they spend money or worry about deeper meanings of what they choose to own. Want it? Buy it! So why do I want the damn house?*

Mayo's cell rang before Martin had even registered that Mayo was expecting an answer. He answered his phone with a puzzled expression that deepened during the twenty seconds or so that the caller was talking. His only part in the conversation was to say "Yes. Give us half an hour." When he ended the call, he turned to Martin and Natalie.

"We need to go somewhere."

Martin asked, "Where?" at the precise moment that Natalie asked, "Why?"

Mayo stood up and moved toward the stairs, clearly expecting them to follow. He turned and said, "Where? The house that we've just been talking about. Why? Because the man on the phone says that he can help me solve five murders. And he wants all three of us to be there."

The Story of Five Murders

Mayo stopped the car in the bus zone directly across the street and he and Martin stared at the ornate front entrance of the Brookings House. It was flanked by a pair of Chinese men dressed in blue blazers, grey slacks and wraparound sunglasses that hid their eyes and – almost – hid the very thin stalks of the headsets they were wearing. They stood almost as though at parade rest in a military formation.

"I don't think those guys are realtors," Martin said.

"Whoever they are, they travel in style," Mayo said, gesturing at four black stretch limousines taking up half-a-block of curb space in front of the house.

Natalie leaned over from the back seat, holding her cell phone. She'd been on it during their short ride. From the snatches of conversation he overheard, Martin assumed she was talking to Janet Li.

"It's a Chinese trade delegation. A group of nine very important people from Beijing. Janet just told me that the city is putting them up in the Brookings House for the week. And she wants to talk to you, Mayo." She handed him the phone as he started to get out of the car.

Martin looked at her. "So, it's off the market?"

She shook her head emphatically. "Mummy specifically said, 'Tell Martin that his offer is still on the table, that this is just a trial balloon.' I think she likes you and doesn't want your feelings to be hurt."

Even as she was speaking, the expression of puzzlement was becoming clearer by the second. He asked, "What's bothering you?"

"She's here," Natalie said. "The mayor." She pointed at the cluster of three men leaning against one of the limos. "The guy in the V-neck sweater …that's her driver."

She looked like he wanted to say more, but Mayo was already halfway across the street, so Martin and Natalie scrambled out of the car. They caught up to him just as he reached the front door.

It was clear that they were expected. One of the two men at the entrance moved quickly to open the door and gestured for them to go in. Once inside, they were greeted immediately by a young Chinese woman, also in blazer and grey slacks, but without the sunglasses or headset.

"Good afternoon. Chao Zhu is waiting for you in the library."

She moved ahead of them down a long and very wide hallway. They passed what seemed to be a large dining room with a group of five or six individuals at a table covered with bound documents. One of them was Janet Li. The woman leading them stopped at an arched doorway into a room that seemed to be all oak and leather. An elderly Chinese man approached them and bowed slightly. He was dressed in a dark grey pinstriped suit and looked every inch the welcoming diplomat.

"I am Chao Zhu. The one who called. Thank you for coming."

The three of them stood silent, each waiting for one of the others to move first. It was Natalie that began. "You don't know me. I am –"

"Natalie Weiss, preservationist and adopted daughter of the mayor." He nodded to Mayo. "And this is Officer Mayo Marsh of the San Francisco Police Department … for a few more weeks before his retirement. And this person" – he nodded at Martin – "is Martin Kline, a billionaire ex-felon."

He smiled, as if at a joke visible only to him. "Forgive me, but you are a strange trio."

Mayo was clearly suppressing his impatience with the whole proceeding. "When you called, you said something about solving some murders? I prefer to have this discussion at our offices, with a police stenographer present, and without Ms. Weiss or Mr. Kline involved."

"I understand your preferences. But they are irrelevant. We can have this conversation here, now, with just the four of us, or not at all. It's your choice."

Mayo didn't like it. *But Janet just told me to go along with whatever goes down with this guy. She said, 'Forget the rule book on this one. You'll see why as it goes.' And she's down the hall.*

Chao smiled, "I guarantee that our conversation will be an interesting one."

He led them to a cluster of upholstered chairs in the far corner, grouped around a low table with a glossy enamel surface. As soon as they were seated, the young woman brought in a stainless steel coffee pot and a set of mugs.

"Normally, these would be fine china saucers and cups. But the house is not yet fully furnished for such affairs."

He actually sounds apologetic. Natalie reached for one of the mugs and poured herself half-a-cup and studied Chao closely. *He looks like a diplomat, talks like a diplomat ...*

What the hell! "Are you a diplomat, Mr. Zhu?"

"Not in the slightest, but I am complimented by your question. I am a businessman, here with a trade group to negotiate contracts between the City of San Francisco and the Chinese government. I assume you saw them working in the large room near the door. We hope to be done soon. If conditions are favorable."

Mayo was brusque. "Your call said something about murder."

The smile disappeared. Chao sat back in his chair and placed his hands together very delicately, his fingertips together and just touching his chin. Once again, he gave the strong impression of someone thinking very carefully about what he was about to say.

"Five murders, actually." He addressed himself directly to Mayo. "Well-known to you particularly, and all of them except one unsolved. And even that one, you got wrong."

Mayo was about to speak, but Natalie stopped him by placing her hand on his forearm and saying to Chao, "You're going to tell us about the Brookings family, aren't you?"

Chao beamed at Natalie as if a very bright student had unexpectedly answered the question posed by a teacher. "Yes. That's why I thought we should meet here, in their house."

And he began to talk.

Chao Zhu spoke as if reading a story from a podium, a story that he had told many times before. He was careful to make eye contact with each of his listeners and he spoke in whole sentences, without any 'uhs, ums' or other verbal pauses.

"I must tell you a story. It is about a man named Ah Yang. He was the descendant of Chinese emperors. He was also my great-grandfather, the oldest of eight children. He was born in the year 1797 –"

At this, Mayo stood up with a sound of disgust. Zhu ignored him.

"As I was saying, he was born in 1797, using your western calendar, with most auspicious signs. When he was ten, his father moved the entire family to Peking and was one of the architects who designed and built the famous Summer Palace outside of the city. Ah Yang was educated there and attracted the attention of court officials who recognized his intelligence and skills. He was trained as an engineer and schooled in languages, both the major Chinese dialects and English.

"When the family returned to their village in the south of China, Ah Yang quickly rose to become a leader, even in a society dominated by elders. He married, fathered children and became a wise and respected man.

"But China changed. Natural disasters and the foreigners with their gunboats, predatory traders and demand for opium were part of the problem. But it was not just the foreigners. The ethnic Manchus who dominated the Qing government were corrupt and despised the Han Chinese in the southern provinces. Ah Yang's village and his family were out-of-favor at court and destitute when news of the American gold rush came, along with the attractive colored pamphlets that shipping companies distributed with pictures of smiling Chinese workers picking up large gold nuggets from streambeds. It was an easy choice for a man such as Ah Yang. He took his three younger brothers, two sons and three other young men from his village with him to the gold fields. When they arrived in San Francisco, there were less than one-hundred Chinese in the city.

"All went well at first. They earned the respect of the other miners. They worked claims that had been abandoned by white miners who did not want to do the hard work required to extract the gold that was still there, because it required too much work. The Chinese worked hard. They kept to themselves and lived frugally, always believing that once they were rich, they would return to China. Some, but not many, sent their gold home to their families, but that was a hazardous venture, so Ah Yang and his community kept their growing wealth close to them, hidden from the white men.

"But gold became harder to find and the white devils took back their claims by force and passed laws against the Chinaman. Your government imposed special 'miner's taxes' on the Chinese and, far worse, Chinese miners and merchants were robbed and murdered with impunity. At the start of 1857, Ah Yang began planning for their return to China. He sent his youngest brother back to their village with the news that they would be shutting down their camp and returning 'with a substantial amount of gold.'

"How much gold? We don't know, but historians estimate that approximately ten million pounds of gold was extracted during the first few years of the gold rush, including individual nuggets weighing over one-hundred pounds. That would be more than fifty billion dollars today. And Ah Yang and his six companions had been digging and prospecting for eight years in the heart of the gold country … 'twenty-four, seven' as you Americans say.

"We know that two groups of Chinese miners from Ah Yang's camp were waylaid on the way from Auburn to Sacramento, even though traveling separately at night on little-used roads. They were killed and the gold they were transporting was stolen. Ah Yang was sure that the killers had been tipped off, so he convinced the other miners – some fifty or so men -- to send their gold to San Francisco in a single shipment, using a date and a route that only he would know about.

"He left the camp with a horse and cart after midnight a few days later. He picked the day because it was his sixtieth birthday, thought to be a most auspicious time for new ventures. That is the last time he was seen until last year.

"Some in the camp believed that Ah Yang stole the gold for himself and that he lived out his life as a rich man in a remote corner of California. Others argued that the thief was the white man who disappeared on the same night as Ah Yang. They did not know his name and had viewed him as a weak, pathetic character, but in their stories, he now took on the shape of an almost mythic villain, the man who had stolen the wealth of an entire community that had labored for eight years to build enough wealth to alter their family's future in China. Both sides passed their version of the crime on to their children from generation to generation. The first story that I can remember being told as a small child was 'the mystery of Ah Yang.' For my grandparents, he was a hero.

"We now know that the white man left him buried on the banks of the Rio de Los Americanos river, what you now call 'the American River.' His grave was part of what was flooded when Folsom Lake was created in the 1950's. Thanks to your prolonged drought, his skeleton was discovered last year when the original riverbank was exposed by the receding waters. Ah Yang's bones now rest in China, with those of his ancestors and three generations of his descendants."

Where, before long, I shall join them.

"Ah Yang's two remaining brothers and his sons did not return to China. They stayed in San Francisco and became important merchants in your fast-growing Chinatown community. They and their sons were also were key players in the Tong system, with ties to drugs, prostitution and gambling operations. It was inevitable that they would eventually encounter and recognize a man as prominent and rich as Hiram Brookings. And for them, it was no mystery where his capital came from that launched his shipping business."

Chao Zhu paused and looked at each of his three listeners in turn. When he was satisfied that they were attentive, that he in fact had made his story a compelling one, he said, "And they did find him. It was a most memorable day for many people in your city."

The Second Murder
(April 1906)

It has been almost fifty years. Surely long enough that none of them would remember me even if they stayed in California. Surely I can live without fear in San Francisco.

Hiram Brookings had lived in Monterey for those five decades, visiting San Francisco only a handful of times during those years. He had avoided Chinese for that entire time; crossing the street to avoid them, refusing their business if they called on him. However, his confidence seemed to grow in proportion to the lines of his new house, as though its completion would finally and forever immunize him from the consequences of his past sins. Surely, that growing sense of immunity was further boosted by being male, white and rich – features that tended toward a feeling of entitlement.

However, the specter of Ah Yang would not leave him alone, appearing in his thoughts and dreams without notice, always with an accusing stare. The mere sight of an adult Chinese male would resurrect vivid details of that fateful boat ride. It was because of those visions that he kept Ah Yang's crates of "women's things" with him, other than those few items that he had used to fund his company, as if they served as some sort of protective talisman. The man who sold him his first two boats said, "Gold is gold. I do not care what form it takes or where it comes from."

He told no one, not even his wife or only son, about his days in the gold fields or that strange night on the Rio De Los Americanos. Nor did he share anything about the contents or location of the crates of women's things.

I am seventy-six years old and tired. I shall hand off the company to Douglas and become one of those stout gentlemen who spend their time with stockbrokers and belong to the best clubs in the city. Learn to play golf. They say the Presidio course will be expanded to eighteen holes shortly. Just get this damn house completed!

What he did not know was that Mr. Hearst's newspaper, the Daily Examiner, delighted in writing about exactly such stout gentlemen as he aspired to be and that a very flattering article and photograph of him had appeared as a major feature article in last week's edition, heralding his move from Monterey to San Francisco and the construction of his new house. The issue was studied intently in Chinatown by one man in particular even though he spoke almost no English and was far removed from the intended readership. His lack of English proficiency didn't matter to him because he was interested only in the accompanying photograph.

Hiram was wrong: fifty years was not long enough to erase memories or make him unrecognizable.

Neither Hiram nor his son Douglas, now a man of thirty years and his partner in the shipping business, were much interested in the idea of a new house. But the pressure from Hiram's new wife and the realities of a suddenly large family finally overcame their reluctance. She was thirty years younger and came with three daughters and the strongly held opinion that San Francisco was the appropriate setting for a man of Hiram's stature. She also required a residence commensurate with his status and, more importantly, one that promoted her own social aspirations.

Even after he signed on to the idea, however, Hiram showed little interest in the project. He was indifferent to architecture and told the builder "It's for her. Do what you like, but I don't want one of those sissified Victorian things. Make it big. And I want it to last." His only aesthetic contribution was to insist, "that it has to have big pillars at the front entrance."

She would have preferred Nob Hill, but the 'Big Four' – Stanford, Crocker, Huntington and Hartford – were already there and she recognized that both her and her new residence – no matter how much of Hiram's money she spent – would be overshadowed. So she commissioned the biggest single structure on Russian Hill. Hiram approved because the location not only provided easy access to the harbor, but enabled him to see his ships at anchor.

There were no actual Russians on Russian Hill. It acquired that name when a number of crewmembers from a Russian warship anchored in the Bay died from disease and were buried in what came to be known as the 'Russian Cemetery,' not very far from where the Brookings house was under construction. Given the prime hilltop location, however, the bodies were moved to the Yerba Buena Cemetery in 1848.

The new house was launched by buying three existing properties that Mrs. Brookings intended to demolish and replace with their new home. The three lots ran from the top of the Hill down toward the Bay in stairstep fashion. They moved into the house furthest down the hill and used it as temporary quarters. Actual construction began early in 1906 by razing the two small existing houses uphill from them to clear a foundation for the first phase of construction. By the morning of April 18, 1906, the new structure was a towering four-story latticework of studs and crossbeams, lacking walls, connecting stairways or a roof.

Today's schedule called for beginning the demolition of the third of the three houses that had stood on this land, the one that had served as temporary quarters and a storage site for their goods until construction was well underway. No one but Hiram knew of what lay beneath the thick layer of dirt at that third level. He had singlehandedly buried Ah Yang's crates beneath the lowest level of the new structure, far away from the street and next to the massive retaining wall that formed the southern foundation and kept the hillside in place. They rested in their own rock-lined vault and were, in his mind, a surety against Ah Yang's vengeance.

The room directly above his hidden crates would house his new wife's collection of dolls and ceramics that she had collected over the last dozen years. She thought his concern for every detail of that room's construction was on her behalf.

The Brookings, along with most of the inhabitants of San Francisco, were awakened at 5:13 AM by the terrifying shaking and rolling of the house and the sound of objects crashing around them. They did not know it then, but they were about to participate in a historic geologic event, one that would destroy and reshape one of the world's greatest cities.

There was surprisingly little damage to the partially completed house. Being nothing more than vertical and horizontal timbers bolted together, it was ideally suited to survive the initial shock and the numerous aftershocks. However, the massive shockwave cracked his new retaining wall and several tons of rock and soil cascaded down and were now covering his hiding place, further shielding the material from both the coming firestorm and curious eyes. The slide also severely damaged some furniture and the several crates containing the extensive collection of ceramic dolls that the new Mrs. Brookings had been collecting.

Hiram walked to the top of the hill to survey the devastation of their city. He paid little attention at the time to the several columns of smoke that were already forming. They were too far away and too insubstantial to be threatening.

But his complacency was short-lived. From the top of Russian Hill, he could easily chart the progress of the fires and calculate the ever-changing odds. Thirty hours later, when it was abundantly clear that the flames were coming, Hiram began a frantic search for wagons to transport his stored goods to safety, but all transport was commandeered for firefighting and, in any case, the streets were mostly impassable. When an army unit showed up and announced that they needed to dynamite his structure to help form a firebreak, he displayed a large revolver and refused to allow them to come near. He sent Douglas to "scrounge whatever manpower you can and send them to me" and began plotting his defenses. His intention was to use the workers as firefighters, particularly to ward off the increasing threat of windblown cinders from where the fire was approaching from the south and east.

He went outside to see how much time he had. *It's halfway up the hill and moving fast. Nothing to be done except get out of its way! At least, the damn house is barely started. And what I really care about won't be harmed by a little heat. The only thing I'll miss is the desk.*

'The desk' was a massive antique creation, quite heavy and with a dozen drawers and cubbyholes. It was the heart of his filing system for his shipping company and the only piece of furniture he had moved from Monterey.

The voice startled him. "Douglas sent us. Said you pay much money for our help."

When he turned, he saw four men standing inside the wooden framing. They were holding shovels, standing wreathed in the smoke that was denser by the moment. They had kerchiefs over their mouths and noses, which made him realize that his eyes were stinging and his throat rasping from the smoke. For the first time, the roar of the fire was quite present in his consciousness.

Too little, too late. But ...

He gestured for them to come with him. "Not much we can do for the house, but you can help me move this desk out of here and to the top of the hill. Somewhere the damn flames won't reach ..."

He pointed to the desk. The four men moved as one, but not to the desk. They formed a square, with him in the middle, an arm's length from each of them.

"I said – "

The smallest of the four held his hand up to cut him off, and said, "I am the son of Ah Yang."

He pulled his kerchief down and, when he did, the other three men did as well. Hiram found himself looking at men only slightly younger than him. They were Chinese, and he knew who they were even though forty-nine years had passed. Each of them held a long knife in his right hand and was looking at him with a pitiless gaze.

"You stole our gold. And you killed my father." The man spoke the short English sentences in the cadences of one who has learned them by rote. One of the others prodded Hiram with the point of his knife and asked, "Where is gold?"

Hiram was not a coward. And he believed entirely in the superiority of the white races over the heathen Chinese. To fear them was to give them a power that they were unworthy of. Perhaps it was also true that he felt guilty about what he had done a half-century in the past and may have welcomed what was coming. Or he may have been momentarily depressed by the destruction all around him and the fiery storm racing uphill toward them. Who knows what one will think about or do when your certain death is staring at you, unimpressed by your achievements, incurious about who you are or what you want, interested only in how you will respond in the final seconds?

He said, "The gold is back where it began. And so is your father." And he pushed past the nearest man and started walking toward the uphill wall, where the redwood planks were already beginning to smolder from the heat.

Sins of the Father

When Chao Zhu paused, Martin said, "You have told us of two murders. Ah Yang in 1857 and Hiram Brookings in 1906. You said there were five. I presume that the others are the subsequent generations of Brookings?"

"Yes. Douglas, Orville and Donald, in that order."

Mayo snorted, "Ancient history! An accident, a suicide and a solved case."

"Uninteresting by your policeman's standards, perhaps. But it is still an interesting story. And it may have some bearing on your remaining career, Mr. Marsh."

Natalie said, "But three killings, over – what – a century? It makes no sense."

Chao Zhu settled back in his storytelling posture, steepled fingers resting on his chin. "You need to know three things to make sense from what happened.

"First, there is one of those accidents of fate, what you westerners call 'coincidence.' Ah Yang was killed on his sixtieth birthday. And his son's sixtieth birthday was on the day after the earthquake, the day when he found and killed Hiram Brookings.

"Second, you need to understand that – in our Chinese culture – the sixtieth birthday has special meaning, more than any other except the first and tenth birthdays. In our astrological calendar, a man's sixtieth birthday completes a full cycle of life and signifies the beginning of a new life. For my grandfather, Ah Yang's son, this *coincidence* between his father's death and his deferred vengeance, both on sixtieth birthdays, took on an almost divine significance. From then on, our two families were locked together."

"The Hatfield's and McCoy's," Martin said very softly.

Chao looked politely at him with a quizzical expression, but Martin just said, "So. Douglas, Orville and Donald are given a deferred death sentence, to be executed on their sixtieth birthday..."

Chao Zhu nodded.

"What's the third thing we need to understand?" asked Mayo.

"That the gold is still out there somewhere."

Mayo shook his head. "But Hiram had it for over fifty years. Hard to believe he didn't use it up. Or his wife or sons after him."

"No," Chao said. "My grandfather was convinced that Brookings hid it. From everyone, including his wife and children."

Mayo scoffed, "So now we have a treasure hunt, a bunch of unsolved murders, and a global vendetta. Beginning to sound like a fairy tale. How much gold was there?"

"Ah Yang was very secretive about just that, so my grandfather wasn't sure. But his guess was several hundred pounds, once it was melted down. That's at least a very large number at today's prices."

"He looked, surely? Your grandfather." More than the others, Natalie was caught up in the story. She was leaning forward, almost reaching out to Chao Zhu.

"Some, but he died fourteen months after the earthquake. In those days, they called it 'consumption.' But what he did do was to make sure that his sons committed themselves and their sons to ritual murder, to killing any male Brookings heirs on their sixtieth birthday. Hence, the deaths of Douglas – *drowned* in 1936, Orville – *suicide* in 1970 -- and Donald – murdered in 1995."

"Did any of the Brookings descendants know of the hidden gold?"

"No."

"How can you be sure?"

Chao was silent, focused inward, clearly thinking about how to respond. "First, they were poor, or at least were not wealthy as they would have been if living off of the gold."

He hesitated. "Second, they were tortured before they died. They knew nothing."

Natalie shuddered and ran through the record in her mind. *Douglas's body washed up on the beach three days later, badly chewed up by fish. Orville was a drug addict, probably perpetually bruised and battered. Donald was beaten during the robbery, quite savagely.* She observed Mayo nodding, probably running through the same history in his mind. But something struck him, causing him to sit up and peer closely at Chao.

"So," Mayo said, "we should look for their killers among your family members – the descendants of Ah Yang. In fact, in Donald's case, I seem to recall a gun registered to a Chinese man."

"My grandson Xi, actually. Investigate my family if you like, but the deaths were long ago and would have to be proven to be murders. Even you, Mr. Marsh, would fail to close such hopeless cases. Your district attorney would think you a superstitious fool … a sore loser."

Martin watched the building tension between Chao and Mayo. It was crystal clear that they were locked in a contest, a duel with uncertain rules. *Mayo's a homicide cop and he's listening to a story of serial killings, told by a person who is not only related to the killers but almost certainly approved of them. This is hard for him.*

Mayo was leaning forward, talking directly at Zhu's impassiveness. "That's true for the first two. But Donald is still an open case, and 1995 wasn't all that long ago. I have a personal interest in that one."

"You already tried – and failed – to convict the person that you thought did it."

"Warren Wah. I presume you know of him?"

"He's my nephew, the son of my wife's sister. And, despite what you think, he did not kill Donald Brookings. My grandson Xi did. And he died two years ago."

Mayo looked at Zhu for a long ten seconds. It started out as a glare and slowly settled into an expression of grudging acceptance.

"That, his dying, makes it hard to prosecute him for murder, doesn't it?"

Zhu shrugged. "I suppose." He stood up and faced the three of them. He stood very straight. "It also means that my family, the name that runs for five hundred years, from emperors through Ah Yang and me, will end when I die."

And what you do not know, nor will I tell you, is how soon that will be. How ironic that I must trust you to finish certain things for me!

Both Chao Zhu's tone and his body language signaled that their meeting was over. The sound of Mayo's phone ringing was like a confirmation of that ending.

Chao Zhu stood unmoving when the three of them left the room. *I called them 'a strange trio,' and they are. So unlike the Chinese. Each of them passionate in his own way, and so transparent about their passions. I like them and wish that I could spend more time with them... tell them more stories about Ah Yang's legacy.*

Perhaps even the story about how I came for the first time to the United States, in 1965, a provincial twenty-five year old filled with purpose. How my cousins brought Orville Brookings to me in the whorehouse and I put the noose around his neck while explaining why this was happening to him. But then I spoke only Mandarin, so he did not understand.

Near the front of the house, Janet Li and Mallory were taking a break from the negotiations. They had found a small sitting room off the entryway and were sitting in facing chairs in a muted conversation. The other three participants in the negotiating session across the hall – all of them Chinese – were huddled in their meeting room, engaged in recalculating tonnages and yields based on the new information that had just been delivered.

"They smile and nod at you the whole time you're talking. Then they present a position that is completely at odds with what you've just said. It's infuriating." Mallory stood up and started pacing, three quick steps and then back again in the small space.

Li was amused by Mallory's irritation. *Put her in the room with a public sector union and she'll behave exactly the same way as the Chinese.*

"It's the diplomatic version of the Chinese water torture. They can't help it; negotiation is in their DNA. And it's worse when Chao Zhu isn't in the room. They're not about to agree to anything unless they know he approves."

"So why isn't he there? We're really close on everything except the question of the operating management."

The question troubled Li. *Which means there's still a very large gap. He wants Gruber and I can't go along with that. At least, I don't think I can.* But she didn't share that with Mallory.

"Zhu's running all kinds of games at the same time. But he told me he'd be back with us within an hour." But Mallory wasn't listening, back on her cell phone.

Li had seen Natalie go by with Mayo and Kline, on their way down the hall. *Probably something to do with Kline trying to buy this house. But why Mayo?*

Even as she was thinking about him, she saw Mayo leaving the room down the hall, clearly in a hurry. At the same time, Mallory touched her on the shoulder and said, "Boss ..." in the tone she used when she was about to convey news that she knew would be unpopular.

Li forgot Mayo and turned to Mallory. *She is really disturbed. Must have been an unusual phone call.*

Mallory held up her phone. "That was the police chief. They've got a murder victim in South San Francisco."

Li waited, knowing there was more.

"The victim ... it's Mannie Gruber."

Mayo at the Garbage Dump

"The last time I was here, I was on an eighth grade field trip. Our teacher was big on recycling that year. He required us to write an essay called 'the world without trash' and arranged for a tour of this place."

'This place' was the hangar-sized Recology Center in South San Francisco, the central dumping ground for the trash of San Francisco. The speaker was Victoria Morrison. She was talking to Mayo, but he wasn't paying much attention and probably wouldn't have heard her anyway, given the caravan of diesel garbage trucks moving past them. He'd sent a uniform out to stop the incoming queue of trucks, but apparently he was having difficulty doing that.

From where he was standing, looking up from the foot of a sloping heap of trash that towered over him, all he could see was the man's arm protruding from the sleeve of what looked like a gray suit coat. The arm was bare from the elbow down and a quite large gold watch stood out against his skin.

Dark complexion, probably Latin. Big chunky-looking gold watch, probably a Rolex. Ten-to-one we've got ourselves a recently deceased drug dealer.

Two white-suited crime scene technicians, waist-deep in trash, were attempting to expose the rest of the body, but it was clear that it was like trying to dig a hole in fine-grained sand. Even as he watched, the trio – technicians and corpse – slid several feet down the slope toward him. A very loud "fuck this!" came from one of them.

Mayo called out to them, "Forget what the book says about preserving the crime scene. Take a couple of photos and then get him down here and let me look at him. He sure as hell wasn't killed at the peak of a garbage pile."

While that was being done, Mayo turned to Morrison. "Who found him?"

She pointed to a fat guy in white coveralls sitting on an overturned pail about forty feet away. "Him. Name is Jose. He was driving a front-end loader that moves the trash from here to a conveyor into a furnace. Scooped him up with all the other stuff. Scared him to death."

"You talk to him?"

"Yep. And he ID'd the victim … along with everybody else here."

Mayo raised both eyebrows.

"His name – the victim – is Gruber. He owns the company with all the trucks. His business card reads 'The King of Garbage'."

Mayo winced and, very softly, said, "Shit!" Morrison looked at him quizzically, but nothing more was forthcoming.

Gruber was fully clothed, but the suit was badly torn and stained with numerous substances. One side of his face was severely scraped and a small patch of white skull was showing.

"Looks like someone beaten to death in the course of a mud wrestling match."

Morrison said, "I think that's because he's just been on a long ride in a compacting garbage truck. His real problem is this." She turned Gruber's head to one side, revealing two neat holes in the side of his head.

"Small caliber. Up close. No exit wounds. Very professional."

"What else do we know?"

"Man left home about eleven o'clock last night after receiving a phone call. A video camera caught him going into the garage where they keep several trucks for servicing. Next time he's seen is when Jose there" – she pointed to the guy sitting on the pail – "picks him up in his bucket."

"You got a theory, don't you, Morrison? Please share it."

She gestured at the trash heap behind them. "This particular batch of garbage was brought in by truck number 317. We've got it pulled out in a corner of the parking lot and a lab guy is going over it. The driver got it from the garage at seven this morning, ran his regular route, filled up his truck and then dumped the load here about two hours ago. We think –"

"Wait! You said 'we'? You and who else?"

"Me, the driver – his name is Hooper – our man Jose, and a couple of the other workers. We think Gruber was killed last night and tossed into the back of the truck. Hooper didn't check the back of the truck – no reason to – just took off and started his route. The truck compacts the stuff as they go, so the body would have been tossed around a lot and be at the very back of the load. That's confirmed by its position at the top of the heap after it was dumped."

Mayo thought about it. "Did the video show him leaving the garage?"

"No. Nor did it show anybody else coming or going. But there's a back entrance that we found unlocked. I think Gruber might have let his killer in that way. A meeting of some sort, maybe?"

"Could he have been killed here and the stuff dumped on top of him?"

"No. This section is scraped clean every night. Checked by the supervisor before the first truck comes in. He came in with the garbage."

She doesn't know how apt that is. Christ! She's already done most of the work, although with a crowd-sourced investigative technique. But they're probably right about what happened.

"Victoria, just how many people have been involved in the last ninety minutes?"

She grinned. "When I got here" – she looked at her watch – "one-hundred-and-eight minutes ago, there were four men wallowing around on the top of this garbage heap trying to pull Mr. Gruber out. I think we have what you might call a 'contaminated crime scene.' Fitting for a garbage dump, don't you think?"

She tried, and almost succeeded, to put on a serious look when Mayo frowned at her. She shook her head. "The real puzzle for me is why none of them took his watch. It's a Rolex and he obviously doesn't need to know what time it is any more. Makes me rethink my basic negative views on human nature."

I can help with that! "Detective Morrison, would you steal a watch from Al Capone or Lucky Luciano, even if they were dead?"

She looked at Mayo, clearly puzzled. He gestured at the corpse, who seemed to be contemplating the brownish stain on his pinstriped sleeve. "Let me introduce you to the late Manfred Gunter Gruber, the recently deceased head of what passes for organized crime in the City of San Francisco."

Personality Sketches

Chao Zhu met Warren Wah at Portsmouth Square, the park in the heart of Chinatown. They found a bench in a relatively isolated spot, away from the chess players and their kibitzers. Chao had brought along a few crusts of bread, which he tore into small pieces and tossed to a cluster of earthbound milling pigeons as they talked.

"I met a policeman yesterday. His name is Mayo Marsh. I think you know him."

Wah was no longer surprised by Chao, and he understood that Chao said nothing without forethought. So he knew that Mayo Marsh was of interest to Chao, not merely an oblique way of tantalizing him. So he did not respond, just waited for Chao's purpose to reveal itself.

"I told him the story of Ah Yang. And how it led to the death of Donald Brookings. I told him that you were not the killer."

Chao Zhu spoke quietly and Wah sat stonefaced, but the words resounded in his consciousness as though they were shouted at him.

Is that what this is? An apology for sixteen wasted years?

Wah played it safe. "Marsh was a good cop. I'm sure that he knew that your grandson Xi was the killer and that I was lying when I told him that I killed Brookings, that I was there alone. The lawyers got my confession tossed out, but he knew that I was part of it, so he went for what he could get. Even then, the best he could do was armed robbery."

Zhu nodded and changed the subject. "I asked you to meet with four people. What have you learned about them?"

Wah leaned back against the bench and thought about the question. Not about what he would say, but how Chao Zhu would respond. He decided on a simple test.

For him, it is always about family, so let us start with some reality.

"Your granddaughter, Donna Yang, is ambitious but careless. I think that is a bad combination in her circumstances. She is over her head."

Chao nodded, thinking about his granddaughter's late night phone call and her bruised face when he visited her.

"So she is at risk?" Chao Zhu asked without much evident interest.

"Yes. There is an expression … 'picking up nickels in front of a steamroller.' She is very good at creating many small schemes to make money, but she does not see that one simple misstep puts her entire enterprise at risk."

"Can she learn?"

"I think so, but she needs to respect the steamroller."

Chao looked off into the distance and Wah knew that he was visualizing the rearrangements to be put in place for the sake of his family members. *I remember his words from so long ago. 'Xi is stupid. But he is my grandson.'*

Zhu asked, "Martin Kline? I also met with him and found him to be … interesting."

Again, Wah thought carefully before answering. *Interesting ... a good word for Kline. A wealthy man who does not act wealthy and seems not to care very much about money. A man that I am indebted to. I wonder if Chao knows about my encounter with Kline – and the other man, the dead one -- on the bridge in that fog?*

He answered carefully. "Like you, I find Kline to be intriguing. He is someone that I would like to know better. His only agenda seems to be helping others, particularly ex-prisoners."

"The Americans have this thing about the wrongly accused –"

"No." Wah's interruption surprised both of them with its abruptness. "He doesn't care if they're murderers or tax evaders, guilty or innocent. I think because he sees himself as some of each."

Mei Ling said, 'He gave James half-a-million dollars. For me. And he asked no questions.'

Chao nodded. "He wants to buy the Brookings house. Just as I do."

"I know that, but I do not know anything about his motives. He seems to care little about owning things. Perhaps it is the woman Natalie Weiss who is influencing him? They are spending much time together."

Chao stood up and walked a few paces away, scattering the pigeons. He spoke without looking at Wah. "And the other man, Manfred Gruber?"

"I talked to him, as you asked. I did not like him. He is arrogant; a bigot who mistakes power for ability."

Should I tell him more?

Wah hesitated and then added, "He wanted me to do some work for him."

"Did you? Do the work?"

Wah hesitated again, but quickly realized that that very hesitation was an answer. He shrugged, "Yes. He wanted me to threaten or bribe both Kline and your granddaughter, which I did because I assumed he was acting for you with regard to the Russian Hill house. He also hinted that he might like me to kill a man named Paul Campos, who he was dissatisfied with."

Chao returned to the bench. "He's dead. Gruber. Did you kill him?"

"No." He returned Chao's searching stare without any change in expression. *He did not ask me if I killed Campos. I wonder if he knows?*

Chao sat back and when he resumed, his voice was less harsh, as if seeking reassurance. "Gruber was the front for the ... for a ... significant investment here in San Francisco. It is very important to me that the project should succeed, but it would have required him to be ... larger, more sophisticated ... than he seemed to be. He's dead, but I wonder if he had that capability."

Wah did not hesitate in answering. *How easy it is to reassure a person when there is no way to test the truth of such comforting thoughts. Like reassuring grieving relatives that the recently deceased is 'in a better place.'*

"Gruber was small time, a big fish in a small pond. His death should be good news for you. He would not do well in a bigger pond."

Chao smiled, a very rueful smile. "Thank you for that. However, it seems that I have *accidentally* created a totally honest business venture for the Chinese and Americans!"

He recovered quickly. "And the last person I asked you to talk with, the woman Emily Connors?"

How to answer this?

"She is ... not right." *That's a start. And it says everything there is to say about her.*

But Chao Zhu wanted more and he waited patiently.

Wah continued, in a tone as though talking to himself. "My aunt would say, 'She has bad chi.' I think that she does not know who she is and wants to be somebody else, but she doesn't know who. She is bad in ways that I am not familiar with."

Chao nodded. "I have never met anybody quite like her." And even as he said the words, he realized that they were true and that his fascination with her had caused him to make mistakes.

"She will be hard to control," Wah said thoughtfully. "I don't think she will be like others. You cannot frighten her and she doesn't seem to care very much about money." *She is like Kline in that way.*

"I agree," said Chao. "But can I trust her to do what she said she would do?"

Wah thought about the question and finally shook his head. "I don't know. She definitely has some internal code that she follows, but I think she has an agenda here in San Francisco that we do not understand. She is spending much of her time watching two houses ... your Brookings house and another one ... a restored Victorian owned by the woman named Natalie Weiss."

Chao Zhu was only half-listening.

Emily has failed me. Her reliance on Gruber was misplaced and that mistake has caused pain to my granddaughter. Perhaps that could be remedied. And her interest in the house is strange, driven by something more than my interests. But her decision to eliminate Gruber – even if she thinks she's operating on my behalf – is a mistake that I cannot tolerate.

They sat silently together on the bench, each of them thinking about Emily Connors. Finally, Chao stood and turned to face Wah.

"If I decide to ... to break off ... to terminate my arrangement with her, could you do that?"

Wah stood up. "She has a driver, a man named Ali who I think is very good at his trade. He would have to be dealt with, but she is out on the streets most of the time."

He paused and then nodded. "Yes, she can be dealt with."

A Discovery

Chao Zhu sat on a high stool at the large plank table in the center of the room. It was the only piece of free-standing furniture in the room, apparently designed as a convenient surface for sorting or folding laundry, high enough for a person to work comfortably while standing. A stack of weathered wooden crates rested beneath the table, taking up all of the space. Another half-dozen crates were stacked against the wall. The table was set as for a very crude dinner, with four dull black dinner plates and four equally black and ugly misshapen mugs without handles arranged symmetrically around the edges. In the center of the table, Zhu had constructed a three-layer structure by stacking a large number of small metal boxes – each of them a two-inch cube, with ornate designs – Chinese characters -- worked into their hinged lids.

Chao Zhu was amused by his own need for drama. *Such an elaborate staging. But, after all, we are at the end of a story that has run for one-hundred-and-sixty years. Not so very long really if one is Chinese and can trace his family's ancestry hundreds of years into the past, and find their origins in royal dynasties. But long enough to justify some small ceremony, especially if one has little time left for ceremonies of any kind. The Americans will not appreciate the subtleties, but it is important to me and that is sufficient.*

He heard them approaching and reached out to correct the slight misalignment of the nearest plate and mug. Martin Kline and Mayo Marsh were ushered into the room by the same woman as before. He gestured for them to join him around the high table.

"Welcome back to the Brookings House."

Martin looked at Mayo, who nodded at him in a way that said, 'This is your show; I'm just along for the ride.'

They sat, awkwardly because of the high stools and the way the boxes prevented them from placing their feet under the table. Neither Mayo nor Martin commented on the table settings.

"Is your trade delegation still at work upstairs?" Martin asked politely.

"No. We are done ... with that and other things."

"Did everything work out as you intended?"

Zhu thought about the question. *My granddaughter is still rebellious, dangerously so. The joint venture was settled, but not to my specifications. I have created and must yet deal with a very lethal enemy. Both I and my family name are coming to an end and I have debts to people that cannot be repaid with money or favors. On the other hand, I have what is on this table before me.*

Martin watched Zhu, wondering what was going on behind those eyes. Finally he said, more harshly than he intended, "Are you trying to buy this house? Is the Petrel Foundation yours? Why do you want to own this place?"

Chao responded promptly, seemingly not bothered by the abrupt change in tone. "I did at one time want to own this house, and I did ask my agent – through the Petrel Foundation – to acquire it. But I no longer am interested."

Mayo could not contain his impatience any longer. "Why did you ask us here again? More stories about ancient times?"

"In a way, yes. But really, I just wanted you to see these things." He gestured at the four place settings and odd-looking centerpiece on the tabletop between the three of them.

"What? Bad pottery?" Mayo was openly contemptuous.

"It is quite amateurish, isn't it? But once you get past the poor workmanship, you've got to admire the quality of the material." Zhu picked up one of the mugs and scraped it across the surface of the plate in front of Mayo. He left a long, bright yellow streak across the center of the plate.

Martin picked up the plate in front of him and looked closely at it, weighing it in his hands and thinking about their last meeting with Chao, in the upstairs room of this house.

"Ah Yang's gold. You found it."

Zhu nodded. "They wanted to bring the gold home with them, but the white people would kill them and steal it. So they melted it down and fashioned ordinary looking objects

– belt buckles, buttons, plates, saucers and mugs – that they blackened and hoped to sneak past the killers and thieves. Ah Yang left camp that night with a cart filled with what looked like ordinary household objects. These crates in this room, plus whatever Brookings used to start his steamer company."

Mayo's hostility had changed to a wondering look. He picked up one of the small cubes from the center of the table. "And these?"

Zhu picked up two of them, handing one to Martin and keeping one for himself. "These little iron boxes are designed for a single purpose -- to hold gold dust and flakes, the result of panning in streams or taken from sluice boxes. Each of them is marked to indicate its owner... the particular Chinese miner that worked eight years to accumulate its contents."

When they looked closely, the markings on the cover were scratched into a wax veneer, not etchings in the metal cover itself. Each box had a tiny clasp and when Mayo opened his, it was filled with the same bright yellow glow as on the surface of the plate.

Martin nudged the wooden box under his feet. "And these boxes? More of the same?"

Zhu smiled. "Ordinary household objects from the nineteenth century camps. More 'bad pottery,' as you say. And other things."

"You're taking it with you, back to China?"

Zhu looked closely at the two men, wondering if he had judged them correctly. *A rich man who does not care about money and a policeman who takes murders personally and is bothered by unsolved crimes, no matter how ancient they are.*

"Yes. It belongs to their families."

Mayo and Martin looked at one another and – after a few seconds – each of them smiled. Mayo gave a slight nod. Chao Zhu relaxed when he saw the smiles.

"How did you find it?" Mayo asked with an evident curiosity.

"Remember my story. About my ancestors. They didn't come across Hiram Brookings until fifty years after the theft, the day of the earthquake. My grandfather and father always assumed that he used up all of the gold in starting his businesses or at the very least converted the metal into a more liquid form of wealth. And they questioned ... tortured ... each of his male descendants and none of the three knew anything about any buried treasure. The last was twenty years ago and the story was no longer important to anyone except a few of my very old family members.

"That all changed when they found Ah Yang's bones on the riverbank last year, and some of us felt that 'face' and 'honor' and other such vague notions should be revisited. And I have always been bothered by Hiram Brookings' last words to my grandfather. He said, 'The gold has gone back to where it started. And so has your father.' I translated that as 'under the ground,' and thought of his excavations for his new house on Russian Hill. Given the difficulty of excavating the foundations of a house you do not occupy, I thought I would buy the house and conduct a leisurely search."

He smiled. "And I have other motives for wanting to buy outrageously priced houses in San Francisco. Even if there is no buried gold in the basement.

"I was not optimistic about finding the gold, but I planned to make the house a museum that would honor the Chinese contribution to the development of the modern San Francisco. That would be a unique – and honorable – form of vengeance for the crimes against my ancestors in the gold country."

"But that didn't work, did it?" Mayo's question had a hard edge to it, and both Martin and Zhu knew where he was headed.

"I made an offer, but it wasn't accepted by the owner."

"But then she died unexpectedly," Mayo said. "Her name was Stephanie Green, by the way. So you tried again, this time through the Petrel Foundation. But that didn't work because of an obstinate bureaucrat. Who also died unexpectedly." Mayo was becoming visibly angrier with each bitten-off sentence.

Zhu was silent, staring at Mayo with an unreadable expression. He was thinking of his talk with Warren Wah.

He talked of steamrollers. A very appropriate characterization of what happens when certain things are set in motion. I visited with Emily Connors in Macao and a sequence of events leads us to this strange meeting, sitting at this laundry table with Ah Yang's gold scattered around us and talking of murdered individuals ... victims of the steamroller.

He chose his words very carefully. "The person who killed Green and your bureaucrat is dead. The man who hired him to do the killing is also dead." *And I shall not talk about the man who hired the man who hired the killer.*

Mayo was standing up now. "Paul Campos, who was working for Mannie Gruber. We have evidence that ties him to both the Green and Alban 'accidents.' The funny thing about it? Mannie had nothing to gain from either death. I think he was working for someone else. Too bad that he's dead too. Hard to ask him who it was that hired him."

Chao Zhu merely smiled and Martin could not help thinking of the word 'inscrutable.'

He asked, "So, this so-called trade delegation that is staying here, is that just a front that gets you access to a search of the house?"

"No, the delegation is quite real. But I did have some influence in getting the city to make the house available to us. Normal business channels with access to the mayor's office. Two members of the delegation that came with me are structural engineers and have spent most of their time becoming familiar with the house. They brought some special instruments with them, very fancy stuff. They found the gold quite quickly, actually."

Martin sat quietly, thinking about himself twenty years ago. *I lived in this house. Wandered through every one of the twenty-three rooms. Oblivious.*

Mayo stood up, saying, "I guess I can retire now. All the killers are dead." He looked straight at Chao Zhu as he spoke. "Except the one who hired them."

Zhu stood up as well. "I understand your frustration. Would it help if I could show you how to find other killers?

The one who was responsible for what you call 'the Mission Murders' perhaps?"

Mission murders!

The words hung in the air, so unconnected with everything that had gone before that it took a few seconds for context to form around them. And even then, it made no sense in this time and place.

Zhu gestured at the wall behind them. For the first time, Mayo and Martin noticed that half of it was covered with heavy plastic sheeting, the kind of weather barrier used on construction sites.

"That's where they found the gold. It was buried beneath the floor level and also beneath a small slide that probably occurred during the 1906 earthquake. Interesting that they also found some quite rare ceramic dolls. Hiram's new wife was apparently a collector."

He walked over to the other half of the wall, made up entirely of built-in shelving. "They also found this."

He pushed on the edge of one of the shelves and a slight 'click' was heard. He then pulled an entire section of shelving away from the wall, exposing a large and very dark hole behind the shelving.

"This was sealed up by somebody a long time ago. They poured glue mixed with sand into the mechanism. Very effective. My engineers cleaned it up, restored it to its original condition."

Martin said in a wondering tone, "It's a secret room!"

Zhu said, "That's what it turned out to be. But originally, it was intended as the entry into an elevator shaft. Would have been the first one in San Francisco if it had been completed."

"We haven't touched anything, just looked in." He took a flashlight from a nearby shelve and shown it into the interior. When the three of them were lined up in the entrance, he aimed the flashlight down into the hole in front of them. The beam picked out three distinct skeletons, partially covered by a bright yellow dress thrown into a corner.

"Detective Marsh, I believe that John and Moira Malloy have finally returned from off-the-grid."

Three hours later, Mayo and Martin had been joined at the laundry table by Janet Li and Mayo's boss, Hector Ramirez, Chief of Homicide. The plates, mugs and wooden boxes were gone, along with Chao Zhu and the Chinese trade delegation. Instead, the table held plastic evidence bags with a large handgun, hypodermic needles, and a stainless steel flashlight. Three dresses in plastic bags were draped over the backs of stools lined up against the wall, along with a badly discolored and curved plank with faded lettering. Crime scene technicians had set up floodlights in the exposed 'elevator' doorway and were working in the pit with the skeletons.

"Tell me what we know for sure at this point." Ramirez addressed Mayo directly. "Just the facts, ma'am," as Sergeant Friday used to say."

"We have three sets of remains, one man and two women. Dead for a long time. All with large caliber gunshot wounds to the head. Recovered these items" – he gestured at the plastic bags – "the flashlight has some pretty good partial prints and the gun is registered to a Dr. Matthew Weiss, who was drowned in 1995 in a boating accident. We think" – he pointed at the piece of wood leaning against the wall near the dresses – "that plank is from the boat."

"Now, tell me what we're 'pretty sure of' at this early stage of our investigation."

Martin started to talk, but Mayo glared at him and overrode. "Two of the skeletons are John and Moira Malloy. We've got their medical records and each of them had a fracture that matches what we see in the pit. The other one is almost certainly the unidentified female teenager that was staying here at the same time as the Malloys disappeared. The drug paraphernalia probably belongs to her. The best we can do is try to match her up with missing persons reports in the late 1980's through 1995. I'd guess that's a dead end. The best bet for the shooter is the other kid who was hanging around at that time."

Ramirez looked at Martin. "You were here, in this house, in that same time frame?"

"Yes, I was," Martin said, "but I didn't kill them."

He answered in a distracted tone, still thinking about himself twenty years in the past. *I could be another set of bones in that hole in the ground. Where was I when he was killing them?*

Janet Li gestured at the three dresses in their plastic wraps, "The dresses?"

"That probably should be in the 'what we know for sure category.' We know that the bright yellow one is the one worn by the killer of one of the three boys in 1990 in the Mission District. We're testing the bloodstains against that of the third victim now, but we already know that the piece of cloth in his grip matches up precisely with the torn sleeve of the dress. There are stains on the other two dresses as well, and I'll bet that they will match up with the other two victims. That's how he got them into the alley, dressed as a woman."

"Natalie … she …"

They looked at Martin, who had maintained the same dazed expression since Chao Zhu had shone the flashlight into the elevator shaft.

"Natalie. It was her dress. And the gun was registered to her father."

Mayo spoke gently. "It wasn't her dress. And the gun had been reported stolen along with other stuff, right after her father drowned. That's who we're looking for, whoever took the gun. And you know him. You lived with him. In this house."

Martin closed his eyes and let a stream of long-ago images run through his mind, most of them involving John or Moira Malloy. Finally, he shook his head.

"He said his name was Ken. That's all I know."

Trade Agreements

The first announcement was at the Mayor's weekly press conference, the day after the Chinese trade delegation had left town.

The City of San Francisco and the government of the People's Republic of China have announced the formation of a joint venture to process and recycle scrap plastic in the U.S. and ship it to factories in China that require high quality plastic as a key input for products such as clothing, furniture and construction materials. The plant will be the first of its kind in the world, using technology developed in Silicon Valley for precisely this application. It will cost an estimated one billion dollars, most of which will be funded through Chinese investment. The facility will be located on city-owned land and will eventually employ up to six hundred workers.

Chao Zhu's call to Janet Li was timed for thirty minutes after the news conference. He was sitting in a Gulfstream G550 on the ramp at the San Jose Airport. It was a ridiculously expensive alternative to the usual commercial first-class flight to Beijing. There was only one other passenger and the cargo hold contained very little -- three suitcases and several exceptionally heavy wooden crates. The plane had impeccable documentation, however, and the reality that it was owned by the Chinese intelligence services was quite undiscoverable.

For Zhu, the personalized travel arrangements made sense, given all of the possibilities. *Emily is a wild card. I think she will be out of play, but just in case ... And the American policeman may get less noble once he has time to think about the gold and who it belongs to.*

"Good morning, Mayor Li. Congratulations on completing the largest joint Chinese-American project ever done in the U.S."

"Thank you, but you know quite well that it was both of us. This was truly a joint effort. And there's a lot of work to do before we can relax."

Janet paused, wondering how far to go. *So much for the polite part. I wonder if he'll bring up what's really bothering him? I figure that his skim would be in the millions if Gruber had run the operation. What the hell! Let's get it out in the open.*

She said, "That last bit was the hardest ... choosing the operating company to manage the facility. I'm glad your team finally saw it from our point of view."

"You left us no choice once our preferred candidate was murdered."

"Chao, Gruber's killing was *not* our doing. *Not.* And, yes, I concede that it made it much easier to get the deal approved on our end and that it will cost you personally, but we do not assassinate people that are merely inconvenient."

Chao said nothing. He believed her, but he could not help recalling her closing comment the last time they met. "Maybe I should use your methods to solve my problem with your candidate?"

She surprised him then with a direct question. "Did you have Gruber killed?"

His reply was instant, his reasoning impeccable. "Why would I do that? His death has cost me a great deal of money."

But I know who killed Gruber. And why. And I must deal with her. In a way that she will understand....

Li's voice hardened, "I'm glad you called. I wanted to let you know of some recent initiatives that I'm launching from, as you say, my high position."

He said nothing, but a proverb popped into his mind.

'Everything has its season.' Lao Tse, I think.

Janet Li was reciting, as though reading from a list. "First, I'm revamping all of our city real estate operations. No more anonymous buyers using shell companies. Full anti-money-laundering procedures with federal cooperation and a special interest in Chinese and Russian flight capital. And I'm going through the Department of City Owned Real Estate with the proverbial fine-toothed comb. I think you know what I'll find."

Zhu glanced across the aisle at his passenger. Donna Yang's badly bruised face looked back at him. *Maybe I would have asked Emily to deal with Gruber in any case.*

He realized that Li was expecting a reply. "I imagine you'll find that you need to hire a new Department Head. But what else?"

"Second, I've asked Mayo Marsh to defer his retirement for six months and lead the investigation on several unsolved murder cases where he has a personal interest. He has a very, shall we say, *flexible,* view of the statute of limitations and I'm sure he will want some time with you. And it may not be voluntary on your part."

Chao Zhu made a circling motion with his index finger, and the pilot who was watching him through the open cockpit door turned to his controls to start the short taxi to the end of the runway.

"I have enjoyed working with you, Mayor Li. And it pleases me that a woman such as you is mayor of your wonderful city ... to see our people rise to such high positions."

Ah Yang would not have believed such a thing to be possible.

"I'm not one of *your people.* And it's called democracy, Chao. Your country should try it."

"Everything has its season, Mayor. I have enjoyed our time together. Please give my regards to your lovely daughter."

Puzzles Resolved

Yellow crime-scene tape was strung between the columns that stood astride the front entrance and a uniformed patrolman was sitting in a marked car directly outside the door. Martin waited while the cop used his radio.

"Go on in. He said to tell you that you'll know where to find him."

Mayo was sitting in the laundry room at the central table typing with one finger on a laptop computer. The evidence bags were gone, but the floodlights were still illuminating the open doorway for what had been intended to be an elevator. Martin took the stool opposite Mayo and waited for him to look up from the keyboard.

Might as well start with the obvious question.

"Isn't there a law about who has salvage rights for buried treasure? Should we have protested all that gold being taken back to China?"

Mayo closed the laptop and gave Martin a very obvious 'Yeah, sure' sort of look, as if he'd suggested a simple cure for homelessness. "So, why didn't you say something? You were there."

"Me? I'm rich. They say a billion dollars, but it's really only seven-hundred million. What's a few ingots here or there for someone with that kind of dough? But you're about to retire on a city pension. One of those ugly plates would have been a nice supplement."

Mayo's expression changed. "I think it was those Chinese characters scratched into the wax on those little boxes. Names of real people. I keep thinking of what it must have felt like for those guys who slaved for eight years to find that stuff and then handed it to Ah Yang because he promised to get it to their parents and children in China."

They sat in a mutual silence with their own thoughts for thirty seconds or so, then Martin asked, "Any new discoveries?"

"No obvious matches for the prints on the flashlight yet. My ballistics people tell me that the gun we found was the one used on the three people in the pit. Not much surprise there. They also dug up a knife and I'll bet my already inadequate pension that it's the one used on the three kids in 1995. We've started DNA testing on the dress fabric, but that will take a bit.

"Lemme see. Oh yeah, the fingerprint crew is sorting out at least a couple of dozen sets of prints from the house. Some of them are from the various Brookings who lived here, some are identifiable for other reasons, but the ones we're interested in are those we can't match up. We're hoping that one of them will be from the kid named Ken and will match up with the prints from the flashlight. The problem is, that was twenty years ago and we don't have anything to compare them against for ID purposes. Your prints turned up, by the way."

"One of the legacies of my time in the justice system," Martin said. "So our boy Ken dumped everything in the pit, sealed the secret entrance and took off. Not very smart."

Mayo said, "It was good for twenty years. It didn't work for John and Moira Malloy, but I think maybe Ken did succeed in getting off the grid."

Mayo lapsed into another silence. This time it was apparent that he was troubled. He finally blurted out, "We may know who Ken is." He said it in a way that indicated it might not be good news for Martin. "Someone who had access to the gun and the dresses."

When Martin looked at him, Mayo said, "Natalie's brother."

To his surprise, Martin looked neither surprised nor offended. He merely nodded as if the disclosure confirmed what he was thinking.

"Gary."

Mayo slid a dog-eared photo across the table to Martin's side, face-down. Martin turned it over very slowly and deliberately. It was a picture of a family of four, including a teenage boy who was holding a very young Natalie's hand and looking quite sullen, as though wanting to be somewhere else.

"That's Ken," said Martin tonelessly.

Mayo nodded and picked up his phone. He punched a single number and said, "Vic. We've got a confirmation. Gary Weiss, now thirty-seven years old. Get started, beginning with 1995 airport and border data. See if he left the country, and where he went."

Martin was remembering his 'how did you get to be an orphan' session with Natalie.

He spoke tonelessly. "Natalie thought he was dead. He disappeared on the day his father drowned. Everybody assumed that Gary was in the boat with him and that the body went out to sea."

Mayo turned back to Martin. "It all fits. He had access to the dresses and the gun. A lot of valuable stuff was missing, taken on the day of the memorial service by someone who had a key to the house."

"But why? Why would he kill six people?"

"Actually, seven. The three boys – our Mission District victims – were pure vengeance. I went back to the files once I had Gary as a possibility. Turns out that he was severely bullied, maybe even sexually assaulted, by the three that were killed. It happened eighteen months before the killings. In a locker room at Mission High. I can't tell you for sure why he killed the Malloys and Jane Doe, but I'm pretty sure it was to cover up his exit."

"You said seven; that's only six." *Christ! I actually said 'only!'*

"I think the other one was the first victim. His father. It was always hard for me to understand how an experienced boatman would fall out of his own boat."

Christ! Does Natalie know this?

Martin hadn't seen her since their session with Chao Zhu in this room, with the story of Ah Yang, Hiram Brookings and the one-hundred-and-sixty year vendetta. She'd rushed off, saying something about 'finishing her history of the Brookings House.'

He voiced his fears. "Have you shared any of this with Natalie?"

"Not yet. It's all happening at once and she hasn't been around. Obviously, we'll need to talk to her. Do you know where she is? She's not answering her cell."

Martin thought about it. "She said something about going to work. She was excited about what Chao Zhu told us about the Brookings."

Mayo popped the laptop open once more. Before he could focus on it, Martin said, "He's really out of reach, isn't he? Gary? You're not going to catch him."

Mayo shook his head. "I think he's gone." He gestured at the hole in the wall. "Our only hope – and it's pretty desperate – is if he came back to do away with the evidence. But that would be really --"

He stopped when he saw the expression on Martin's face. "What?"

"Maybe he did," Martin said. "Come back to get rid of the evidence."

"And why would he do that, after twenty years?"

"Because the foundation was going to be torn up for an earthquake retrofit. That would expose him for sure."

"Yeah, but – "

"Think about it, Mayo. Nothing happens for twenty years. Then the city requires that the foundation be redone on the next change of ownership. Suddenly, we've got a mysterious offer to buy the house, which is rejected by the owner. Then she dies – very convenient timing -- and the house goes on the market, with two hot bidders for the property.

"One of those hot bidders was you," Mayo went on impatiently. "And you're threatened and warned to back off, presumably by agents of the mysterious other buyer … Who turns out to be Chao Zhu, and his interest – we now know – is in money laundering, fronting for Chinese flight capital, and looking for buried treasure, not to destroy evidence of past crimes. He's the one who handed it to us."

The rapid fire back-and-forth came to a halt and the two of them looked at each other.

Mayo shook his head. "So if it's Chao Zhu and you bidding for the house, where's the connection to Gary?"

Martin continued, speaking softly as though to himself. "Chao Zhu operated through a front -- the Petrel Foundation... founded by a woman named Emily Connors."

He spoke even more quietly, so that Mayo had to lean forward to hear him. "Matthew Weiss's boat, the one he fell out of? It was named 'The Petrel.'"

It was Mayo's turn to stare, but Martin was still talking. "And there's something else. At our first meeting with Zhu, when you charged off after you got the call about Gruber, Natalie and I walked back upstairs with Chao. The last thing before we left, Natalie asked Chao if he would withdraw the Petrel Foundation from the bidding for the Brookings House. He said 'I have nothing to do with the Petrel Foundation. You should talk to a woman named Emily Connors. She's here, in San Francisco.'"

Gary disappears off the face of the earth, then Emily Connors shows up twenty years later. Natalie has the feeling some one is following her, spying on her. Sergei can't find any digital traces of either Emily Connors or of a Petrel Foundation. He called them 'fictional creatures.' Chao Zhu has some weird need to tell us stories and help us solve the Mission murders. And then he points us at Emily.

Mayo stood up, ready to move. "So Emily Connors is our connection. She's working for Gary as well as Chao Zhu. She's more than ..."

He broke off, struck by the expression of horror on Martin's face, and knowing that he was missing something important. "What? Tell me!"

Martin sat extraordinarily still, with a frozen expression. *Three kids killed by someone posing as a woman. Natalie talking about her brother and how he didn't fit in. And the other thing Chao Zhu had said ...*

Martin said to Mayo, "Do you know the play, M. Butterfly?"

Mayo looked at him as though he were crazy.

"When Zhu showed us those skeletons? You rushed out, leaving me with Zhu. I was in a daze, wondering why I wasn't the fourth set of bones in that hole in the ground. I mumbled something about feeling like being in a horror movie. Zhu said, 'Not a movie. A play ... M. Butterfly.'

"I looked it up. Most people think of Puccini's opera, Madama Butterfly. But *M. Butterfly* is actually a play that was inspired by the opera. It is a story about a French civil servant in China who falls in love with a beautiful Chinese opera diva, Song Liling. But she is actually a man masquerading as a woman. Very sad ending.

Mayo stared, trying to work out what Martin had already gone through.

"Chao Zhu was trying to tell us something.

"Emily isn't working for Gary. She *is* Gary."

Mayo looked at Martin with an uncomprehending expression. "But Emily is –"

He stopped himself, suddenly aware of the absurdity of what he was about to say. When he spoke again, it was a savage mockery of his own innocence.

"But Emily is a woman. Gary is a man."

Martin added the obvious, "Or *was* a man."

Martin grabbed his phone. "I've got to get Natalie. She went looking for Emily Connors!"

Mayo was about ten seconds behind him in hitting speed dial. "Victoria. The prints on the flashlight ... See if they match up with a woman named Emily Connors. She may not be in our system, but she came into the country recently, so there should be something out of the passport system or San Francisco customs. I need to know where we can find her. And run her name through whatever databases we've got, including Interpol. And while you're at it, do the same thing with the name 'Gary Weiss.' This is urgent. I repeat: urgent! Call me back as soon as you have something."

He looked at Martin, who was just finishing his call. "Natalie? Did she answer?"

"Nothing. It rolls to voice mail."

Emily

This whole thing started with me looking out a penthouse window at a world-famous harbor. And that's how it's going to end. Just a different harbor – San Francisco rather than Singapore. A lot prettier, but not nearly as many ships in sight.

From where Emily was standing in her Nob Hill penthouse looking out at the Bay, it was easy to visualize a straight line running from the main pier on Alcatraz Island to the Berkeley Marina and to focus on its imagined midpoint.

Right about there. A nighttime sail with the son that he so wanted to set straight. Pushed overboard in very cold and very rough water with strong currents. With a lot of heavy clothing. Not much chance of making shore even if he had been a good swimmer, which he wasn't. And his precious thirty-foot "sloop" – the Petrel -- sailing indifferently with its flapping sails toward its eventual collision with the southern anchorage of the San Rafael Bridge.

An end for him, but – for me – the beginning of a new person. What I thought of as a virtual rebirth ... until I did it for real.

Other than going from alive to dead, it is the most transformative act one can engage in – from male to female. They call it a 'transition.' Such a gentle-sounding word, signifying the movement from one place to another place, implying an orderly progression, a 'becoming.' In reality, it was one year of hell, with nausea, pain and confusion as the only constants. The 'special' hospital outside of Bangkok filled with patients of indefinite gender and uncertain sanity. Men becoming women, women becoming men. Attended to by surgeons and pharmacists when what we needed were psychiatrists and counselors. I had everything the surgeons could offer: voice feminization, breast & buttock augmentation, tracheal shave, vaginoplasty -- twice, because of tissue rejection issues the first time. And I would have insisted on ovaries and a uterus if they would have suggested it.

The first surgery was called 'facial feminization' but we did so much more than that. I wanted not only to change gender, but to become unrecognizable to people I grew up with, even my mother and sister.

But it is so gradual, one is so preoccupied with the biological misery of the process that you are unaware of the changes. They should take out all the mirrors, so that your new self can appear all at once, when you're done and you walk out into the unsuspecting world. But even then, there are the pills, injections and estrogen creams that are required to maintain what has been constructed, like dikes to keep an unrelenting nature at bay.

What changed after all that? The appearance, of course. The absence of pretense. The sheer fun of trying on dresses and buying a wardrobe for yourself rather than 'for my sister.' The simple thrill of pronouns. The awareness of men – and women -- looking at me in new ways. The shedding of every part of my past, enabling me to reinvent not only who I was but to rethink what I wanted and was entitled to. It was conscious reincarnation.

Then the cosmic joke is played. I am now a woman, manufactured to taste so to speak, so I am visited with hyperthyroidism, a woman's disease and its disfiguring symptom, and another medical term – ophthalmopathy. They called it autoimmune inflammatory disorder, a fancy phrase for swelling eyeballs, so prominent that they dominate one's entire face and are the first, last and – perhaps – the only features that one sees when we meet.

"Oh, was that a woman? All I could see were those gigantic protruding eyeballs!"

Did it even matter? Is either me or the world any different because Gary became Emily? Maybe all we've done is make a few purely cosmetic changes. A change in form, but leaving the substance intact. Certainly, neither of us fit in, before or after. We both have killed people, done horrible things that 'normal' people don't do, things that cannot be justified by any code.

When did Gary stop becoming Gary and truly become Emily? Is he still in there and wanting to assert himself, to take over once again? Or have the scalpels and hormone replacement therapies erased him entirely? Would I even know?

Was it worth it? Such a nonsense question given that it's so irrevocable, so final. Unless I stop the injections, pills and chemical therapies and let nature run its course, although maybe 'nature' doesn't apply in the face of such unnatural processes or intentions.

It was a mistake to come back to San Francisco, to this place where I was confused and unhappy. To where I had a family. Have a family. And to the place where the worst of my crimes are so close to being discovered. So stupid! Throw everything into a hole in the ground and assume – assume! – no one will find it. Too big a hurry.

And Natalie! I was so sure that she didn't matter to me, that I couldn't be made to care. Even that she deserved to be an orphan as part payment for what they did to me.

The phone rang several times before she heard it.

It was Ali, calling from the security desk in the front lobby. "There's a woman here to see you. Name's Natalie Weiss." She could tell from the tone that Natalie was in range of his voice.

Emily sat down on the largest of the several suitcases sitting in the middle of the floor. *So I must make a choice after all; I can't just run away. Do I want this to happen? Where do I want it to go ... or end?* And then she was struck by the most obvious question of all. *Does she know? Is that why she's here?*

"What does she want?"

Ali's voice was muffled as he turned away from the receiver to talk to Natalie. After a few seconds, he said, "She says it's about the Russian Hill house. Says she works for the city's 'department of preservation,' whatever that is, and wants to discuss – and I'm quoting here – your intentions if the Petrel Foundation acquires the house."

"OK, send her up. And Ali? As soon as she leaves, bring the car around."

"You sure this woman is OK?"

She could hear the concern in Ali's voice and felt a little bit sorry for him. *He's a professional bodyguard and all he knows is that 'someone' may try to put me away. Hard for him to leave me alone with strangers. Should I tell him 'Beware of Chinamen?' Best not to. Right now, all he knows is that I'm doing a lot of reconnaissance about a couple of real estate properties. No reason to give him any data that he doesn't need to know.*

"She's fine, Ali. I'm sure. Send her up." And then she added, "I know her."

She looked around the room. Other than the luggage in the middle of the room, it looked exactly as it did on the day of the tour with the obsequious real estate agent. There was no sign of her having been there, and she knew that there were no residual fingerprints. She had spent two hours wiping down every surface within reach. *Can't do anything about chemical trace elements, and even less about DNA, but it's unlikely to come to that. And, anyway, the real threat is Chao Zhu, who certainly doesn't care about forensics.*

The project was a failure. His granddaughter is a lost cause. The next audit of her department is certain to turn up 'irregularities' that will lead to an internal investigation that will lead to a criminal indictment. There is nothing that I can do about that except tell her to run. The Russian Hill house remains in the hands of the city and probably always will. Whatever Zhu needed it for, he isn't going to get. And all of that might be chalked up to bad luck. But Gruber? He'll consider that an overreach , an error of judgment that calls for an object lesson; killing his golden goose, the person that was his conduit to an annuity of several million dollars a year of easy money.

Time to disappear for a while. Australia, I think. Some smaller city on the south coast where a Chinese face would stand out among a sea of white faces. I'm like Hiram Brookings, afraid of my past.

Natalie stood in the open doorway looking at the woman sitting on the suitcase. *Those deformed eyes. She's the journalist who was interviewing the Brookings woman at the CCR. Her name was Lee somebody-or-other, but it sure wasn't 'Emily Connors.' That's interesting.*

She cleared her throat and the woman looked up, startled out of her thoughts and back into the present. She stood up and gestured to a pair of upholstered chairs near the window that overlooked the Bay. "Please come in."

They sat and each of them regarded the other quite openly, more so than would be correct for two professional women in their supposed circumstances. However, their mutual inspection was neither hostile nor competitive; it was mostly curiosity.

It was Natalie that spoke first. She nodded to indicate the cluster of luggage. "You're leaving?"

"Yes, I'm done here."

"I saw you at the Rose Brookings residence. We passed each other in the lobby." It came out as a statement halfway between a polite question and a challenge.

Emily nodded. "Yes. That was the last part of my due diligence on the Brookings House. I wanted to do it myself instead of through my agent."

"You —"

"Used another name. Yes, I am quite serious about staying anonymous. In fact, I'm surprised you were able to find me. How did you do that? And why?"

"By accident, really. There was another buyer for the property – a man named Chao Zhu who I thought was operating as the Petrel Foundation. He gave me your name. For no apparent reason. He said that I should talk to Emily Connors about the Petrel Foundation, and he told me where you were staying."

Emily nodded. *A mild form of revenge, by Chao's standards. He's made me visible, therefore vulnerable. Not enough for him, I think. I wonder what else he's got in mind?*

Natalie continued, looking at Emily even more closely. "He also said that I should be careful, that I might find out things that I really didn't want to know."

Yes, he would do that. He knows that once questions start, they will cascade and that everything will unravel. That

I will have to create a new identity. A third re-creation of who I am. I wonder if that will be enough for him?

She watched Natalie closely and asked, "If I told you that I am no longer interested in buying the Brookings House, would that be sufficient for you?"

Natalie hesitated long enough to signal that the formal answer she was about to give would be incomplete, or even untrue. "Yes. I have no other reason to talk with you." But even as she said the words, she was thinking about the strange story of Ah Yang and his vengeful descendants.

People have been killed to enable a real estate transaction, with this woman as a principal. This is more than about the preservation of a historical site.

Emily watched Natalie thinking. Without warning, an image of her as an eight-year-old came to her. *She was sitting in the middle of her bedroom floor, surrounded by a dozen Barbie dolls, each with a different wardrobe. I wonder what happened to the Barbies? Did she ever wonder what happened to Gary?*

Then, without any warning, she was struck by a tsunami of emotions – envy, regret, anger and wonder all rolled up in an inseparable tangle that washed over her. *This is my sister. And she's a woman. Always has been. Always will be. So easy for her.*

Incredibly, at that instant, Natalie asked, "Have we met before? I have the strongest feeling that we have."

A moment of truth if there ever was one! Is it an act of cowardice if I deny who I am? Who I was? Or would it be an act of compassion?

She responded instantly and in tones of absolute certainty. And as soon as she heard herself speak the words, she knew that their very spontaneity was the proof of their rightness.

"No. I'm sure we've never been in the same place at the same time. You're mistaking me for someone else."

That last part is certainly true.

In the lobby, Ali was distracted by his own calculations and at first did not notice the man standing outside the locked glass doors watching him.

The woman Natalie Weiss is the one who lives in the Victorian we've been watching. So we may be having some kind of showdown upstairs. It'll have to be quick; there's a plane to catch. The question is, should I stay? I like San Francisco and she's prepaid for this place for the year. But who knows who's chasing her and for what? High potential for guilt by association. Probably better to cut all the ties. With her and with this city.

The tapping on the glass got his attention. The man was wanting in. He was new to Ali, mostly Chinese but something else as well. It was also clear to each of them that they were of the same profession and therefore could be dangerous to one another. That realization did not necessarily call for hostility, but did require a respectful wariness.

Ali pushed the button on his side of the door, sounding a buzzer. At the same time, he stood back and put his right hand into his jacket pocket, making sure that the man outside the glass saw the motion.

Warren Wah pushed open the door and came inside, careful to keep both hands in plain sight. He stopped ten feet away from Ali and the two men looked directly at one another. Not in a challenging way, but the way two men who had each divorced the same woman might upon first meeting.

Wah inclined his head to indicate Ali's hand in the jacket pocket. "I'm on parole. Not allowed to carry."

Ali smiled, "Sure."

Wah studied Ali intently, as if deciding whether to lie or tell the truth, whether to impart bad news or search for euphemisms. Finally, he nodded as if listening to some internal voice and said, "About your client, there are some things you need to know about the woman ..."

When Mayo and Martin showed up five minutes later, the lobby was empty and Martin had to use the intercom system to dial the building manager to gain entry. Mayo was on his cell phone with Victoria Morrison and finished the call as they entered the building.

"Morrison matched the prints on the flashlight with those of Emily Connors, taken from a passport application in Singapore. Ken, Gary and Emily are all the same person."

Martin nodded, no longer capable of surprise. "And Natalie's here. That's her car outside. She's up there with her."

"Or him, or them!" He added in a savage tone.

Mayo was carrying a handheld radio and used it to make sure the four exits from the building were all covered. When the elevator came, he threw the "off" switch and the two of them used the stairway to the penthouse floor.

The double doors were standing open and they could hear voices from inside; normal tones, as though in a conversation. As they went in, Mayo drew his Glock and kept it in his hand, pointing at the floor and slightly behind him.

Natalie, Warren Wah and Emily all turned to look at them when they came through the arched doorway into the vast living room. Natalie and Emily were sitting in two facing swivel chairs near the floor-to-ceiling windows with their view of the Marina and, out in the Bay, Alcatraz Island. Wah was standing facing them, his hands in the pockets of his jacket. It was a casual pose, but to Martin, he seemed to be focused entirely on Emily, with the intensity of a predator.

Emily turned in her chair to face them and her disproportionate eyes were all that Martin could see, taking up so much of his attention that it was a second or two before he realized that she had taken a handgun from between the cushions and was holding it in her lap. He saw Wah stand up straight and the definite outline of a gun take shape in the fabric of his jacket pocket. Beside him, he could sense Mayo's sudden rigidity. Natalie was open-mouthed, her hand reaching out towards Emily, frozen in midair.

The tableau held for three seconds. Then Emily smiled and said, "Time for one more transition. The last one."

She slowly raised her hand, bringing the pistol up and – even more slowly – swiveled her chair to bring the gun to bear on Mayo. The smile remained in place the entire time.

The things that impressed Martin the most, the images that would stay with him for years, were the smile and the deliberateness of that turning motion.

Mayo fired three times, slamming her back into the chair. Natalie screamed, just once, then covered her face with her hands and began sobbing, her long hair hanging down over her face. Even as he started toward her, Martin saw Warren Wah take the gun that he had brought out of his pocket and drop it behind the credenza next to him, looking at him the entire time.

Emily's protruding eyes were even more prominent, seemingly lidless and devoid of life. But even then, Martin's first thought as he looked down at her would become an epitaph that she would have approved of.

She would have been a beautiful woman except for those eyes.

Epilog

Martin was glad for the interruption. He had misjudged both his aptitude and enthusiasm for painting walls. And Bartholomew was hinting that the work would go faster and turn out better if Martin found something else to do.

"Didn't they offer you *any* vocational training when you were in Folsom Prison?" was one of his kinder comments.

Neither of them noticed Warren Wah standing behind them until he spoke.

"James Lee told me to tell you something. I'd forgotten until now. You paint like shit, by the way."

"Bartholomew is of the same opinion, but he's an employee, so he can't tell me that." Martin put down the brush he was holding and asked, "What is it that James wanted you to pass on?"

"That he changed his mind; that pastel is probably better than a darker shade for those walls. Something to do with seratonin and mood inhibitors. He lost me there."

All three of them looked at the wall. They'd covered about half of it so far in alternating vertical stripes of black and various pastels. Natalie had suggested the compromise and promised Martin that, "No matter what it looks like, I can find you an art critic that will say it's consistent with the aesthetic spirit of the Mission District."

Martin gestured toward the back of the room. "Want some coffee?" he asked Wah.

When they got to the table with the coffee urn, Martin reached up for two mugs, but Wah shook his head when he offered him one. He said, "I brought my own." He took a very crudely shaped, coal black mug from his jacket pocket. Martin had last seen it or one like it in the middle of the laundry room table at the Brookings House.

"Man gave it to me. Said it was a family heirloom."

Martin looked at the mug. *So, the first of the promised distributions to the extended family of Ah Yang. Mayo will be pleased, I think.*

Wah set the mug down on the table and pushed it toward Martin. "James was a hundred thousand short on your loan. I looked up today's commodity prices and this makes a pretty good dent in that."

Martin pushed it back. "I can't accept heirlooms. Too hard to sell."

Wah stared hard at him, searching for something. Before he could speak, Martin said, "But I could use some help with this place. Maybe you could work off the balance of that 100K? Give me a year and we'll call it even."

"Painting walls?"

"That and other things." He gestured at the seven or eight individuals grouped around the pool table. "Some of these guys think five years at Folsom for manslaughter doesn't count for much. Pansy time, they call it. Show 'em sixteen years with the last six at Pelican Bay, they'll probably pay close attention."

Warren Wah went off in his head for a long thirty seconds. Then he picked up the ugly black mug, put it in his pocket, and said, "OK, but you can't make me paint any of those *pastel* stripes. I'll do the black ones."

The Mayor's scheduled weekly press conference was devoted almost entirely to the new waste management processing plant. The combination of US/Chinese collaboration in the cause of environmentalism and hundreds of new jobs was headline stuff. Among other things, it would make Janet Li's reelection campaign a walk in the park.

The printed press release also contained a page devoted to her strategy for city-owned real estate. The core of that strategy was to privatize most of the city's holdings, leaving out only the historically important sites. She was commissioning a consortium of real estate firms to begin the marketing process and – effective immediately – abolishing the Department of City Owned Real Estate.

The very last part of the press release stated, "In keeping with the new strategy, the Brookings House on Russian Hill has been sold to a private buyer who has committed to restore and preserve the house in its original state."

Mayo rapped on the door of Martin's Presidio house and was only mildly surprised when Natalie opened the door.

"Hi. Martin's not here. Doing some urban renewal at the hangout, mostly painting, I think. Probably be here before long though."

"I'll wait, if that's OK. Don't have a whole lot to do, what with all the homicide cases being solved these days."

Natalie waved him in, reciting as he went by. "Alban, Campos, Gruber & Green. Sounds like a white-shoe law firm. Oh, yeah. Four generations of Brookings. And the three Mission kids, two Malloys, and Jane Doe. Makes our City By The Bay one of the bloodier sounding ones, doesn't it? But we know who did all of them, don't we?"

Mayo said, "You forgot the one that started it all – Ah Yang."

But her casual tone had told Mayo what he wanted to know. *You still don't know. That your father should be on the same bloody list. Or that it was your brother that killed most of them? Or should I say 'your sister?'*

Then Mayo saw the shadow flit through her eyes and guessed at its cause. "Natalie, it's not your –"

"Relax, Mayo. No therapy required." She went to the refrigerator, grabbed two bottles of beer, opened them and handed one to Mayo. "Both Martin and I have had a few decades – almost – to get over our childhood losses. And all that bullshit about the need for closure is just that – bullshit."

"So you and Martin –"

"Are getting married this weekend. At City Hall. The Mayor will officiate, you'll be best man and the Chief of Police will be maid of honor. Most of the guests will be felons of one sort or another. Definitely not one for the society pages."

Mayo tried to look hurt. "You haven't asked me yet. To be best man."

"Will you be best man?"

"Yes."

"Well then."

They grinned at one another and sipped their beer.

She turned serious. "Are you OK?"

They both knew what she was referring to. And his response was immediate and casual.

"Me? Yeah, no problem."

Natalie kept staring, needing more, so Mayo continued. "Early in my street career, I had a 'suicide by cop' incident. A paranoid schizoid pointed a gun at me from six feet away. It turned out to be unloaded. That was tough.

"But this time? Emily not only wanted to die, but she deserved to. I just happened to be handy at the time. And her gun was loaded."

And she had a Plan B. Wah would have done it if I hadn't. And if neither of us had done it, she probably would do it herself. In front of Natalie. So, am I OK? Yeah, I'm quite OK.

He changed the subject. "I also heard a rumor that the two of you have bought a house together."

Another grin. "Just something basic. Twenty-three rooms, with big ugly columns at the front entrance. Got it cheap because they say it's haunted. Something about an ancient curse."

Natalie pointed her beer bottle at him. "I hear you're deferring your retirement?"

Mayo grimaced. "Six months. Just to make sure all the loose ends get tied up. Ramirez threatened to subpoena me as a material witness. Seems to think that Chao Zhu shared all those facts with me for a reason. In the police world, we'd call it a confession."

"Can you get to him?"

"Not unless Obama agrees to invade China."

Natalie cocked her head and gave Mayo a quizzical look. "Chao didn't tell you, did he?"

"Tell me what?"

"He's dying. Cancer. Incurable."

Mayo shook his head, a sign that Natalie interpreted as his sudden awareness that he had missed something important.

What she could not know was that the cause was his concern for her.

Martin will have to tell her. Sooner rather than later. But after the wedding!

Chao Zhu would have commended the Mayor's commitment to the preservation of history if he had known of it. However, at the time of Janet Li's press conference, he was in a very small village on the banks of the Yangtze River, not far from the hillside where Ah Yang's bones were resting and where he would be very soon, along with his ancestors. He was distributing belt buckles, buttons and very small inscribed iron boxes to the eldest surviving member of carefully chosen families. At each house, he would drink tea and retell the story of Ah Yang.

The house on Russian Hill sat mute, as it always had. Stolid and inanimate in the moonlight, indifferent to the view and the curiosity of the tourists. Emptied of its treasure and skeletons. At peace, finally, with its history and attentive only to the vibrations transmitted from deep within the earth.

Other Books by Thomas Hofstedt

A Conspiracy of Patriots
A Convergence of Evils
Once Upon a Time in LA
The Hundred Year Storm
A Small War in a Far Off Place

About the Author

Thomas Hofstedt is engaged in approximately his fourth career, each of which is partially reflected in this book. He has worked as a professor, an international banking consultant and finally as advisor and board member for not-for-profit organizations. He lives in San Carlos, California with his wife and most diligent critic, Sharon.